Donna & Nik,
Thank you for your
support & friendship.
I love you!

a life less perfect

A Life Less Perfect
Editor: Rainy Kaye
Cover Design: Wendy S. Russo
Cover Photo: © rocketclips - stock.adobe.com
ISBN (Print): 978-0-9908973-3-0
ISBN (eBook): 978-0-9908973-4-7

To my son, Daniel.
Question everything that's "true."

a life less perfect

a grunge era romance

by wendy s. russo

Rotten Apple

January 2, 1996

Two apples—one green, one mottled—sat on a glittery black granite countertop. In the dim glow of the under-cabinet lighting, they appeared like misshapen planets in a field of stars.

It was just before three in the morning in Phoenix as Ofelia "Marie" Baez slouched at Tia Sarita's kitchen island, her arms crossed and chin resting. She shifted in her seat and freed one hand to touch the Granny Smith and lazily turn it. Light rippled as the uneven edges passed into shadow.

She should be sleeping. Her own bed waited at the end of a twelve-hour trip if everything went well, but she doubted it would. The weather forecast for northwest Wyoming promised snow. Lots of it. However, the moment her head touched the pillow of her cousin's trundle bed, her train of thought was chugging along at speed.

Grasping the green apple, she rolled her wrist so it sat in her palm. *He's got the whole world in His hand.*

Innocent words, but they shoveled more coal into the boiler. Her thoughts raced faster. Her heart thumped half-notes to the tempo of the crazy cat clock on the wall above the sink. Its eyes flicked one way and its tail swished the other, counting down seconds she could be sleeping through.

She sat up straight and picked up the Fuji apple in her other hand. *As man now is, God once was,* Lorenzo Snow revealed long ago. *As God now is, man may become.*

"What's bothering you?"

The soft voice coming from the dark doorway belonged to Tia Sarita.

Marie returned her attention to the "planets" in her hands. Her Heavenly Father earned dominion over her world through perfect righteousness. She assumed He was not the first, the only, or the last.

"You'll think it's absurd," she said without looking up.

Her aunt sat down on the barstool next to her. "Things that keep a woman up at night rarely are."

Marie had to disagree. Earlier in the evening, Marie and her cousin, Erin, had watched an episode of *Star Trek: The Next Generation*. A member of the *Enterprise* crew died on an alien world. She didn't think much of scene at the time, but as the night progressed, she had difficulty thinking about much else.

Unable to sleep, she'd come downstairs and focused her distress onto these two apples—analogues for the world Tasha Yar was born on and the one on which she died.

She couldn't admit to her aunt. Instead, she said, "Erin wants to go to Mars."

Of course, the odds of the now-sixteen-year-old ever actually leaving Earth's orbit were slim to none, but it wasn't the possibility bothering Marie. It was Erin's desire. Her concerns were not shared by Tia Sarita, who smiled wide enough to brighten the kitchen and Marie couldn't imagine why.

"It would be a one-way trip, tia. Why would she want to leave us knowing she'd never see us again?"

Tia Sarita raised eyebrows chastised Marie. "Says the young lady who put a gun to her head."

"It wasn't loaded!" She let the apples roll to the countertop and covered her hot face in her hands. "How many times—"

Faking a suicide attempt hadn't been her best idea ever. At the time, she needed to get out of town and explaining why would ruin more lives than just hers.

"You wanted Ash. You couldn't have her. You couldn't bear to let her go. You wouldn't hold her back either. I understand, *mija*." Tia Sarita's voice was soft but the words squeezed breath and tears from Marie. "You'll discover soon enough that's what motherhood is. Letting go when your heart desperately wants to hold tighter."

"If the girls were sealed to you..." Anger flashed in her aunt's eyes and she stopped. *Uh oh.*

Children born under the New and Everlasting Covenant were "sealed" to their parents for eternity, promised their families would be together forever if only they lived according to the gospel. Thus, Tia Sarita's choice to marry and have children with a non-member was a source of consternation for their extended family. Marie included. It hurt to know her cousins would not be with her in the Celestial Kingdom, even more so knowing it wasn't their fault. Their father would not join the Church and their mother chose him.

The subject was always on Marie's mind when visiting her aunt but she'd managed for years to never bring it up. Now the words were out there and she couldn't take them back.

She didn't want her aunt to misunderstand her. "I love Uncle Carl, truly, but—"

"Good *rarely* ever comes after a 'but', Ofelia."

Duly warned by her aunt's interruption, Marie kept the rest of her opinion to herself. The swishes of the cat clock's tail became unbearably loud as the silence stretched on.

"Do you know why I left the Church?"

Because she fell in love. Marie also knew her aunt's choice drew a line in the sand, one that to her knowledge, no one crossed except her father and her. And didn't *that* make holiday suppers fun. Tia Sarita could make their family whole by coming back but, seventeen years later, she still refused. She'd been stubborn from the womb, Marie's grandmother said. Passed her due date by two solid weeks.

"Because of Uncle Carl." Blaming him was wrong, but it was easier. "You wouldn't raise your children in a divided house."

Tia Sarita's frown told Marie clearly as words the story as she knew it was incomplete.

"Carl read the Book of Mormon. Cover to cover. He met with the missionaries.

Then he learned he'd never be given the priesthood. We couldn't be sealed. No matter what he did, he'd never be worthy."

Goosebumps rose across Marie's skin. She straightened on her barstool and pulled in her arms to rub the chill away. It didn't help. "But why?" Baptism washed away sins. She'd seen new members ordained with the priesthood minutes after they were blessed with the Holy Ghost.

A weak laugh slipped from Tia Sarita. "Because he's black."

Marie frowned. "Our church doesn't—"

Tia Sarita's index finger cut her off. "Now. It doesn't *now*. The ban was lifted in '78, and my phone started ringing off the hook with the *great* news that Carl could take me to the temple and we could be a family again."

"Why wouldn't that make you happy?"

The cat clock ticked off seconds her aunt held her gaze steady, giving away nothing. Already anxious over a dozen other things, every stretch of silence between them weighed heavier.

"You are a good Mormon." Tia Sarita gently fanned her fingers through Marie's hair and pushed it back over her shoulder. "You look at the world gospel-forward. You defer to it without question, and when it changes, you adjust. You move on. You forgive and forget, because healing the family is always more important than yourself."

"Isn't it?" Marie's voice broke at moment she should have felt pride. Her aunt's words were true, but it was judgement, not praise.

Tia Sarita dropped her hand and brushed her thumb over Marie's cheek, taking away rogue tears. "My mama—your *lita*—said it would be best if I didn't bring my husband to family gatherings. He wasn't welcome there. When the policy changed, they didn't understand why we declined their invitations. They expected him to catch up so that we could get married in the temple and be a family again. The turmoil was always my fault. Before, because I offended them by marrying an unworthy man, and after because I wouldn't just forgive and forget what no longer mattered."

Marie had never felt as hollow as she did with those words flowing through her and echoing off her bones. She resisted the knowledge her family could be so callous, even as such comments returned to her from the past.

Yet, she was compelled to defend them. “They were following the prophet, *tia*.”

“And I chose to be offended.”

The bitterness in her aunt’s voice hurt Marie’s heart. “Is that why you left?”

“That was the last straw.” Tia Sarita’s voice rose loud enough Marie feared she’d wake others in the house. “It wasn’t just black people, and it wasn’t just the ‘70s. I had a woman tell me I was pretty for a *Lamanite* a week ago.”

As Marie puzzled out why a Mormon woman with Native American ancestors would be disgusted by such a statement, her aunt’s frown deepened.

“You do know what the *Book of Mormon* says happens when *Lamanites* are truly righteous, right?”

Marie had read the scriptures three times, cover to cover. “The Lord blesses them.”

“With *white* skin.”

“That’s…no, I’ve never heard that.” Tia Sarita didn’t react at all, angering Marie more. “That’s an ugly lie! Why are you saying these things?”

“I live my life as the Church taught me.” Tia Sarita pushed away from the island. “Do what is right. Let the consequences follow.”

· ❄ ·

Sixteen hours, two planes, and three take-off delays later, Marie sat in her father’s truck as he drove down State Highway 14. He turned left two blocks earlier than she expected onto Main Street. Downtown Coulter, Wyoming, looked like a Rockwell painting. Snowflakes big as quarters floated like down feathers between antique street lamps. It was calm now, but it wouldn’t last. The winds they’d left behind a few miles back were only the beginning of a storm the DJ on 103.1 FM called a monster.

Main Street was marked for angled parking, so when he pulled to a stop in front of Blessed Beans, he illegally occupied at least three spaces. Not that anyone was around to care. The street was mostly deserted.

The coffee shop’s windows radiated gold. The scene on the other side of the glass—Ashley Clark polished the chrome pieces of an espresso machine—filled Marie with joy. And regret. And longing. *Oh, heart, make up your mind.* She jerked away and whipped around to face her father with mallets hammering on her ribcage in time with the soft throb of rock music penetrating the truck's door.

"She's still here?"

His gaze turned wary. "Why wouldn't she be?"

"She was supposed to move to San Francisco like two months ago." *Why would she stay?* "Did something happen to her while I was gone?"

Her father shrugged stiffly. "Not to my knowledge. She calls once a week to ask about you."

No, no, no. She was supposed to get on with her life!

"Figured, we're passing through…storm's coming…she might need a ride home."

Ash got stuck in Coulter on a night like this two years ago. Marie and her boyfriend, Jason, pulled her out of her car after she slid on black ice and crashed into a light pole. A year later, Jason confessed he was going to be a father and married Marie's "best friend." Ash helped her pick up the pieces while weeks passed her in an angry blur.

Somewhere along the line, the wires in Marie's brain had gotten crossed in the process. By summer, she didn't care a bit for Jason anymore, but her fondness for Ash grew into the space he left behind and tested the limits of the walls. She knew Ash had plans to continue her move to California. All Marie had to do was keep her attraction hidden and let her friend go when the day came. In October, when she doubted her ability do either, she looked at her father's gun and saw a way out.

Her aunt's rehab facility in Phoenix put a thousand miles between Marie and the object of her sinful affection. The weeks that followed, though, were heavy with talk of life and death. The clinic apparently had a policy to tell her suicide was a permanent solution to temporary problems. Grasping the concept was a simple task. Convincing a dozen people she never actually tried, less simple.

When her father showed up the day before to take her home, the staff wasn't comfortable with her leaving. They cautioned her father about "repressed aggression" she needed to confront before she tried to hurt herself for real next time. But, money talks, and, ready or not, patient walks. She voluntarily committed herself, after all.

Marie pushed open the truck door. The scent of ozone and wood smoke pooled in her lungs, and the voice permeating the brick wall of the coffee shop became clear. Eric Clapton. "Sunshine of Your Love."

One of her black leather boots stomped a thin layer of powder, followed by the other. The crisp air seized upon every bit of skin not protected by two layers of fabric, which was most of it. It had been sixty degrees when they left Arizona. Marie reached into the truck and grabbed her coat before shutting the door. It was only six or so paces to the shop, but at the volume Ash listened to music, Marie wasn't counting on her hearing a knock at the door.

Marie had stayed in rehab to make sure Ash had moved to San Francisco before coming home. How naïve she'd been to think *not* seeing Ash all those weeks was hard. On the other side of the glass door was the object of desires Marie had never felt before and didn't understand. Knowing Ash stayed…*for her*…didn't help keep those feelings where she buried them.

I should leave.

Ash hadn't noticed her yet. Marie could go back to the truck and tell her father to go home. Maybe he didn't see Ash. She could tell him another barista was closing and he had a car of his own.

Instead, she placed both hands on the door and thumped the meaty part of her fists on the glass. A lukewarm voice of caution aside, there wasn't a part of her willing to go without seeing Ash first.

Just as the frigid air had succeeded in changing her mind about that, Ash finally turned away from the espresso machine.

Ash's eyes widened and her jaw fell agape. A split second later, she rounded the counter, reaching for the lock well before she approached the door.

The decadent scent of coffee with a hint of chlorine wafted out and enticed Marie inside. She rubbed her feet on the welcome mat, ridding her boots of what remained of the snow she'd tried kicking off outside.

"Turn it down." Marie couldn't hear herself yell.

Ash grabbed the remote from the glass display case beside the door and pointed it unnecessarily toward the stereo. The café fell silent.

"Holy geez, Ash." Marie wiggled a finger in her right ear, trying to scratch an itch she couldn't reach. "How are you not deaf yet?"

Ash grabbed Marie by the shoulder and pulled her into an unexpected hug. Her friend usually avoided touching people. Every hug they'd ever shared had been solely for Marie's benefit. This one felt personal, though, and the warmth of it was lovely. Marie rested her chin on Ash's shoulder and melted into it. She couldn't help snuggling into Ash's neck a bit, even if the ends of her unruly, honey blonde hair tickled.

It had been much shorter once. An hour after they met, Marie still hadn't been sure if her new friend was male or female. It was a rude question to ask, wasn't it? She gleaned the clues she needed and came away with a stronger impression of "boy" than "girl" but only just. Logical deductions had been a strength in school, so she felt mild shock when Ash later walked into the ladies' restroom.

As time passed, Marie had begun to see in Ash parts of herself that were missing. Courage when she felt afraid; confidence when she doubted. They passed from Ash into her like ghosts summoned through her by an invisible hand. Often, Marie had a desperate urge to cuddle somewhere quiet, to wrap her body around her friend and stay tangled together until she absorbed a bit of Ash into herself. The fire always left her cold, breathless, and terrified when these moments flickered out.

Marie had never told Ash about these thoughts. She'd never told anyone. How would she even start?

"You scared me."

The exhaled words hurt Marie's soul. She squeezed Ash harder, and she returned an embrace so tight Marie could hardly draw breath. It wasn't nearly snug enough.

"I'm so sorry."

"You don't have to be."

Kind words, but so untrue. Her plan to leave town had backfired. Time would tell how badly she'd messed up. For now, though, if she cut away everything but

Ash's arms and just breathed, the moment was perfect.

The bell jingled as the door was pushed open again. Marie backed up as Ash abruptly released her. A blush stained Ash's cheeks and she cast her gaze low. A chill filled the empty space. Heavy hands settled on both of Marie's shoulders, completing her father's interruption of their reunion.

Ash shoved her hands into her jeans pockets. "How are you?"

"Fine. I'm fine." Marie pushed away her separation anxiety and embarrassment. "Momentary lapse of reason."

Frowning, Ash barely glanced up. Trying to assure her again could only make things worse, so Marie crossed her arms, looked at the floor, and kicked the melting snow on the rug with her foot.

"Can I get you something warm for the road?" Marie glanced up again. Ash was looking out of the storefront windows with concern. "Might take you a while to get home in this mess," she said.

The wind picked up and the snowflakes tangoed in the glow of the street lamps, while the blue-gray sky hung low. Even without the espresso machine, making drinks would take time she didn't have with snow falling heavier by the moment.

"Were you planning to walk home or get stuck here?" Her father wasn't in the habit of dropping in unannounced a her friend's workplaces to give them rides. The concern was genuine.

"Don't worry about me." Ash shrugged. "Got it handled."

She meant a friend of theirs was supposed to pick her up. Marie scoffed at the very idea. "Neil won't get out of his driveway without crashing. What do you have left?"

"Sweep and mop."

"Rock, paper, scissors." Marie held up her fist.

Ash flicked a reticent gaze from Marie's hand to her father behind her. Marie held her hand steady though, prepared to argue until the blizzard trapped them all. There were pastries in the case to keep them fed for days.

"Three of us." Marie's father walked a few steps farther inside the coffee shop, panning the room. "Should take ten minutes. Tops."

Outnumbered, Ash sighed and held up her fist near Marie's.

One...two...three...

Marie won with paper. "I'll sweep." She turned on a heel and walked to back of the coffee shop.

As she opened the restroom door, she flicked a sideward glance toward the utility room and caught Ash looking her way at the same time. Ash's lip tugged upward in the smallest of smiles. Her eyelashes kissed her cheeks and lingered there a moment longer than natural. The flash of Ash's amber eyes burned Marie in a dozen hidden places.

Marie ducked into the dark restroom and lay against the door. Her face burned beneath her frigid hands. If she didn't move a muscle, would she suffocate?

· ❄ ·

Ash lived in the basement apartment of her employer's house, so the three drove there after they'd finished closing the coffee shop. The heavy snowfall blew sideways through the truck's halogen beams. The white curtain was so thick now. Marie could barely make out the yellow, mid-century home when they pulled into the driveway. Ash exited the truck and rounded the front, plodding through inches of fresh powder.

Each step her friend took away from Marie hurt like...a thumb pressing a bruise on her heart.

No, it's not pain. And it wasn't only in her heart, either. All of her internal organs were bothered. Anxious. *Guilt?* Not quite. *Regret...maybe.*

Her mind scrambled. Her heart danced with the wind. A tender spot between her legs protested sharply when her body shifted but her underwear didn't. She'd think her period was due if she wasn't still spotting from the last one. The itch had been relentless since the coffee shop. And she could. Not. Scratch.

She wanted—*needed*—out of the truck. And her father wouldn't budge until Ash was inside Signy's house, safe and sound.

She wished he never would. She wanted to turn back time thirty seconds and freeze it, so Ash would be at her side forever. Or speed up the clock, to when she'd see her friend again. These desires scared her.

She'd hoped rehab would smother whatever this was in its cradle, but when Ash had hugged her, her urges had come back with a vengeance. They dredged up the daydreams of kissing Ash she'd meant to put away for good.

If her father hadn't been standing right there…

Ash bounded up the steps of the home's side entrance. She yanked open the flimsy screen door and pushed the heavier exterior door inside of it. At the last moment, she paused and looked back at the truck. *Good-bye.* Or *thank you*, maybe. The light above the door cast a gold halo on Ash's head. A small smile pulled at her lips and disturbed a bird trapped in Marie's tummy. The beat of its wings rippled through her flesh and ended abruptly as the screen door slammed shut.

Marie tucked her foot under her. She was alone with her father again, with a mixed bag of emotions and weeks of prayers God chose to ignore.

"Are you alright?" Her father reached up for the gear shift lever.

"Yeah." The hard heel of her boot relieved the itch but not the burn. To explain her sudden squirming, she said, "Felt like spiders just walked up my spine."

"Probably the dry air."

Sure. Dry air. Never mind all the snow filling in Ash's footprints as they sat there.

They hadn't even gotten home yet, and the problem she'd run to rehab to escape had come screaming back. Ash was supposed to be starting a new life in San Francisco. Not *here.* Not teasing out feelings Marie shouldn't still have. Should *never* have had.

When her father finally backed out of the driveway, Marie shoved her heart at another want. She couldn't wait to shut two doors between her and every other living thing on Earth, sink into a hot bath, and *maybe* breathe freely again. She leaned against the ice-cold window and chewed on her thumbnail as snowflakes raced to the edge of the headlight's cone.

Ash would ask her why she wanted to die sooner or later. But if she ever found out—if *anyone* found out—it could destroy *everything.* The bishop might discipline her. Her parents would disown her. Ash might hop on the first bus out of town without another word.

Marie could hardly blame any of them.

Forty minutes after they left Ash's house, they turned off the highway and plowed into a field of snow, following the sweeping driveway by feel and memory. As they neared the house, motion-detecting lights illuminated the outside of the mansion she'd called home since she was eight.

As the glow brightened, her mind was flooded with memories of growing up in this house. She'd assembled thousands of tamales at her mother's side and listened to her father read books to her at bedtime. They'd celebrated the end of swim seasons with the team in their great room and welcomed home missionaries at their formal dining table. Happier times.

The front door opened as her father parked the truck in the driveway. Her mother stood in the doorway wearing a plush white robe over a long nightgown and fluffy slippers. Her thick black hair fell about her shoulders, styled as if she planned to go out. She never did after seven pm, but if there was ever a fire—*¡dios me libre!*—her mother would be presentable.

The truck rolled slowly, and ever closer to the home, her pleasant memories gave way to the unfinished business she'd left behind when her father took her to rehab.

A mission application incomplete. Amends not made. Forgiveness withheld.

Motherhood delayed.

She'd wondered since landing in Salt Lake City why her father would pick *now*—amidst blizzards and holiday traffic—to yank her out of rehab against doctors' advice? If she were a betting woman, motherhood was where she'd put her money. Twenty-one years was too long to keep her mother waiting for a grandchild, and ten weeks was too long to make her father bear the complaints alone.

Marie stepped from the cab and shut the door. She shoved her hands into her pockets and scuffed her feet through the snow as she rounded the truck. Seeing Ash again made her anxious; her mother's presence filled her with shame.

She swallowed against the ache in her throat and fought to keep from blinking, because she had no right to forgiveness or pity. The last time they saw each other, this woman thought her child—the only one of her many babies to survive the second trimester—would kill herself if left alone. Together again, Marie expected her mother to let loose with all the things she didn't dare say two months ago.

Her mother's frown softened and her posture relaxed. Marie grabbed onto selfish hope they wouldn't have to talk about rehab tonight.

"You look tired," her mother said.

Marie was going on forty hours without sleep, and she couldn't say what had been most taxing in the meanwhile. The trains of thought? Two planes and three take-off delays in Salt Lake City. Driving through a white out. Pretending to be okay when she wasn't.

The tears she was holding back spilled. "I am."

Her mother brushed her wet cheeks with soft hands and opened her arms. Marie accepted her welcome home. As the embrace around her tightened, she hoped they wouldn't talk about the gun tomorrow either. Or ever.

"Go on up to bed." Her mother kissed her head. "We can talk tomorrow."

Marie shoved her gloves and hat into her pockets before handing her coat off to her mother. The ache deep inside had subsided, and she was grateful for it. She wanted to go to sleep and trudging up the stairs would be hard enough without the burden of answering questions her mother had been waiting weeks to ask.

She walked into her darkened room and shut the door behind her. Blindly, she flipped the light switch.

Her room was gone!

The once coral walls were dove gray now. The butterflies stenciled under the crown molding were painted over, too. Her striped balloon shades were gone, as was the worn shag carpet she'd dropped nail polish on when she was ten.

She gave the room a quick pan and identified the new bookshelves as the ones from her father's home office. The books were his and so was the desk. It was her room. And it was temporary storage. And it was becoming something new and unknown to her. All at once. Her mother's message cut through her wearied body and bothered soul like a cleaver through bone.

You are a guest in this house.

Marie shut off the light. She kicked off her shoes and stripped out of her clothes as she crossed the distance to the bed in the dark. As her shin found the hard wood frame, she stifled a curse and dropped to her knees to pray.

"Dear Heavenly Father. I thank Thee for bringing my papa and me home from Phoenix safely. I ask Thee to look after the pilots and the flight staff of the airlines who are working in bad weather and keep them safe. Also, please watch after my Tia Sarita and Uncle Carl, and my cousins Erin, Tricia, and Stefanie, and the staff at the clinic. May they continue to bless the lives of all they touch. I ask for Thy strength in the days to come, Heavenly Father, that I can overcome the trials Thou hast given me and be prepared to receive the blessing of Thy divine plan. I ask these things in the name of Thy son, Jesus Christ. Amen."

Exhaustion fell over Marie in ever heavier layers as she crawled between the cold linens. There, she curled up into a ball, craving the warmth prayer had once placed in her chest. Sleep did not come quickly. A discussion of the fertile years she'd already wasted loomed on the horizon and it filled her with dread.

Help

Somewhere under the thick white blanket of snow surrounding the Baez home was a highway. Coulter lay at one end, on the other, the Montana border. It was convenient on days Marie had plans to leave home, but on this particular Thursday the road was merely a promise. A tease.

Her bedroom was on the southwest corner of the second floor. Her father had designed the room so two window seats met in an "L." It was the perfect place for two people to watch the sunrise over the Big Horn Mountains if they caught the moment.

In the winter, even with the double-pane glass, it was a cold place. A shiver prompted Marie to pull the blanket she huddled under tight around her. The comforter still smelled of its plastic packaging. Not an offensive smell on its own, but it reminded her it was new.

The sun crested the peaks just before eight in the morning, casting pale rays through tattered clouds. Wisps of snow danced on the breeze across the virgin field between the horizon and Marie. The light caught the flat planes of snowflakes, setting them on fire. The landscape shimmered with glitter.

This time, when she shivered, it wasn't from cold.

Marie loosened her down cocoon and pulled out the pile of mail she'd found on her bedside table. A dozen Christmas cards, give or take, all from college friends who'd moved away years ago, and one blue and red striped envelope mailed from Brazil.

Sam.

Marie's family had moved to Coulter when she was eight years old. Sam

Rigby was one of the first people she'd met. He was best friends with Jason Swing, the boy she'd lost her heart to years before she was allowed to date. She spent more time with Sam than Jason, though. Like her, Sam was a diver, and they joined each other's teams as managers, so for four years, from August to February, they were together every morning and afternoon for practice, and most every weekend for swimming meets.

Jason didn't mind. He trusted her, he'd reply whenever she asked. Sarah, though—at the time, Marie's best friend and Sam's girlfriend—minded quite a bit.

Sam was nearing the end of his two year mission in Sao Paulo. Marie had written him off and on, less so after Jason married Sarah than before. It had been a while since she'd heard back from him. This envelope was postmarked in October and arrived after she left for Phoenix.

She put aside the cards and opened Sam's letter. He usually just answered the questions she asked in her last letter and told her about the day he was having. This letter was different from his others the start.

My companion suggests that our Heavenly Father has a great blessing in store for us both. I believe this to be true. I am hopeful that you will consider that we are on the same path. We always have been, and if it pleases you, we can continue together.

The storm clouds blew east as the sun moved west. Daylight softened and faded to gray. Without shadows, the snowy shroud on Marie's world became shapeless and deathly still.

She shrugged off the comforter and walked to the bathroom. She flipped on the vanity lights and read the letter again. Laying the paper safely aside on the counter, she drew a bubble bath and sat on the toilet lid. She reached across the sink and caught the letter between two fingers. A third, fourth, and fifth read confirmed the words she read in the first two reads through.

Yes, Marie. I am asking you to marry me.

The proposal struck an odd chord within her. Not unwelcome, but wholly strange. For half of the years they'd known each other, Sam had been her boyfriend's best friend, and her best friend's boyfriend. But neither condition rendering them mutually off-limits applied now, and she could not argue with his bullet points. They had shared goals. Values. Pain, too.

She read the words a sixth time and saw in them an answer to many of her prayers. If there was such a thing as the *right* man, it was Sam Rigby, and Heavenly Father was sending him home any day now.

A craving for saxophone and bass took root bone deep. Perhaps it was the window of opportunity that had opened. Or the humidity rising in the bathroom. The cause didn't matter when the fix was simple.

Marie left the letter in the bathroom and went to the chest of drawers serving double-duty as a base for her boom box stereo and storage unit for her CD collection. Morphine's *Cure for Pain* would be in the top drawer.

She pulled it open. Her heart stopped.

"What the..."

It was filled top to bottom with *Ensign* magazines.

She closed the drawer and opened the one below it. Magazines again. This time *The New Era*.

The third drawer was full of excess art supplies from Marie's college classes, and the two below held random stuff.

Of her once vast music collection, she found four discs. A Mormon Tabernacle Choir Christmas album, case missing. A collection of Baroque classics. The Beatles Anthology 2. And the soundtrack to *Swing Kids*.

Marie slammed the drawer shut and gave her room a once over. Why move her CDs to store old magazines and junk?

Weary as she was, she hadn't noticed the night before the upstairs hallway was different. Pale hardwood and rugs lay where shag carpet used to be, and her bare feet registered *hard* where soft had always been.

Change was occurring around Marie and without regard to her. Every new piece of evidence made her angrier.

She stalked into the kitchen. There she found her mother poking whole cloves of garlic into a pork roast. A crockpot sat on the counter next to her. From childhood, this would be a welcome site for her. Her favorite comfort foods were on the menu. Having given up meat months before, it only added to her growing list of burdens.

Her father was also in the room. He sat at the breakfast table reading a book titled *View of the Hebrews*, his half-eaten ham and cheese omelet apparently forgotten. *This* relaxed Marie a bit. *This* was normal.

"Where did you move my CDs?"

"Good morning to you, too."

Her mother's biting reply reminded Marie of her manners. "I'm sorry. Good morning."

"Breakfast is on the stove."

"Thank you. Where are my CDs?"

Her mother's slimy hands froze on the pork roast. Her father flipped a page in his book. To Marie, the world seemed to have stopped and restarted.

"I threw them out." She pushed another clove of garlic inside the roast.

Marie felt the poke of those fingers in her stomach and gasped for air. "You *what*?"

Her mother continued her meal prep.

Being ignored enraged Marie more. "I bought those CDs with my own money, Mama. You had no right!"

"Right?" Her mother pounded one fist on the granite countertop. She turned away from the roast. The tears welling in her eyes tempered Marie's anger with guilt. "You dare speak to me of *rights*? You brought *the devil* into *my* house."

"Devil?!"

"That garbage Jason got you hooked on damaged your soul. You gave me no choice!"

The guilt she felt over her mother's tears evaporated in a brand-new flash of rage.

"Unless you intend to flood the house, might I suggest you turn off the faucet upstairs?"

Her father's calm interjection disarmed Marie. She stopped and listened for a moment and heard the flow of water through the pipes in the house. The bath was still filling.

Marie bolted from the kitchen, climbed the stairs two at a time, and ran the upstairs hallway at top speed. As she entered the bath, the water was just reaching spill stage at the lip of the tub.

She turned the water off. The bath tempted her with a promise of warmth and peace. But it wouldn't be the same without Morphine and none of the options her mother left her with were substitutes for saxophone and bass.

Marie plunged her arm to push the drain plug lever. The water overflowed onto the floor, soaking the floor mats and her socks. For a moment, she panicked about soaking the bedroom carpet but the water simply poured onto hardwood.

Towels from her cabinets made quick work of the mess. She sat on the side of the tub and listened to the gurgle of the water as it drained. Bad days were familiar to her. Still, this one had started out good and the flip-flop stunned her.

She needed to get out of the house.

She left the bathroom and retrieved the Beatles Anthology from the bottom drawer of her dresser. Popping the case open, she found two disks with apples on them. Green skin on one, cut side on the other.

Her brain played the *Star Trek* scene again. A tar creature flicked Tasha Yar like a bug. She was dead before she hit the desolate alien soil.

It was just a TV show.

Marie removed one disc and fetched her snowsuit from the closet.

· ❄ ·

Marie stood in the open threshold of the garage. While inserting earbuds, she imagined the landscape in front of her as it appeared in spring. The driveway extended for 125 feet before gracefully curving right for 300 paces, straightening for 500 paces before curving left for 100 paces before meeting the highway.

Over the earbuds, Marie placed her gun range earmuffs and settled on a strategy. The snow blower was good at its job but bad at turning. She'd push until she hit grass. Turn and push. Turn and push. Until she ran out of gas or rage, whichever came first.

She pressed the play button on the CD player in her snowsuit pocket. The dreamy electronic melody of The Beatles' "Real Love" tickled her ear. She turned up the volume until she couldn't stand it before backing off a bit.

The fuel tank was half-full.

Her dad leaned against the work bench at the far end of the garage. The gas can sat on the counter beside him. The keys to the dually dangled from his hand. The old truck had a plow blade attached to it six months out of the year for the purpose of moving snow.

Whatever.

She didn't want to move snow. She needed to vent rage, which she usually did by diving or singing grunge rock at the top of her lungs, but neither was an option at the moment.

After topping off the snow blower's tank, she grabbed hold of the plastic handle and ripped back the starter cord. It never worked on the first try. Or second.

You brought the Devil into my house.

Marie grabbed the cord with both hands and yanked. *Three. Hundred. CDs.* The machine rumbled to life. Paul and John sang like angels. Snow flew as she shoved out under the gray sky and mild winter wind.

Eleven tracks later, the Beatles serenaded her arrival at the highway with a melancholy *Yesterday.* Coulter lay to the right. Montana to the left. When she pushed her palm flat to the ground, snow covered her arm up to her elbow. She was truly stuck where she was.

She turned the snow blower to make her next sweep toward the house. Her dad stood about ten feet away and in the snow, within two feet of the strip she'd cleared and directly in the way of her next pass. The keys to the dually dangled from his left hand. His right swept across his throat, pantomiming "kill."

Marie looked skyward and exhaled frost. With a grudge, she turned off the snow blower, removed her earmuffs, and pulled out the earbuds. Paul McCartney and John Lennon begged for help getting their feet back on the ground. The music sounded thin and raspy from the tiny speakers hanging from her neck.

"If you want to get out of here, the dually would be much faster," he said.

"Except three things." She raised her right hand. "One, the dually has AM radio. Two, an 8-track player..." She tugged her glove off to free her fingers. "Three, you own zero 8-track tapes...that's more of a problem with you, though."

Her father's lips flattened into a thin frown. "You've had enough time to think, *Ofelia.*"

He wasn't talking about the time she'd spent blowing snow.

Marie silently begged God's forgiveness for her bitter thoughts. He deserved better from her. Last fall, on the day she took the gun out of the safe, the only thing he had said to her was "get in the truck." She had expected a lecture while they drove. Instead, he had bought plane tickets to Phoenix. They had boarded without bags, met Tia Sarita at the airport, and checked her into a rehab clinic an hour later.

That was ten weeks ago. He still hadn't asked her why she wanted to die. She could never say he was stingy with his time or patience.

And he wasn't talking about the gun now either. He was talking about her mission papers, which he'd insinuated before leaving her at rehab would be the best use of her time there.

She *had* entertained the idea of going on a mission a few months back, after Jason broke her heart and the future planned together crumbled to dust, but she'd never felt *called* to the task. Now, on the list of things she could do with her life, eighteen months of knocking on doors with the *Book of Mormon* came in near the bottom, between prostitution and taking calls at a customer service desk.

She pulled her mitten back on her freezing hand and folded her arms tight against her body.

Top of the same list was "get my old job back."

To the man on the other side of the snow blower, that was a wrong answer. Her father believed a woman operating machinery took work away from men. Her mother believed a woman with resources should not work at all.

Her former boss believed Marie's parents might have less of a problem with their daughter working than consorting with lesbians. There were three at Valkyrie Press and Copy, including the owner.

"I'm waiting, *mija*."

Her parents, her bishop, her therapists in Phoenix…they all agreed her life had gone off track. She wasn't blind to it. She didn't deny it. And after four years of putting off marriage and family, mostly while waiting for Jason to get his act together, the thought of disappointing her father now caused her actual pain. But, her heart wasn't into righting the train. The things troubling her about her life were also things she *loved.*

When you're ready to be an adult, her boss said, *call me.*

If only it could be so simple. Being an adult, in her case, broke the fifth commandment God gave to Moses, and defying her Earthly parents also defied her Heavenly parents.

"Ofelia."

"I don't want to go on a mission." The words fell off her tongue without a shred of grace and hung in the icy air. She paused to calm the spike of panic seizing in her chest. "I don't have it in me."

"Have you thought of alternatives?"

One. Two if she counted marrying Sam, but if she mentioned that, her mom would call his mom and he would come home to wedding plans already made. So, for now…one. She had but one blessing to count right now. Her mother wasn't standing there to wail and moan about what they were going to do with her.

"I want to go back to work."

"Ofelia—"

"Papa, stripping is—"

He groaned as if he'd touched something slimy. "I wish you wouldn't call it that."

"It's an industry term."

"Could you please come up with something that doesn't give me a mental picture of you dancing with a pole?"

Rolling her gaze skyward again would only annoy him further so she restrained herself. "Okay. How about…*solving puzzles.*"

"If you want to solve puzzles, try church history. You've got all my books in your room, just waiting."

"*That's* a puzzle? Church history?"

"You'd be surprised."

"And give up playing with razor blades?"

Her father's eyes narrowed. "Care to try again?"

Maybe it was tactless to joke about sharp things while fresh out of suicide intervention, but she needed humor. Without it, the lump she was fighting to keep down in her throat might choke her.

"I know you don't approve, Papa, but Valkyrie is where I'm happy."

With his hands on his hips, he cast a lingering glance in the direction of Montana. He exhaled deeply before returning his attention to her. "Happy enough to forgive your mama for the CDs?"

Marie studied his face for signs he was joking. His eye contact was steady. His posture relaxed. A spark of warmth ignited in her chest. She nodded eagerly.

"Stop screwing around with the snow blower." He tossed the truck keys. She caught them in her gloved hand. "Clear the driveway like you mean it."

It was the best possible outcome, but Marie tried not to be too excited. She left Valkyrie short-staffed when she left. Would her job still be there? And even it if was, would her boss even want her back?

Gotta Get Away

Marie woke on Friday with a mission to get her job back.

The weather called for a lasagna-worthy combination of layers. At twenty degrees below zero, every drop of moisture remaining in the air became a microscopic dagger flung at the whims of the wind. Driving unfortunately required a bare face and hands nimble enough to steer, so she let the car run a full half-hour before daring to leave the garage.

Before going to Valkyrie, she had to make a stop by her father's car dealership to drop off his lunch. That caused her a bit of consternation. Not the dropping off lunch part. That was no big deal at all. But her mother hadn't forgot to give her father lunch at the door once in Marie's lifetime memory and she had been oddly nonchalant about her slip-up.

Dropping by the dealership would give Marie a chance to catch up with her brother, Neil, so she simply took the plastic-wrapped bowl of *chile verde* from her mother and left.

Even though warm, the drive was miserable. Her hope her mother had forgotten the CD changer in the car was crushed when she pulled the magazine and found it empty. Alice in Chains had been in there. Tori Amos and Nine Inch Nails, too. She preferred road noise to the assorted misery crooned about on the local AM stations, and no thanks to the ice on the highway, she got to listen to it twice as long.

Clear skies left nothing between the winter sun and miles of uninterrupted snow to bounce off of, and she had no idea where her sunglasses were. By the time she reached Baez Ford-Chrysler-Toyota, the service garage was a sight for literally sore eyes.

The walk into the building required negotiation between the opposing opinions of her body parts. Her face demanded her feet run to get out of the cold, and her butt insisted doing so on ice was ill-advised, Doc Martens or not.

A man her father's age put his cigarette in his mouth before pulling the door open with one hand and tipping his cap to her with the other. She thanked him and entered the building.

Even while cold, the garage was a living thing with a pulse of metal banging metal. Country music radio played in the background, interrupted frequently by bursts of profanity, off-color jokes, and the ear splitting pops of pneumatic wrenches.

Minding the safety markings on the floor, she strolled through the garage while scanning the maintenance bays looking for a mop of messy black hair streaked with red. She found Neil elbow deep in the wheel well of a Nissan Sentra. He'd pushed his curly locks back with a rolled bandana, which exposed half of his pale, acne-scarred face to her as she approached.

"What are you doing to that innocent car?"

He froze at the sound of her voice. A smile pulled his lips. "Thyroidectomy," he replied with a rasping, and utterly butchered, Southern drawl.

As she chuckled at his joke, he pivoted away from her to cough into his elbow and resumed working his wrench. The top of his overalls was unbuttoned; the sleeves were tied around his waist, leaving a thin layer of cotton knit as his last defense against the cold.

The garage could safely store meat according to the thermometer on the wall. They had heaters running twenty-four/seven, but with the sub-zero temperatures outside the corrugated metal building and twenty foot ceilings inside, refrigerator cold seemed a decent outcome. It boggled her brain to see him work in a t-shirt.

But work, he did. Each move of his ironically tattooed forearm was accompanied by the clickity-clack of a torque wrench. The exquisite cursive black script read: Leviticus 19:28.

Ye shall not make any cuttings in your flesh for the dead, nor print any marks on you. I am the LORD.

Neil in a nutshell.

"Alternator's dead." His natural voice, clear and precisely enunciated, popped her out of her headspace.

"Don't those usually come out of the top?" Her father had replaced more than one with the tools in their garage at home.

"In this lovely piece of—" The pop of a pneumatic wrench drowned him out. When country music radio once again reclaimed the garage, Neil continued as if he hadn't been interrupted. "They decided the *armpit* would be a better place." He groaned while straining with a bolt deep inside the wheel well. "They...be...*wrong*."

A moment later, he slammed his hand on the car body, dropped the ratchet wrench, and blurted a curse. Shoving the injured knuckle into his mouth, he turned away from her and stomped his work boot on the concrete.

Marie put her father's lunch on Neil's rolling toolbox and ripped a sheet from the paper towel roll. He sucked his finger as he pulled it out and then shook his hand. "Geez, that's smarts."

She grabbed his hand and grimaced at the peeled skin. It made sense to clean the wound before wrapping. After a quick scan of his toolbox supplies, she grabbed the bottle of glass cleaner and sprayed his bleeding wound. Neil hissed.

She cringed for having caused him more pain. "Sorry!" She wrapped the paper towel around his finger.

Neil wasn't, in fact, her brother. Immediately after moving to Coulter, her father had brought her along to look at a dually pick-up truck. While a price was negotiated, she played London Bridge with the seller's sons, Neil, and his three-year-old brother, Josh. Neil introduced her to Sarah, Jason, and Sam at church, making him her oldest friend by three days. Since then, he'd played the role of older brother, protecting her from other kids and teasing her relentlessly.

Of everyone in Coulter, excepting the one who should have left weeks ago, Neil was the friend she missed most.

"So, what brings you here today?" Neil's breath hitched as she pressed into the wound too hard. "Or did you anticipate needing to play nurse?"

"Papa forgot his lunch." She dipped her head at the dish. His face scrunched in disbelief. "I know, right? It got me here to see you, though, so I didn't ask questions."

"You look good, M." Neil's cognac eyes smoldered as his smile grew wider.

"Did you expect anything less?"

"I was worried about you."

"Sorry." She placed her hand over the loose end of the ridiculously huge wad of paper on his finger and surveyed the room. "Who else knows about…?"

"Why you left?"

She nodded.

"Everyone here thinks you were hanging with your cousins for the holidays, but…your mom told the bishop, who grilled Jason, who vented to Sarah. She told me. And I…"

"Told Ash?"

His cheeks took on a surprising shade of red. "I shouldn't have but—"

"It's okay."

News traveled fast in Coulter. And Ash deserved an explanation for why Marie wouldn't be around to say good-bye. She just hadn't anticipated her sticking around for one.

"If you didn't know…Sam's home."

Her breath caught in her lungs, and her heart thumped harder, faster. She knew he'd be home soon, but already? She picked up her father's lunch. "This is getting cold. I should go."

Neil winked at her. "Stay strong, *manita*."

She smiled at the nickname he'd given her years ago. *Little sister.* But as she turned away from Neil, her thoughts did as well, refocusing on Sam as she approached the doors that lead into the service center's business office.

Two days after Christmas, 1993, Elder Samuel J. Rigby, Jr., then nineteen-years-old, boarded a long flight to São Paulo, Brazil, via the Missionary Training Center in Provo, Utah. Two years and ten days later, the Lord had delivered him safely back home to his family. And to her.

Marie's heart beat hard against her ribs and reverberated in her neck and temples. She expected him home soon, of course. His proposal combined with her father's blessing to go back to work made for the best morning she'd had in months. Her life was starting to make sense again. But Neil's news that Sam had already returned home shocked her. She had been ready before he said it, but now she doubted.

She forced a smile for the finance manager who greeted her with a hug. As she walked through a waiting room, she fist-bumped a chipper salesman as they passed each other. Half-a-dozen of the dealership's staff welcomed her home. True to Neil's word, none of them looked at her as if they knew why she left. It calmed her some.

Until she saw a man in a black suit.

He sat with his back to her on the other side of the glass wall that separated her father's office from the showroom floor. She didn't need to see his face. She'd stood behind him at the ladder of a diving board for years; she'd recognize the port wine stain behind the right ear of her father's guest anywhere.

Sam.

Neil said he was home. He didn't say he was in the building.

Why hadn't her parents told her? The Rigbys had her parents' phone number on speed dial. There was no way Regina didn't call the moment she knew her son was coming home. Yet, there the man was, and her parents didn't say a word! Not one!

Her heart beat maintained its crazy race to nowhere as she stared at the back of his head, this time with the knowledge he'd been waiting for her to respond to a letter since October. She was positive he was going to want to talk about it.

I'm not ready.

She looked down at the bowl in her hands. Drops of condensation dangled from the plastic wrap, distorting her view of the now-lukewarm meal. She'd come to town to get her job back. Her mother asked her to go to the dealership first.

To bring her father his lunch.

Which her mother *forgot* to give him.

For the first time in *nineteen* years.

Oh, she smelled a set-up. A pork and Anaheim chili ambush.

Marie looked around for someone to pass the meal off to, and as her gaze crossed the glass windows of her father's office, she found both men on their feet and facing her. Sam's arm was mid-reach for the door. There was no backing out now.

She forced another smile as the door opened. "Hi, Sam."

Her father took his lunch at the door with a kiss on the cheek and backed away. Her head barely met Sam's chin, and when his arms wrapped around her, they warmed her shoulders. A light and familiar cologne wafted past her nose. The scent took her back years to diving practices and rowdy road trips. As she became comfortable with him there, she remembered missionaries had rules and stiffened.

Sam let her go. She took a step back to put distance between them because he wasn't supposed to touch her.

"You okay?"

"I—uh…I don't want to get you in trouble."

Until the Stake President released him from his mission calling, the only thing Sam was allowed to do by himself was use the restroom. Glancing around, she looked for who he'd left home with. His mother. A brother or sister. A friend of theirs from church. There was no one around but her and her father.

"I was released on Sunday." He pushed his hands into his pockets and rocked on his heels. "Got no strings on me."

As the words settled, they explained her father's unexpected arrival in Phoenix on Tuesday. She wasn't the only person who saw Sam as the right guy at the right time and knowing that stifled her ability to draw breath.

Marriage had always been in the future for her. Ready or not, the future was now.

Her father pulled back the plastic wrap on his bowl and the savory aroma of *chile verde* filled the office. "There's a staff meeting at 7:45 am. It is mandatory. And I'd like you to learn everything there is to know about *that* truck before your shift tomorrow." He gestured at the black Tacoma on the other side of the glass.

"Yes, sir," Sam said. "Thank you for the opportunity."

Her father shooed them out the door and left his office with the bowl.

When he was out of sight, Sam pulled her into another hug. Unlike the first, he didn't let this one go after a moment. He wrapped both arms over her shoulders, almost around her neck. His nose and lips nuzzled her hair, completing more of a trap than an embrace.

"Hello to you, too." She spoke brightly despite her trepidation. She placed her hands on his ribs and pushed a little, hoping he'd let go.

"Why?" One of his hands cupped the back of her head. Nerves connected to a few hair follicles protested. Shivers rumbled down her spine. He held her tighter. "What did he say to you?"

Ugh. Here we go. "He who?"

Sam withdrew his arms and took hold of her shoulders. "Your dad said you had talked to Jason that day…you know, when you uh…"

Marie stiffened again, shifted her gaze away, and mentally filled in the blank. *Put an unloaded gun to my head.*

"He either didn't know what you two talked about or wouldn't tell me."

She crossed her arms between them. "He said too much as it was."

Finally, Sam let her go. He took one step backward. Only one, but she silently thanked her Heavenly Father for the small mercy.

She turned and fled.

Wrong direction, of course. The showroom's exits, strategically placed for the comfort and safety of customers, were not convenient to the employee parking lot. She stopped after only a few steps.

"Please," Sam said. A hand took hold of her arm. "Marie."

She considered the -20°F air outside and decided she wasn't annoyed enough to walk around the building to where her car was parked. As Sam tugged on her arm, she allowed him to turn her around. She kept her gaze purposely low and answered his question.

"Jay said nothing wrong."

"Why do you defend him?" Sam guided her chin upward. She closed her eyes. "After all he's done?"

"Because what I did is one hundred percent on me."

When she opened her eyes again, Sam lips were pulled tight and flat. His dismissal angered her. There wasn't a cell in her body still in love with Jason Swing the day she picked up her father's gun. She may as well have been talking to the mailman.

She was perfectly capable of falling down all by herself. Getting up, too.

Sam, of all people, should know.

I'm being unfair again. She relented. "We talked about Carmina. That's all."

"Who's Carmina?"

She met his scowl with utter disbelief. "His daughter."

"I didn't know her name."

Marie wouldn't have thought much of him forgetting if not for rubbing his face and groaning, but his reaction gave her a moment too long to consider the words he'd used. *Didn't know.* Sam was released the previous Sunday, at church, no doubt. The girl he dated for *years* was in the same building as him with a newborn baby, along with at least a dozen or so of his own extended relatives. How could he not know?

He dropped his hands to his hips. His gaze was leveled over her shoulder, toward but not at a column of plaques the community had awarded the dealership.

Painful subject, she supposed. She hadn't wanted to talk about Jason's sudden courthouse wedding when it happened almost a year ago.

"Good. That's good. Sarah always wanted a little girl."

Of course, she would be the one to get what she wanted out of all this.

Again, Marie mentally slapped herself for her thoughts. She'd put in a lot of effort into leaving her anger at Sarah and Jason behind. No one was dragging her back into it.

"I'm over them, Sam. *Over.* Like, it doesn't even hurt anymore. So, if you must talk to them, please…I'm begging…please don't mention me."

Sam's lips pulled tight with annoyance, but nodded as he opened the passenger door of the showroom's brand-new Tacoma. "I won't."

With his promise made, she felt lighter. She climbed into the truck, ready for the subject to change. Sam stepped closer. He rested one arm on the door and the other on the truck's frame.

"So…" Sam's smile became cartoonish. "You're single now?"

"Get behind the wheel and do your job," she ordered. Her shove on his chest drew a hearty laugh.

Sam shut her door before sauntering around to the other side of the truck. He kept eye contact with her through the windshield the whole way, pinning her to her seat with intensity. By the time he climbed into the driver's seat, a desire to get out and leave the building had taken root bone deep within her.

"I'm sorry. I know you've been waiting months for an answer to your letter." She hoped by broaching the subject, they could get the conversation—and the awkwardness—out of the way.

"Actually, I haven't." Sam fiddled with the adjustment lever under the truck's steering column. "Well, I *have*, but Mom told me in October not to expect one soon. Said you were out of town and your parents were holding your mail until you got back."

His words almost relieved her. "Our parents talked. Mine must of had told yours about a letter from you."

"I assume so." Sam shrugged. "How else would they know?"

"Did your parents tell mine what's in the letter?" She couldn't imagine they had. Her mother would have said something, *but*....

"Shouldn't have." Sam slipped his hand under hers. "I specifically asked them not to say anything unless you did."

Wow. He managed his parents better from the Southern Hemisphere than she did hers while in the same house.

"About your question," she said. His palm was warm, almost moist. The urge to wash her hands chipped away at her confidence. "It makes sense, you and me, but—"

He let her hand go and grasped the steering wheel. His lips pursed with irritation. She discretely tucked the hand he'd released under her thigh.

"I've accepted that Jay will never be my husband, but welcoming another man in his place..."

He huffed and shook his head. "Another man."

Marie steeled herself. "This is important, Sam. I need you to *listen*."

In an instant, his rigid body deflated, transforming an aggravated man into a remorseful version of the boy she remembered. "I'm being a jerk. I know, and I'm sorry. I've just been hoping I might mean more to you after thirteen years."

"You do, but there's—" She grasped for the appropriate words. "I've never thought about...being *with*...you."

He half-nodded slowly before turning to face her again. "After all the time we've spent half-naked on pool decks?"

She didn't blame him for sounding surprised. A lot of girls from high school would ask her what's wrong with her. Maybe even out loud. Maybe they were right to, because Sam was the cutest guy ever—and right now, he was sun kissed in the middle of winter—but, no. Making out with him felt as wrong to her now as it always had.

"Until I read the letter…" She shrugged and shook her head. Sam shifted his attention from her to a tiny lever on the door. The mirror outside her window moved.

As a teenage girl, sex had occurred to her about once a year, when her bishop had asked her if she'd ever touched herself, or anyone else, in inappropriate places. And hadn't *that* been a lovely talk to have one-on-one with her boyfriend's father? She hated worthiness interviews, but it was the bishop's duty to ask and hers to answer. He had confessed he didn't like the questions any more than she did, so she had done her best not to squirm too much.

Outside of the bishop's office, Marie had only ever thought about sex in the abstract, as a part of her life with a future husband. Boys didn't tempt her. Not even Jason, whom she *adored* and hoped to marry. She never daydreamed about classmates or actors or rock stars. She couldn't say for sure she'd ever been aroused.

The bishop's questions were mortifying by virtue of existing at all, but unlike other kids in the ward, having the right answer for him had required no real effort on her part. Now, as she consciously considered having children with a man who'd been crushed on by all the girls on her diving team, her indifference to sex became revulsion.

What's wrong with me?

She hoped the shrug she gave him was good enough to appear unbothered. "And to be honest—"

"Always."

"You, Neil, Jay…you're like brothers to me."

"You got past it with Jay."

"He and I never—" Marie caught herself. She had enough to worry about in the present and the past was none of his business. "My relationship with you has always been very casual."

"Do you trust our prophets?"

He questioned her faith? "Of course, I do."

"President Kimball called the idea of 'soulmates' a fantasy. He said that any man and any woman can find happiness in marriage if they're both willing to make it work. And I know this is true. My parents built their family on respect and trust. Love came later. I've watched it grow between them every day of my life."

Her own parents were once crazy in love. She hesitated to call their marriage cold, now, because there was love there. But, her mother liked her "me" time, and her father was happiest when visiting Tia Sarita and Uncle Carl and the girls. Marie didn't doubt President Kimball was right, but she worried all the same. What price would she and Sam have to pay to find happiness together?

"You are so much like your dad, Sam, but I am nothing like your mom."

He grinned and shook his head at her, as if her concerns were preciously small.

"Marry me, Marie." He reached across the cab and tickled the inside of her wrist to coax her hand out from where she'd hidden it. Her teeth ground together as a shudder flashed through her. She prayed for the strength to hold steady. He lifted her hand and pressed his lips softly to her fingers. "We'll make a life together we wouldn't trade for anything. I promise."

She'd waited her entire life for a worthy man to ask her to be his wife. Her decision was made already. Yes, was on her tongue. The fear in her made no sense. Every moment the question hung in the cab between them, her cheeks burned hotter and her stomach grew angrier.

This is the right choice.

"I..." It's what her Heavenly Father wanted her to do. She was sure. If He didn't, the Adversary would not be working so hard to convince her to run. "I believe you, Sam, but I just got home. And so did you. I need..."

"The spring temple trip is what...four, five months away?"

The nearest temple was on the other side of the Rocky Mountains, so the ward planned its trips to perform by-proxy ordinances in May to avoid road closures. Sealings were also scheduled during these trips for convenience sake.

She answered his question with a nod.

"I'm happy to give you time, Marie."

She didn't realize how heavy the weight on her chest had become until he released it. "Thank you, Sam."

"I won't wait forever."

· ❄ ·

Marie and Sam agreed to meet up that afternoon at the high school swim practice, and she left the dealership to continue her primary mission. Minutes later, she entered Valkyrie's front door to the jingle of sleigh bells. A familiar female voice called out a welcome as she rubbed the snow and the salt from her boots onto the doormat. Lana raised her head above a display rack near the cash register. Her whole face lit up like the sky on the Fourth of July and she erupted into a squeal.

"Holy crap, Marie Baez. Back from the freakin' desert."

Lana was Cowgirl Barbie, county queen of barrel racing. Might have gone pro if she hadn't broken her back in college. Due to her injury, Lana walked with a slow, stiff gate. A hard brace lay under the woman's uniform shirt to support her torso. Beneath it was scarred skin, and deeper, a spine held together with screws. She was lucky to be alive, let alone walking.

"How's the cold treating you?" Marie asked.

She groaned mightily. "Doing its darndest to break me."

"I doubt there's a power on Earth that could." She knew Lana to be half-grit, half-bubbles, and a hundred percent unsinkable.

The woman's hug relaxed and Marie backed away.

"Ash is on break," Lana said. Ash opened the copy shop and closed the coffee shop. Two salaries to get her to California quicker. "That dumbass Neil is here on his lunch break, too. I can go get them if you—"

"Thanks." She smiled and held up her hand. "I'm here to talk to Sig."

Lana straightened as well as one in her condition could. "I've got stocking to do." She gave her another hug. "It's so good to see you."

"You, too." Marie really did miss seeing her. Being back in the building, with the smells of toner and ozone, she wondered how she could have let her parents bully her into ever leaving.

Lana returned to the spindle of greeting cards next to the cash register. Marie made her way toward the office. She let her hand trail across the copy machines and gazed longingly at the bank of PowerMac and Windows desktops and printers made available to customers. She found the place mildly intimidating, even, like now, when it was empty.

As she neared Signy's open office door, the Norse Goddess got up from her desk and greeted her with arms open. Marie accepted the embrace and breathed in the soft leather and iris notes of a Chanel variety she couldn't name. It wasn't No. 5. Signy was never so obvious.

"How are you, honey?"

"Better."

Signy hummed, and to Marie's ears, it sounded doubtful, but the woman said nothing more.

Signy wasn't alone. Jeannie Praetor sat in a chair deeper in the room, one denim-clad leg crossed over the other. The soles of her boots were dry and fairly clean. She'd been here for a while.

"I can come back later," Marie said. "I don't want to intrude."

If she was going to crash a conversation, she'd rather talk to Neil and Ash. Jeannie was Neil's stepmother. He called her "The Shrink" as an insult. Marie didn't like her on his behalf.

"Nonsense," Signy said as she put her hand on Marie's lower back and guided toward the couch. As Marie sat down, Jeannie turned in her chair. She picked up a short glass and rolled her wrist a bit to swirl the golden-brown liquid within.

Drinking at one in the afternoon! No wonder Neil's mother kept her boys away from their dad until she legally couldn't.

Signy plopped sideways on the couch, leaving a cushion between them. Then she drew her legs in close. Marie cringed inside at the woman's footwear on the upholstery but held back her urge to scold. Shifting her gaze toward Jeannie, she saw compassion in the woman's face, and felt a little guilty for judging her.

Neil's mother got full custody of her sons after the divorce, no surprise given the circumstances, but she kept them away from their dad out of spite. Home-wrecker or not, Jeannie couldn't be blamed for another woman's spitefulness. Neil had spent years since turning eighteen rebuilding his relationship with his dad. He'd even made peace with Jeannie so he could ask for her advice without feeling her rendering it would obligate growth between them personally.

And it was no more Marie's place to judge her drinking habits as it was to tell Signy to get her feet off her own couch, however much she wanted to.

With her arm propped casually on the back of the sofa, Signy rested her head on her fist. "Now, don't get me wrong, but your dad was the last person I expected a call from this morning. I just gotta know how that came about."

Papa called her? "Why did he call?"

"Shop hours. He said you wanted to talk to me. Didn't want you driving in if you didn't have to."

More like he wanted to know whether to "forget" his lunch or not.

"Well..." Marie took a breath and exhaled heavily. "Yesterday started well. I got up, watched the sunrise, read my mail, and went to sink into a bubble bath but my Morphine disc was gone, along with the rest of my CDs. They're renovating. My stuff is packed and Papa's stuff is *everywhere*, so I went downstairs to ask Mama where my CDs were. She threw them out."

"How many discs?"

It was Jeannie who asked.

"Like, three *hundred*."

Signy's eyes widened.

"And not just CDs. Books. Posters. Photos...."

"That bitch!"

Marie grimaced at Signy's outburst.

"Sig." Once Jeannie had Signy's attention, she shook her head. "Language. It's her mother."

A wordless conversation took place between the two woman, and it became obvious Jeanie hadn't come for a visit.

Marie flicked her hand lightly at the arm supporting Signy's head. "You called her to talk to me?"

"I'm not giving you razor blades until I know you're okay. That's her area of expertise, not mine."

Right. How many more things was the stupid gun going to make more complicated than—

"Wait. Give me razor blades? I haven't even asked for my job back yet."

Signy's eyebrow arched. "It *is* why you're here, right?"

"Yes, but—"

"You're the best stripper I've ever known. *Of course*, I want you back." Signy shifted on the couch and crossed her arms. "What's changed at Casa Baez?"

"Papa didn't know about the CDs. He felt bad. Call this an apology."

"A decent one." Jeannie swirled the bit of liquor that remained in her glass. "Have to give him that."

"I won't play his games, M." Signy held Marie's gaze firm. "I won't hire you only to have you back in here a week under family pressure to quit again. The Strip Club deserves better."

I won't hire you. She pressed her lips together and steeled herself. "I understand."

"If you did, you wouldn't be upset about it," Jeannie quipped.

Marie scowled, but Jeannie had tipped her head back to drain her glass and didn't see it.

"You will leave my employ when *you* are ready to." Signy paused and grinned. "Or I get tired of your shit. What are your plans? And how will they affect your working here?"

"I'm getting married." Marie's smile stiffened as Signy's eyebrow raised. "Maybe. I haven't said yes."

Signy frowned. "You're not giving me a lot of confidence in your decision making."

"He's an old friend. I just didn't know he was back in town until an hour ago."

"Ah." Jeannie's tone was dry. "Sam Rigby."

"Is he that obvious a choice?" Marie had thought it herself. Her parents set her up with him. Now a once-professional psychologist tossed his name out on a bare hint.

"No…" Signy drew the word out. "I'd say a conspicuous one."

"The difference is...?"

"Obvious implies *right*. My jury's out."

"You don't like him?" Everyone liked Sam. Except Neil. Something happened on prom night senior year and the two stopped talking. Marie still didn't know why. But everyone else loved the guy.

"I never got the impression *you* liked him. Not like *that*."

"I don't." She'd considered his proposal because he checked all the right boxes. Knowing him most of her life was a bonus. "But, we have shared interests and values and he can give me the life I've always wanted. He's the right man at the right time."

Jeannie uncrossed her legs and sat forward in her chair. "If he's truly the right man, time doesn't matter. Why not date him for a while? See what happens?"

A reasonable suggestion. And she would like nothing more than getting to a place where it felt like he never left, *but...* "I'm twenty-one. I've already wasted years."

"Correction..." Jeannie punctuated her rebuttal with a lazy finger point. "You're *only* twenty-one."

Signy touched Marie's leg, getting her attention back. "Eternity is a *long* time to be with someone you don't like."

Her Heavenly Father had eternity in His hands. It was the *present* she was concerned with. Her life-long goals were in reach *now*. If she managed to lose the opportunity He'd given her, would He ever open another window?

"I do like him, Sig. We've been friends for twelve years."

"You were *in love* with a very different kind of boy for six of those years."

Signy was close to her nephew, Jason, a connection Marie credited with getting her a job in Valkyrie's Strip Club in the first place. She was right. The differences between Jason and Sam were stark.

"What about Ash?" Jeannie's gaze burned and froze Marie at the same time.

Ash had problems in need of a trained ear; Jeannie Praetor was a doctor with a revoked medical license. They filled each other's needs, one talking and the other listening. Marie had never wondered what they talked about, until the mention of Ash hinted they might have been talking about her.

She swallowed hard. "What about her?"

"Nothing, I suppose." Jeannie sighed heavily, as if disappointed.

"I've been where you are. Young. Single. Under pressure to marry and have children." Signy had rolled her Young Women's lessons into a ball and squashed them under her boot long ago. "I just want you to know you can come to me… if you're working here or not. If things ever get ugly—"

"I know." She appreciated the offer, but she'd never need it. Sam would never hurt her. That much she was certain of.

Signy pinned her to the couch with a stare. "Can I trust you with sharp objects?"

"I promise." She drew an X over her heart. "I swear I'm okay."

Signy looked over her shoulder at Jeannie Praetor.

"I wouldn't go that far, but…" Jeannie sat back in the lounge chair again. "She's telling the truth. As she knows it."

"Come in tomorrow." Signy stood up from the couch. "Mitchell could use your help."

Marie was an employee of Valkyrie Press and Copy again. She hugged her boss. "Thank you, Sig."

· ❄ ·

Coaching the high school divers should have been the perfect activity to reconnect with Sam, to get back to the comfortable place they'd occupied before he left. Getting away from her mother and the herd of white elephants at home had been a plus.

Playing *Twister* had not been part of her plans for the day and neither had Sam's insistence to play after she said no. She gave in on the assumption two years in Brazil would affect his skill, but his muscle memory kicked in. In minutes, he was back in his groove.

Was his smile always so grotesque?

When sophmore Josh Praetor called out dive number 407—an Inward dive with three and a half somersaults—the diving coach vetoed it on the spot. Sam seconded with an offer to skip it. They both knew she was afraid of it.

"After you." She punctuated her overrule with a gesture toward the ladder.

Sam had bullied her into this game; she desperately wanted to punish him and didn't care how much it cost.

He rolled the flip as tight as he could but he didn't jump high enough and landed hard. His gasps for breath joined the ghosts in air, tormenting her with memories of sharp pain and past failures.

I should have taken the out.

It was too late now.

I can do this.

The dive was not impossible. Her size gave her an advantage over him. She could roll the somersaults tighter. She'd never completed it with grace, but the one time she *needed* to succeed, four years ago, she hit the water like a 100-pound Sunday roast dropped onto concrete.

Breathe.

Marie drew the heavy, chlorinated air into her chest. She willed her hands to release their death grip of the high dive's ladder and climbed the rungs. The pumice texture of the board bit into the soles of her feet, step after lingering step, as she walked the plank.

Below her, the water shimmered like a sheet of living glass. Rosettes of fresh water rippled at intervals across the length of the pool. The movement sent waves of water toward the deck's gutters. The overflow swallowed by the filtration system reached her ears as a soft gurgle.

The steady stream of water falling into the drains and the vacuum of air into the dehumidification system combined into a soft *hush*. The topaz sheen of the water, the concrete floors, the glossy white masonry walls, and the glass windows high on the wall to her left...every surface amplified the sounds of the room into a dull roar.

The pool had always been a safe place for her. A second home. As fond memories swirled around her on the air with the echoes, the room transformed into a house of ghosts.

She blinked. The walls disappeared, and she stood under a cloudless summer sky on a diving board a thousand miles away. A second blink brought her back to Coulter.

Stretching out her arms for balance, she turned and faced the west wall of the pool. She ground her toes into the edge of the board, left foot first. She exhaled the air growing stale in her lungs, dropped her arms, and waited for the board to still.

Fall down seven times, get up eight.

The words, painted in blood red, taunted her from the wall behind the diving board.

She sucked in the thick air again. She lowered her heels below the board and stood up on her toes. The shift of her weight down and up again built the momentum to toss her upward.

Fall down seven times, get up eight.

Her body recalled her last fall. The open air on her wet skin. Her paralyzed lungs. The pain.

Get up.

Behind her on the pool deck, the swim coach ordered his boys into the pool and barked instructions for a 100-yard set. Five, four, three, two… The shrill sound of the coach's whistle jarred her.

"Marie."

She whipped her attention to the spectator deck. Neil had come to watch his brother dive. Ash sat beside him. Leaning forward with her arms resting on her knees, Ash nodded once.

A vote of confidence.

She refocused her attention on the dive.

Get up.

The coach blew his whistle again. She breathed in, wiggled her fingers, and breathed out. Two more shrill blasts followed as she stood upon the wavering board, tears blurring her vision.

Get up. Get up, get up, get up.

After the fifth whistle, she blinked tears. She took a step back and fell from the board. The cool water wrapped around her as she sunk through the depths to the tiled floor. She could hold her breath longer than most, but not forever, so she kicked off the floor and swam for the shallow end.

At the opposite wall, two of the swimmers took her hands and pulled her out of the water. Sam called her name across the pool. No, she was done playing today. She ducked into the women's dressing room where she turned a shower as hot as it would go before going into the changing area to get her shampoo.

She caught movement in the mirror as she passed and stopped. The girl in the glass stared back at her with glistening but splotchy skin and blood shot eyes, chest heaving like she'd run for miles. She pulled the elastic bands that held her hair back but still didn't recognize her reflection.

Where was the girl who laughed at competition and dominated diving boards? When had she become so afraid?

She covered the face in the mirror with her hand. It wasn't her.

"Marie."

The voice squeezed her chest. "Go away, Ash." She cringed at her sorry reflection and hated knowing Ash saw the real thing.

"Not happening, M."

A hand settled on her shoulder. Soft warmth soaked into her wet skin. She obeyed its summons, abandoning the mirror. As Ash's arms closed around her, Marie tightened her embrace.

Ash's hand pushed into her wet hair and pressed Marie's head to her shoulder. "You're okay."

Her body disagreed with trembling. "No I'm not."

"You're cold." It was a kind lie. The room was hot enough to incubate eggs. "Let's get you into a shower."

· ❄ ·

Marie followed Ash out of the shower room a half-hour later. Her first breath of fresh air was cool, but its relief was short-lived. Wide-eyed and anxious, Sam pushed off a nearby wall and hurried toward her. The sight of him fueled her need to leave. She caught Ash's hand and pressed her car keys into it.

"Destination?"

"Anywhere but here." She shoved an exit door into the frozen dark outside.

Ash had espresso duty in an hour, so they drove to Blessed Beans. At the coffee shop, Marie chose a table in the farthest corner of the café and leaned her chair backward against the wall with front legs off the floor. She closed her eyes, let her feet swing, and made believe she was enjoying a summer evening on the porch swing watching the sun set over the Beartooth Mountains. No expectations. No betrayals.

It was a feeling more than a sound that disturbed her reverie. She opened her eyes as Ash placed a cappuccino mug of hot chocolate in front of her. She sat on the opposite side of the table with a cup of black coffee.

Marie pushed a swipe of whipped cream and chocolate shavings into her mouth. Ash's eyes darted away. She sipped her coffee while noticeably giving the room a lingering once-over. People had a habit of whittling down homosexuals to their sexuality, Marie had learned over the past two years. Although Ash treated most men with suspicion, her preference for the company of her few male friends in public made sense. It created less gossip to get around.

Two people had left since they arrived. Three new people stood by the register, staring up at the hand-chalked drink menu. No one took an interest in her and Ash at all.

A mercy.

A curse.

An urge to kiss Ash had been simmering since the shower room and the complex rhythms of the African tribal music playing now wasn't helping her behave at all.

"Hey, Dee!"

At her call, the barista on shift glanced away from the cash register.

"Can you put on The Offspring or something?"

Dee picked up the remote from the counter and tossed it to Ash. A few seconds later, skate punk replaced the abrupt silence between CDs. It helped, until Ash lip-synched "sitting on a bed and lying wide awake" and Marie's want for a kiss morphed into something less innocent.

Gotta get away from me.

It was good advice. It was also the last thing Marie wanted.

Ash abandoned the song at the second chorus repeat for a drink of coffee.

"Why does the dive scare you so much?"

"It's hard." She traced a line in the table's wood grain as if reading the tree's story by touch. "Really hard."

"I was a cheerleader in high school, M. Did I tell you that?"

Marie nodded.

"I've spent hundreds of hours spotting girls while they did dangerous shit, so when I watch you dive, I don't see some God-given gift. I see hard work. Failure. *Pain*." Ash pointed her finger over her shoulder, in the general direction of the swimming pool. "The shit you and Sam did on that board today, I've only ever seen that on TV. At the fucking *Olympics*. Why does that one dive scare you so much?"

"Los Angeles."

Ash looked at her blankly. Marie hadn't thought about it in years. Until Neil's brother called out the dive on the pool deck, she hadn't had a reason to. She supposed she believed Ash knew because everyone else did.

She had trouble remembering a life without Ash, now.

"I was invited to compete in the 1992 US Junior Nationals qualifier meet in Los Angeles."

Ash's eyebrows arched high. Marie had too when she got the letter.

"Huge honor. Total shock. My high school career must have impressed someone because Wyoming doesn't compete on that level. I put the hardest dives I know how to do on my entry card. The dives Sam and I fool around with."

"No guts, no glory?"

She nodded slowly. "Anyhow, before the meet started, Papa found out that none of the girls put dive 407 on their sheet. He wrote it in for me."

Ash's brow creased. "Did he ask you first?"

"It literally didn't matter. There were a few others on the list I'd never done in competition either."

The annoyance on her friend's face didn't go away. "What happened?"

Marie breathed in sharply as the memories returned. "I remember a slap in the face and a punch to my chest and a girl telling me to cough. I woke up on my back after a trainer blew air back into my lungs."

"You lost consciousness?"

She traced the lines in the wood grain. "For twenty-three seconds." A trainer's breath brought her back out of the dark, ruining green apple Jolly Ranchers in the process.

"Come with me to California."

Ash's request was a part of her now, pressed into her fingertips by wood grain the way music used to be carved into vinyl. The words were organic but hard. Rigid. Not like water on her skin or the air in her lungs or fire scorching her as she denied herself the touch she wanted.

She watched her own hand move across the table. Her fingers laced through Ash's without her consent. An apology formed on her tongue as her friend glared at her in shock.

"I wish." Her words were reckless although true.

A veil of determination dropped over Ash. "I'm serious, M. Come with me."

Break off the engagement she wasn't ready for? Leave Sam behind? The tempting invitation filled her chest with a soothing warmth not unlike the cocoa when it was fresh.

Marie timidly grazed her friend's jaw with her fingers, prompting a rapid check of the room. She waited until Ash's eyes met hers again and flattened her palm against her cheek. Ash's eyelashes floated to her cheeks like the wings of a fallen angel. Mildly crooked teeth raked across a bottom lip kept supple with Chapstick. Marie's curiosity demanded to know what flavor.

With her heart pounding in her neck and temples, she leaned in and pressed her lips to Ash's cheek before bolting to the restroom. She locked the door, yanked the faucet handle, and splashed ice cold water on her face.

It was official. Ten weeks of rehab were totally, utterly, completely wasted. She'd been alone with Ash for less than hour and she was losing control.

"I don't like girls." The ghostly whisper escaped her mouth almost too quietly for even her to hear above the running water. She repeated it louder. "I've *never* liked girls.

No. Her therapist in Phoenix had shaken her head in puzzlement and curiosity when Marie had made the comment there. *But...you don't exactly like boys either...do you?*

Crazy talk. She dated one for six years and she *really* liked him.

The therapist had pushed her to go deeper. *One. What was it about that one boy?*

She stood up straight and grabbed two paper towels from the dispenser on the wall. Sorting this out on her own had gotten her nowhere good. And she wasn't the only person with future plans to screw up. Ash delayed her move to California. Sam wanted to get married in four months. Her parents wanted grandchildren, sooner preferable to later.

"You're going to go out there and lay everything on the table." *Just as soon as you look like a woman and not a drowned rat.*

She ventured out of the restroom with hope Ash could give her perspective on her problem. Turning the corner to return to the café, she caught a flash of her father sitting in her chair. She ducked back into the hallway.

Did he see me?

If she stayed in the hallway, she might have to explain why she was hiding. If he didn't see her, he might send Ash to the restroom to check on her and she'd have to explain to her. She couldn't. Not in the time they'd have with her father waiting.

Maybe it's not him.

She peeked around the corner again. *Ugh.* Her eyes weren't playing tricks.

After a deep breath, she rounding the corner and feigned surprise. "Papa! What are you doing here?"

He and Ash both stood up. Marie took her father's hand as he reached for her and let him pull her in for a kiss on the cheek.

"Sam called and told me what happened at the pool. He was concerned about you driving home."

Her teeth ground together. She was a good driver. The insurance company gave her father discounts and everything. She didn't *like* driving when she was upset. It didn't mean she couldn't.

Ash stood nearby with her hands pushed deep into her jeans pockets. "My shift starts in a few minutes, so I'm going to go clock in."

She caught Ash's elbow as she stepped away. She held out her keys to her.

"No, I can't take your car, M."

"Yes, you can." When Ash didn't accept them, Marie placed them on the counter by the cash register. "I'll get them back tomorrow."

And then you and I are going to talk.

Wonderwall

The next morning, Marie entered Valkyrie Press and Copy through rear entrance. The space was dark, lit only by safety lighting. She flipped the light switches as she passed through and the shadows transformed into equipment. There was a trimmer with a heavy guillotine blade that could cut through several inches of paper in a single pass. There were paper folders, hole punchers, spine stitchers, staplers, and binders.

Beyond the finishing area, Valkyrie had three presses. The business Signy bought from one of her college instructors came with two offset duplicator presses. They could handle pages legal and smaller, so she didn't invest in copy machines immediately. Now, most jobs that size were handled in the print shop. The duplicators were reserved for small format jobs that required "full bleed," or ink running off the side of the page. Signy also used them to interview potential press operators and train new staff on her press room procedures.

Opposite the duplicators was the work horse of their shop, a single-color sheetfed offset Heidelberg. The graphic arts lab Marie studied in at the local college had the same model. Signy's was newer but they functioned exactly the same.

Past the presses, Marie walked between the machines that burned and washed printing plates and flipped the light switch. A large, unfamiliar object occupied space on the right edge of her peripheral vision.

She almost ignored it, but her curiosity compelled her check out the new thing in the shop. She regretted her choice immediately. While still wrapped in plastic, she could see the word AGFA on one of the panels and it sucked the air out of her chest.

Signy bought an imagesetter.

Marie knew Valkyrie would have to acquire one of these sooner or later to remain competitive, but she didn't expect it now—Wyoming was slow to adapt new technology—and she certainly didn't anticipate Signy leading the change. Valkyrie had always been committed to traditional process.

Now, she wondered why Signy would bother hiring her back when this machine could take work from a *client* and print it directly to film with much of the work Marie did already complete.

It was too much to think about just then. She pushed her hands through the hanging, clear vinyl curtains that separated the plate area from the Strip Club, where work was waiting for her.

It was too quiet. She needed music.

In addition to three light tables, the Strip Club had a wall of cabinets that stored supplies and stereo. The speakers were positioned in this room and the dark room on the other side of the wall. Mitchell Barnes, her direct supervisor, kept several shoeboxes of CDs, labeled by genre. She walked her fingers across the spines of CDs in his *Metal* box, found the disk she wanted, and plucked it out. After opening the case by feel, she removed the disk and laid the case face down. The image of blindfolded Justice lying abused and broken on the ground had been burned into her brain for years but still she avoided seeing it.

She pressed play.

The guitar bloomed out of silence. High notes, straining toward shrill but held in check by distortion. The shallow melody they made gradually descended an octave as it grew louder. A hard rhythm took command. On most days, her brain submitted to *...And Justice for All's* marching orders. It put her in a productive groove she could maintain for hours, even in silence afterward. Today, though, too many concerns demanded her attention. She needed to clear her head first so she pressed the button to skip tracks.

Two, three, four.

She stepped away, sat on the nearest stool, and closed her eyes.

The haunting melody of *One* coaxed her brain out of chaos to tell her a story. A terrible testimony of a soldier trapped between living and dying, praying for death. And by the time the song ended, her thoughts were purged of anything not a guitar or a drum, free to be redirected.

Ash. Soon as she got to work, Marie would get talking to her out of the way. Afterwards, she had a pile of manila envelopes about six inches high she had to work and get back to Mitchell. The five jobs on the top of the pile had a sticky notes with "Pronto" scrawled on it.

She opened the first of the envelopes and pulled out a piece of film with columns of type on it. Also in the envelope, the laser printed original. It would be easier and faster to shoot another piece of film. But, it was one hairline scratch and repairing it would easily kill half-an-hour.

She flicked on her light table and laid the film emulsion-side up. While James Hetfield sang about short straws, she gathered supplies and a cup of water, and sat down to paint out the scratch. The process was not unlike watercolor. A drop of water onto a pigment, but this paint snuffed out light. The task was precise. Delicate. And when filling in the edge of type, she dared not even breathe.

Metallica played behind her. Jingling bells, soft and distant, came from the copy shop. Ash usually stopped at the coffee shop for a cup of coffee so she entered Valkyrie through the front door instead of the back. Marie glanced at the time clock. Another reason she chose to repair the film rather than reshoot was time. If she was in the dark room when Ash clocked in, they might miss each other. Instead, she got to see her friend walk in.

"M!" Ash pulled her card from the rack on the wall and punched in her time. "What are you doing here?"

Marie leaned into her work and blotted out the tiny stars in the black emulsion. "Working."

"Let me rephrase." Ash folded her arms on the steel border of the light table and rested her chin on them. "What possessed you to leave your warm bed at the ass-crack of dawn to perform manual labor at a job you quit three months ago?"

Ash's mop of honey blonde curls was unruly on most days, but today, she might have used her fingers to brush it and gave up when she couldn't untangle it. The room was dim, which helped Marie see the light shining through the film better, but also cast a shadow around Ash. The fluorescent bulb in her table had a slight pink cast and it radiated onto Ash's pale skin in the loveliest way. No freckles. No acne. Rosy pink lips with a satin sheen. Shadows under her eyes. Did Ash have a restless night?

Her eyes were clear though, and they glowed like the sun through amber glass. Ash had the discipline of a machine, and beneath the surface, she was working for her day in the sun.

Should be *today*. Should have been *weeks* ago. But Ash stayed. *For me.*

"My dad had an early staff meeting at the dealership. And you have my car, so it was come in when he did or not at all."

Ash dug into the pocket of her jeans and pulled out Marie's keys. She placed them on the glass next to a dispenser of red tape and leaned with her hands on the corners of the table.

The silence between them gave Marie an opening.

She stood up straight, hooked her foot around the stool behind her, and pulled it closer. Ash blew air into her bangs. The focused exhale moved her stray lock aside and upset the butterflies sleeping in Marie's chest.

Would Ash be happy if she knew? Would she be flattered? Freaked out?

The words Marie planned to say waited impatiently on her tongue. Things would change the moment she said them. Her stomach was angry at her for even thinking about it.

"So...your parents changed their mind? You're back?" Ash asked.

"Not *exactly*." Her father was indulging her and her mother wasn't speaking to him because of it. "I mean, yes. I'm back, at least until Signy gets tired of me and my complications."

Ash pulled her arms in, caressing the table in the process. She touched her fingertips, both hands, to her lips and barely pulled them away. A floated kiss rather than blown. "Welcome back."

She left to open the Valkyrie copy shop, each step taking Marie's opportunity to get her feelings off her chest with her. Marie rounded the light table.

"Ash, wait!"

She stopped and looked back at Marie with raised eyebrows. "Yes?"

"Last night." Marie fidgeted with her fingers. "You helped. You always do, and I feel like I never tell you enough."

Of all the things she wanted to say, the words tumbling off her tongue weren't even on the list.

"And I'm sorry. About the thing at the pool. I know you don't like to be hugged, and I was soaking wet, and—"

"It's okay."

No, it's not! How was anything she had done…*in months*…okay? For either of them.

Ash drew an "X" over her left breast. *Cross my heart.* Marie raised an eyebrow, still not believing her. Ash closed the distance between them and hugged her.

I need to tell you…

While pulling away, Ash's hands brushed her shoulders and held Marie's upper arms. Did Ash struggle with the same urges she had? To run. Hold on. Get closer. Push away. As the pause stretched out, with their gazes locked, warmth spread through Marie's flesh like she had stepped out of a shadow into sunlight. It lurked under her skin, while her pulse thumped in her veins.

I could just show her.

Marie bit her bottom lip and shut her eyes tight against the temptation to close the distance remaining between them. Bowing her head, in defeat, she prayed for strength while her nerves twitched every moment she continued to deny herself.

Cold seeped through her sweater as Ash's hands left her arms. Warmth surged upon her cheeks as the touch resettled there. Soft lips pressed to her forehead. Coffee had never smelled better to Marie.

Would I like the taste of it?

No. Not once. Not ever.

"Is your coffee getting cold?" Where the words came from, she had no idea.

Ash's breath tickled her skin. "What makes you think I have coffee?"

Marie pulled away. "You usually stop across the street first thing."

Grinning, Ash pinched two loose curls falling loose from Marie's sloppy pony tail and pushed them behind her ears. "You know me well."

Ash backed away two steps, pivoted, and walked out of the room. Marie was alone again, with all the words she needed to say still paused on her tongue.

· ❄ ·

Marie pulled open Jade Garden's door and a fragrance of ginger, garlic, and soy washed over her. Her mind was too busy for food, but when Sam asked her to join him for lunch, she couldn't bring herself to say no. They'd gotten off to a rough start and sitting down to smooth things over should be done sooner than later.

Resisting Ash left her vulnerable to other temptations, and she sensed the subtle, yet awful harm the Adversary's sweetly whispered lies were causing her soul. Twice in two days, she had set her mind to confront a fear, and twice she'd bowed to it. And giving up was easier the second time.

If she could reconnect with Sam, find that comfortable place they had occupied before he left, she could break the disturbing trend.

Or, lunch could go sideways. *Again.*

Leaving herself an out was a habit born of an awkward silence after Jason confessed his affair with Sarah. Marie gave her credit card to the hostess and had her press the carbon copy charge slip. After adding gratuity, she passed through the curtains into the dimly-lit dining room.

Sam stood at the sight of her and pulled the back of a chair opposite him. She thanked him as she sat. The words she needed to say to him punched at the back of her teeth as they placed their drink and entrée orders with the waitress.

When they were alone as they could be during Saturday lunch rush, he leaned forward in his seat. "I'm sorry."

She raised her eyebrows, wondering which decision from yesterday he'd chosen to give further reflection.

"I shouldn't have called your dad, but…I was worried about you."

"I left the pool with a friend."

He held his palms toward her. "I know, but I don't know anything about her—"

"I do."

His eyes snapped open wide at her interruption.

"I have a father, Sam. I don't need another one."

His eyes relaxed, but then narrowed. "Taking care of you will be a responsibility I assume from him when we marry."

"*If* I say yes."

His tempered anger became bewilderment. Was he so certain she'd agree? Had he acted on his assumptions? Told family and friends? Made plans?

He smiled and laughed. "You've changed. You know that?"

Marie's world didn't reflect his observation. Of all the Mormon friends they had in common, she was the only woman still in Coulter who was unmarried and childless. He spent two years in Brazil. Other men from their ward were still out on their missions. Free of his mother's stern thumb, Neil *looked* much different. Everyone had changed but her.

While she puzzled through his comment, his expression changed again, this time from amusement to sadness.

"What's wrong?" she asked.

"Nothing."

The reply came too quickly, too sharply. A lie, she assumed, but who was it for? Her, or him?

"I was just. I had this idea in my head of what coming home would be like. It's not happening that way." He stared at his hands while folding his chopstick wrapper into a small triangle, the way he would the American flag. "I feel shut out."

His words hollowed her and filled her with bile. He thought he was coming home to a friend happy to see him and amiable to a marriage proposal. She was neither. And, looking back on the past two days, she had been adversarial.

She reached across the table and squeezed his hand. "The last few months have been difficult. It's not your fault. It's not fair. I shouldn't take it out on you. I'm sorry."

He smiled and nodded.

"Are you sure you want to work at the dealership?" She hoped a change in subject could lighten the conversation. "You get on my papa's bad side and he could make your life miserable."

"So, I won't get on his bad side."

She snickered. "Good luck with that. Do you *really* want to be a car salesman?"

"I'm not planning to be one forever, but...your dad was hiring. I needed a job. And how hard can selling a car to someone who wants one be?"

It was meant to be a joke, but it didn't amuse her at all. A friend she'd have been comfortable teasing for being cocky or lacking imagination—she wasn't sure yet which problem was his—but he wouldn't be just a friend if she said yes.

He reached across the table. His open hand was an invitation. She pushed aside the weirdness and her concerns over his seriousness. This was a *lunch date*, after all. She was here to talk. To connect. To consider the possibilities of a future with the man on the other side of the table.

She placed her hand in his. As she enjoyed the warmth of his touch, she gazed deeply into his eyes and daydreamed about the temple within which they'd be sealed together. Children. Scouting and Girl's Camp. Holidays at the Rigby Farm and family vacations.

"Are you okay to return to work?"

His words swept away everything light and lovely. She recoiled and pulled her hand away.

"I mean, I doubt your dad would let you if you weren't, but you did just get back from rehab."

It was a perfectly reasonable thing to ask. And, if he was going to commit to a future with her, it was his place. Still, the fact he did prickled every inch of her skin.

She shouldn't be so sensitive. *Try harder.* "It's good therapy, actually."

"How so?"

"It commands my full attention."

His tight lips suggested he wasn't convinced.

"I don't think about much else while I'm stripping."

If his eyes opened any wider, they might fall out of his head. "Stripping?"

She laughed a bit and plucked her paper placemat from the table. It was white with scalloped edges. The Chinese zodiac was printed in red, explanations in green. She flipped it around so the ink faced her date.

"To make this, someone started with black text and clip art. They arranged it onto a pasteboard and photographed it onto a sheet of film. Then, they took that film and cut two rubylith masks to isolate the elements they wanted in each color. Those masks were used to burn the art onto one aluminum plate and the text onto another. This placemat passed through a press three times, once for each color and once again for the die-cut to make the edges. It was one of eight, maybe sixteen copies cut from one larger sheet of paper."

She placed the placemat back on the table. "I create printing plates."

"Did you create *these* plates?"

His interest pleased her, and sharing her knowledge lightened her mood. "Two inks and a die-cut is too expensive for single use, unless your labor is cheap and you're running very large numbers. Like millions of copies. These came from China."

"I see. And how are your parents? I remember they didn't approve of your major at all."

The cold weights pressed on her shoulders. Sam showed her his palms again. "You don't have to answer that if you don't want to."

She was being unreasonable. It was a question. One they'd talk about freely if they were only friends. She was about to answer when the waitress arrived with two plates. The tendrils of steam rising from the food sparked a memory.

"Our last double-date was here." She pinched a cube of tofu with her chopsticks. "Remember? It was before you were set apart for your mission. We went back to Sarah's house and watched the *Princess Bride*."

"I remember dinner. Your dress matched Jason's shirt. Blue looks good on you. Which one is the *Princess Bride*?"

She raised her eyebrows. "The pirate. The princess. Andre the Giant."

He shook his head with a shrug. Sam remembered what color she was wearing but not the movie?

"It's your ex-girlfriend's favor—"

"I don't remember it!" There it was again. The anger. He dropped his fork. "I'm sorry."

"No, I'm sorry," Marie said, wishing she hadn't mentioned Sarah.

"Don't, M. It's not—I'm sorry I snapped. It's just—" He stabbed a nugget of chicken with his fork. "Sarah and I…we did a lot more kissing than watching."

Ah. His emotional baggage contained some dirty laundry. "Well, that settles it, Elder Rigby. I won't marry a man who can't navigate the Fire Swamp."

His frown twisted into a smirk. "So, that's how it is?"

"Girl's gotta have her standards."

"Will you watch it with me?"

She fought to reign in the grin but failed horribly. "I will *watch.* You come near me with those lips, and I'll bite you."

"That's what guys like to call incentive, Ms. Baez."

Her bottom jaw dropped in shock.

Sam laughed out loud. "Oh, bite this."

He shoved a bite of General Tso's chicken into her mouth.

She dropped her chopsticks and spit out the unexpected bite into her napkin. As he watched perplexed, she washed the taste out of her mouth with half of her lemon-lime soda.

"Marie?"

She put her glass down. "I'm a vegetarian."

"Really?" He scrutinized the squares of tofu nestled in her Buddha's Delight. "How long?"

"Almost a year. I wrote you about the piglet Josh Praetor raised for 4H. Even sent you a picture."

"I'm so sorry." His face squished inward. He shook his head with a groan. "I didn't think it would stick."

She resisted the urge to cut her losses and walk out of the restaurant. Instead, she pinched a square of tofu between her chopsticks but paused before eating. "Are you sure you want to marry a woman with weak convictions?"

"No—I mean, yes! I mean—" He groaned. "I didn't mean—"

"You know what's worse than a dead chicken, Sam?" He shrugged. "A *wasted* dead chicken. Eat."

Marie regretted agreeing to have lunch as she watched him half-heartedly pick through his meal with his fork. She'd been harsh. Unfair. It was her place to break the ice. The bruise on his hand was impossible to miss. It seemed an innocent enough subject.

"How'd you hurt your hand?"

Sam froze. Glistening brown sauce dripped from a piece of broccoli paused half-way between his plate and his mouth. The blood drained from his face and congealed into a clot in her chest. As he stared through her, she had the impression she was dining with a corpse until his cheeks bloomed deep red. Embarrassment giving way to shame.

"What have you done?"

"I—" The broccoli dangled forgotten at the end of his fork as he rubbed at the knuckles of his right hand with his left.

She hadn't given the bruise there a moment's thought until now. She noticed it, but it meant little. The Rigbys were farmers. All ten kids were up before dawn with all manner of chores, and he used to come to school with cuts and scrapes and bruises more often than he didn't.

"I'm not proud of it."

Stress thumped in her fingertips, ticking off seconds as he squirmed but said nothing. "What did you do, Sam?"

"I uh…I went to the bishop's house after I was released from my mission. It was the first thing I did."

She clapped her hand over her mouth as the hard spot in her chest seized. He was released at church and the bishop would have been there. The only reason Sam would have to go to the house after he was released would be to confront Jason, the bishop's son. Or maybe Sarah. They lived in the family's basement apartment.

"Jay did what any decent man would do. He looked me in the eye. He answered my questions. Apologized."

She shook her head. As if watching a glass drop, she knew the shatter was coming. She couldn't stop it, only wait.

"He seemed relieved when I said I was over him and Sarah, and he said that he hoped we could still be friends. I don't know what came over me, but I hit him."

She stared, wide-eyed, slack jawed.

"Right hook." He spoke slowly, distantly. It became evident he was holding back. She wanted to scream at him. *What else could possibly matter?* "With his mom and kid watching from the window."

Marie gasped in disgust. "Sam!"

"And I told him it was for you."

· ❄ ·

Tears born of fury begat more spawned by pain. The crisp, dry air burned Marie sinuses. Her tight fists ached, and her lungs begged for mercy. She channeled rage and agony into her arms and legs, pumping air and smashing salt crystals beneath her boots.

The crunching of snow and ice echoed. Heavier. Faster.

"Marie!" Sam's voice bellowed behind her. "Please, stop!"

She didn't.

Jade Garden was almost exactly half-way between Valkyrie and the dealership. A five-minute walk. It was a joy in the Spring but seemed to stretch on for miles at sub-zero.

She slammed both hands into Valkyrie's glass door. She stormed through the shop, rounding Xerox machines, racks of merchandise, and the odd person as they stepped into her way. She passed the cash register before the jingle bells fell back against the shop door with a rude clash.

"Marie?"

She shoved her palm in Ash's direction to silence her and passed through the Strip Club door. Behind her, the bells jingled again. Mitchell looked up from his light table and paused his stripping work to track her with his eyes but, mercifully, he said nothing.

The spinning doorway in the back corner opened into the dark room. She stepped into the dim, red space beyond. Her lungs protested breathing. The warm air agitated her skin.

She shrugged off her coat and tossed it onto the broken couch on the opposite end of the dark room. She placed her hands into the final rinse basin. The water was hot to her cold flesh. The gentle lap of the water and the sound of the excess trickling into the drain comforted her with memories of the swimming pool. The sharp corners of floating film kept her from drifting too far into her thoughts.

Bending at the waist with her wrists hooked on the lip of the sink, she stretched the back of her legs. She dropped her head between her arms and let her hair hang in curtains toward the floor.

The linoleum tiles appeared white with black specks. Her eyes perceived a shade of pink, but her brain made an adjustment for the lighting. Her eyes were wrong, and so was her brain. The walls weren't white. Neither was her coat. In the right light, even something as obvious as ripe tomato red could be rendered invisible.

Was Sam the right man? Or even the man she remembered? Would he keep stunning her as the circumstances changed?

The spinning door spun on its track and stopped. Marie glanced over her shoulder to check her company.

Mitchell Barnes, her once and present supervisor, was the poster child of Wyoming sheep ranching. He'd be well-suited for posing for calendars shirtless with a Stetson and a lariat if he cared to. Instead, he was stripping film and burning plates at Valkyrie, all while unaware of his rugged sex appeal because he only had eyes for Signy and she was utterly immune to it. *Poor guy.*

"Are you okay?" he asked.

"I will be." She squared her shoulders. "Lunch date. With a plot twist."

"Ah. I've had few of those myself. I need the art for the pharmacy job."

She shuffled through the film floating in the wash. "Got it. It'll be right out."

"Thanks." The door spun on its track.

After delivering the requested art, she set about drying the rest of the film in the rinse basin. The door spun once again while she fed a large sheet of clip art into the drying machine. A loud snap-crunch sounded behind her, followed by the distinct sound of chewing.

"How was lunch?" Ash asked.

Marie groaned. "Small talk over General Tso's chicken. What's not to love?"

"General Tso's?" Ash was with her when she quit meat and never needed to be reminded. "How'd that happen?"

"Sam thought it would be funny to shut me up by feeding me." She laid the dry sheet of film in the box with the others.

Ash leaned against the sink, one arm folded across her chest, the other hand holding an apple. Tasha Yar's dead body flew like a rag doll. Marie shook off the rerun in her head and refocused on the fruit.

The lights in the room erased the red and changed the green to gray. She imagined they bled a blush from Ash's cheeks as well, but it couldn't do anything about her disgust on her face.

Marie had convinced herself she'd overreacted. It was a bite of chicken. She told Sam a year ago, in a letter, while he was doing the Lord's work in another country. Was it fair to expect him to remember?

"Gross as that is, it can't be what sent you running."

Yes, she objected to eating meat, but she wasn't one-hundred percent vegetarian. She couldn't be while living in her parents' house. There was only so much she could pick out of her mother's cooking.

It occurred to her the Rigbys were farmers. They supplemented the meat they raised on the farm with game and fish. When she took their name, she'd trade one carnivore's kitchen for another.

"What else happened?"

Her thoughts of butchered meat on the Rigbys' kitchen table was wiped away by her future husband's fist striking her ex-boyfriend's face, bruising an eye and two knuckles. She imagined Sam shaking off the pain in his hand while watching his childhood friend land awkwardly in the snow.

"Can you ask Mitchell to change the CD?" She pulled a few smaller pieces of film from the rinse and turned away from Ash to push them through the film dryer.

"What are you in the mood for? Grunge? 80s? Country?"

"Pretty Hate Machine."

Ash uttered a faint, "Oh, fuck."

"And crank it."

"Yes, ma'am." Ash backed toward the spinning door. "Coming right up."

· ❄ ·

When Marie followed Ash out of Valkyrie's front door hours later, she drew fresh air deep into her lungs to banish the lingering presence of her work. The scent of film processing fluid and press wash was wiped clean by the cold and replaced by ozone and wood smoke. Ash led the way, walking between angle-parked cars and looking both ways before crossing the street. For a Saturday, the street was quieter than usual. The weather, most likely. The bands of compacted snow had become rails of ice on the asphalt.

Ash pulled the door of Blessed Beans open and gestured for her to go in. She thanked her with a smile, greeting the warmth gratefully but the scent as a cost of admission. The coffee smell wasn't horrible, but it reminded her of so much more that was forbidden to her. Ash. The kiss she wanted. The words she feared saying more than holding inside.

"I thought for sure Sam would be waiting for you when you got off work, anxious as he was to talk to you."

Marie knew he wouldn't be. "Why run into Signy again when he can just catch me at church tomorrow?"

Knowing he left Valkyrie with his tail between his legs, Marie was now dreading what he and his parents might say to her. What her own parents might say was mostly to blame for her crossing the street to sit in the coffee shop when she should be on her way home for supper. She'd leave when she absolutely had to.

Ash took a cup of black coffee from the barista and panned the room, as if taking mental notes on who was in the room as they sat. Marie followed her gaze. A few customers in the café gathered near the stage. A girl in a crocheted hat was picking out *Wonderwall* on the shop's guitar decently enough for her friends to sing along.

"Was Signy really as mean to him as Lana said?"

"Mean?" Ash snickered. "She all but literally grabbed his balls and twisted."

What Lana had told her during an afternoon break was that Sam had entered the copy shop about fifteen seconds after Marie and argued with Ash about getting her out of the dark room to talk to him. When Ash stood firm about not interrupting her in the dark room, Sam blurted, *It's not like it's a real job!*

Unfortunately for him, Signy's office door was open and she didn't appreciate his lack of respect for her profession, her employees' time, or the operation of her shop. Lana didn't repeat what Signy said to him, but when Sam walked out of the shop, she said he appeared four inches shorter and white as a ghost.

Signy Swing had a reputation for kicking ass first, apologizing never. Rumor had it, she once caught a man staring at her corseted chest. She broke his nose and went home with his girlfriend. True or not, *Thor with Tits*, as she was sometimes called, had a dark side anyone with half-a-brain was loathe to cross.

Seeing the Rigbys at church was going to suck. She just knew it.

"Care to tell me what happened at lunch?" Ash asked.

Marie blinked, and for a moment, it was Sam sitting in front of her, rubbing his bruised knuckles. *I told him it was for you.*

She pinched the bridge of her nose and prayed the headache coming on would fade away. "He said something..." Sam's eyes had quietly begged her for understanding. She had none. Not about this. "I just couldn't look at him after."

"After what?" She met Ash's stare wearily. "Hey, the last time a guy said something you didn't like, you thought a gun would make it better."

"That wasn't why—" She caught her protest. There was too much she had to say before she tried explaining. "Sam punched Jay."

"Understandable."

"In the face."

"Good choice."

"At the *bishop's* house."

"Amateur."

Marie frowned her disapproval at Ash's quips, but she paid it no mind.

"Clergy members' homes rarely make good fight venues." Ash raised her coffee but paused. "Well, unless the pastor's wearing gloves. In that case, bring out the ref and the ring girl."

Resting her chin in her palm, Marie leaned a bit on the table. "I just don't get how he could do something like that."

"It's not hard." Ash made a fist. She swung slowly and placed her knuckles to Marie's left jaw. "Well, the bone is hard, but...you know."

"I'll take your word for it. But Ash...Sam's never been in a fight. Like...in his *whole life*."

"Can't say I blame him, M. The dude did knock up his girlfriend."

Marie understood betrayal. Been there, did that. Had two matching t-shirts. "If that's why he did it, I might not have gotten mad."

"It wasn't?"

"He says he did it for me!" She touched her hand to her chest as she revealed the source of her disgust. "What the frick, right?"

Ash's left eyebrow rose. Her gaze shifted upward. "Well, you have the diving thing with him. That's special." She bobbed her head back and forth. "I can see how he got over Sarah's betrayal while remaining angry about Jason's. Maybe he's wanted to punch the dude for months and this was just his first opportunity."

"So you think I should forgive him?"

"Why would you?" Ash stared at her. "You're not the one he hit."

The words popped Marie in the sternum. Was Ash right? Sam admitted a wrong, but he didn't hurt *her*. Did she have a right to be mad at all?

Maybe not. She tapped her fingernails against her cheek. "But he asked to talk to Jay. *Talk!* And then he *punched* him in the *face*? It's *so* not like him!"

"Are you sure?" Ash asked while lifting her coffee cup. "You used to eat meat. Now you don't. Habits change."

"That's not a comfort. He asked me to marry him."

Coffee sputtered from Ash's mouth and all over the table between them. Marie scrambled out of her chair and around the table to pat her friend's back while she wheezed between coughs.

"Are you okay?"

Ash waved off Marie's concern. She leaned forward, hands on her knees, and forced several coughs to clear what coffee remained in her windpipe before finally excusing herself to go to the restroom.

Marie settled in her chair. She barely noticed the wet cloth mopping the coffee from the table. Distantly, she assumed it was the barista, until someone other than Ash sat in the chair across from her.

"May I sit?"

"You already are."

Jason handed the coffee stained towel to the barista, who left behind a cup of espresso. A double-shot, if she wasn't mistaken.

"Since when do you drink coffee?"

"When I started feeding a newborn every two hours." Jason sipped the steaming beverage with a grimace. He didn't enjoy it. "She's a freakin' clock."

It surprised her. It shouldn't. Chastity meant nothing to him. Why would the Word of Wisdom matter? Still, she'd hoped he was hanging on to some of the principles they'd shared while they were together.

Ash was wrong, she decided as she zeroed in on Jason's bruised left eye. She did owe Sam an apology for getting mad. Yes, he'd punched someone, in her name. It was uncool. But, Jason had it coming.

She doubled back on the bruise. It was green. Six days old, if her memory of biology class served. She couldn't believe Sam had picked a fight at the bishop's house on a Sunday. Would Monday have really been much better, though?

Did her dad know about this when he flew to Phoenix to get her?

"I overheard." Jason's voice ripped her attention away from his eye. "Sam asked you already."

"Why is that your business?"

He frowned harder. "It's really not."

What was the harm in talking to him? "I told him I'd think about it."

"And?"

"He's…the right guy. For all of the right reasons."

"All?" Jason pushed his empty cup away and folded his arms on the table. "Do you love him?"

"Again, not your business." She shrugged. "But yes. I have for most of my life."

He breathed deeply. Deliberately. "Of course. He's an old friend. But…not the way you loved me."

"How *dare* you?"

Jason's face twisted horribly, as if he were the personified love child of bewilderment and offense.

"What I had with you was *magical*. Like starlight. And I watched it die," she said, her voice breaking.

He flinched as if stabbed. Part of her felt bad, but not nearly enough to stop.

"What Sam's offering…it might not sparkle, but I can trust it."

"Really? Then why are you still thinking?"

She pushed away from the table and pulled her coat around her. "Tell Ash I'm sorry I couldn't wait for her. I have to go."

· ❄ ·

Thirty minutes later, Marie turned off J.M. Rigby Road and rolled under an archway of sun-bleached antlers with a woodcut sign. *Manasseh, Est 1905* was burned into the surface.

Sam's great-great-grandfather had twin sons, both named Joseph after himself. One went by Ephraim. The other, Manasseh, settled on this plot of land west of Coulter. He grew older as the windbreaks grew taller until finally he outlived his purpose and they matured into theirs. On his deathbed, he gave the homestead to his eldest son, Sam's grandfather.

Usually, she'd have Enigma's *Sadeness* paused. She would hit play as she turned off the highway and listen to the monks chant this last leg of the drive. But, her mother tossed it along with the rest of her CDs. Tonight, she still drove slowly, but to the sound of ice and snow crunching between her tires and the gravel bed below.

The private drive was lined on both sides by spruce trees. Strings of white Christmas lights shined through the snow resting heavily on their branches, beckoning her toward a winter palace at its end. A log cabin, in reality, but the effect of light and snow was magical. Her nine-year-old self had felt the presence of the Holy Ghost here. At twenty-one, it filled her being and she wept.

She had ben praying since Jason left her—almost a year—begging her Heavenly Father for direction. Now she was here and she could see the ways in which she'd been guided to this place. The home of a farmer prince.

In the years between nine and twenty-one, she had come to consider the Rigbys as Mormon royalty, if there was such a thing. Their worldly wealth was modest, but they had rich family history. Sam and his nine siblings were part of the *sixth* generation born in the Covenant, and their genealogy was littered with apostles and *Seventies*.

The Rigby family was everything her own had always wanted to be but wasn't. It was everything *she* wanted.

So, why are you still thinking. Her ex-boyfriend's words were meant to sting, and they had. In more ways than he probably intended.

She slowed to a stop as the trees cleared in front of the house. There was a large space between the house and the garage and it was mostly occupied with cars. Four counties were represented in the license plates. Montana, too.

For Sam. She eyed his truck parked in front of the main house. The extended family had gathered to welcome him home.

She second-guessed her decision to come out here. She needed to talk to him, but did she want to crash a party to do so?

Tori Amos would be helpful right about now.

She let out a long sigh and parked her car in an open space. No time like the present.

The Rigby's "garage" was built to perform maintenance on their farm equipment. Its doors were large enough to steer a tractor through, and inside, it was outfitted with much of the same equipment as in her father's dealership service center. And Sam knew his way around all of it. In fact, he and Neil used to work on dirt bikes in there. Cars, too, back when they were still friends.

What happened between them? She recalled them horsing around at prom, and the next morning at church, Neil wouldn't speak to him. He wouldn't say why, and Sam claimed to have no idea. It made no sense.

She paused at the door of the garage and stood on her tip-toes to look through the square window. Inside, dozens of people sat at folding tables and chairs they'd borrowed from the church.

Her hope of slipping in and pulling Sam away without attracting attention was snuffed by the welcome home banner. It was on the far side of the room, directly above his head, as he sat between his parents at the head table. There were plates of food in front of the guests nearest the door. It was a *dinner* party.

Of course, it is.

She shouldn't be here and she mentally kicked herself for letting Jason get under her skin.

Knowing she would talk herself out of her decision by morning, she took hold of the steel knob. She had to tell *somebody* something she needed to say to them, or she'd spew the wrong thing to the wrong person. A failure compounding on twenty-four hours of failures. She twisted the knob and pushed.

Laughter and commotion and the smell of roast beef erupted from the breach. It calmed her a bit. She slipped inside and silently closed the door behind her.

The air inside of the garage was delightfully warm. She swallowed hard and stared in Sam's direction, catching the eyes of several cousins instead.

When he did notice her, a smile pulled his lips wide. He excused himself from the table. She pushed her hands into her coat pockets, and his apparent delight at her arrival faded as he approached.

"Would you like dinner?"

"I'm expected at home." Which was twenty-seven miles away and she was already late. "Is there somewhere we can talk?"

He looked around and pointed toward a far corner of the garage. She followed him as he led her away from the makeshift dining room and navigated a maze of equipment and storage boxes. The Rigbys had made a lounge area away from the noisiest of the machines. There was a fridge, a microwave, and several old couches surrounding a pool table. Also, a television. They'd gathered here back in high school…Sam and Sarah, Jason and Marie, and Neil. On the weekend, it wasn't unusual to have a dozen or so kids back there, playing pool and munching on popcorn.

She sat on one end of a threadbare couch. He sat on the other side with his forearms on his knees, hands clasped. "I'm sorry about earlier. Seems like all I'm doing is saying sorry."

So far, he'd apologized for crowding her personal space at the dealership and for calling her parents and making them worry about her. This time, she wasn't sure where his guilt lay. For punching Jason? Or for barging into her workplace and demanding to speak with her.

Signy had properly chastised him for the latter.

"I understand your anger at Jay, but I won't have children with a man who can't control his temper."

"You know me."

"I knew you this morning. Now, you're asking me for benefit of doubt." Red bloomed on his cheeks. "Tell me why I should consider punching my ex as an exception?"

"I saw him and feelings I didn't know I had just—" He ran his hands over his face. "I guess I'm not as over what he did as I thought I was."

What Sam did made sense to her, but why he did it remained a problem. Jason betraying *him* wasn't what made him mad. Losing Sarah didn't drive his fist into his best friend's face.

I told him it was for you.

"Why aren't you mad at Sarah, too?"

He cast a scowl sideward. "I don't hit women."

"Not what I asked."

"I love you."

"Sam." She drawled his name with annoyance. "Don't change the subject."

"I'm not." He reached toward her but withdrew his hand when she turned away. "I always have."

"Digressed?"

"What? No." His indignation faded. "Well, I suppose, but—I'm in love with you." His gray eyes twitched in their sockets, as if tracking a shivering object. "I have been for a very long time. And they hurt *you*." This time, she remained still as he reached for her. His fingertips were warm. Soft. And touching her face. "And I wasn't here to help you through that."

"I made it through okay." *With Ash's help.*

He brushed her hair over her shoulder and stroked her cheek with the back of one finger. "Of course, you did."

Stand up. Walk away. Panic swirled in her heart as she yanked the leash on her instincts. No, she needed to connect to him. If they were going to have children together, she would have to let him touch her.

"I don't approve, Sam."

He froze. His hand fell away slowly.

"I want you to leave Jay and Sarah alone. I mean it."

He scooted closer on the couch. Blindly, he found her hands. "As you wish."

She frowned. "Are you kidding me?"

"What?"

"As you wish. That's like the most famous line from—Sam, I've always believed in you, but…one moment, you're the boy I remember. The next, you're a stranger. Punching Jason. I need to know I can trust the man I'm marrying."

"*If* you say yes."

She nodded.

He dropped his head and shook it slowly. "I've lost your confidence with actions. Let me earn it back through them."

She raised her eyebrow at him. "Um…how do you mean?"

"Give me a task. And don't say 'hammer a stake through a board with my—'"

She gasped with alarm at his suggestive glance downward. "Why would you ever think I would?"

"'Girl's gotta have her standards'. You said that at lunch. I *do* remember *Real Genius*." He rolled his eyes as she applauded his memory. "It has to be possible."

"Body parts as hammers?"

He laughed. "No, your confidence."

Of course. "Have you told your family about me?"

"Just my parents."

"Don't tell anyone else until I'm ready."

"I wouldn't."

"And…" She pulled her hands out of his. "I'm still uncomfortable with the touching. I need space."

He raised his hands as if surrendering. "Following your lead, then. Anything else?"

"It's probably best if you don't drop by Valkyrie—"

"I plan to avoid Signy for *the rest* of my life."

"Well…barring some unforeseen complication, I will marry you."

He reached for her and abruptly stopped. "May I kiss you, Ms. Baez?"

Jason used to ask her too. Every time. It was endearing now as then.

She nodded. Sam combed his fingers into her hair behind both ears, then leaned forward. His mouth on hers wasn't unpleasant. His kiss held a cautious expression of the love he'd professed to feel for her a minute ago. It was as if he'd never kissed at all, let alone missed six viewings of *The Princess Bride* because he was fused at the lips with Sarah.

She found his timid clumsiness sweet, but as their first kiss stretched on, it died on her lips as an act of flesh smooshing flesh.

Twenty-four hours down. Eternity to go.

High Hopes

Marie's future lay beyond two sets of glass doors. Her father held the first open and ushered her and her mother through. As she reached for the second door, her mother grabbed her arm. The scolding hand fell away as her father took the task on himself. Marie cast him an exasperated glance as she followed her mother into the foyer of the church. He returned a puzzled gaze, either having missed the exchange or not seeing anything wrong with it.

Either could be true. Opening doors for ladies was what men were supposed to do.

After passing her coat, and her mild annoyance, to her mother, Marie filled her lungs with the generic "clean" scent that made every Mormon ward house a familiar place. The brothers in dark suits and sisters in modest dresses clustered about the foyer in hushed conversation. At their feet, little boys in dress shirts and sweater vests played tag with girls in skirts over knit stockings.

The sight of her ward filled her with security and warmth, and a little apprehension. The benefit of close fellowship was, of course, being noticed when absent. Someone in the ward would seek out the reason. Food would be brought to the sick. Comfort to the depressed. Help for the injured.

People had asked about her, if not the first Sunday she was missing, then definitely by the second. She anticipated gossip. Prepared to answer questions. Made a conscious choice to be teflon and let any judgement slide off of her.

The employees at the dealership believed she was visiting her cousins. She'd assumed her parents told the ward members the same. Or, at least her father had. Mama...? She wasn't as confident her mother wouldn't discuss her troubles with her girlfriends. What were girlfriends for if not to bear such burdens?

Jason could keep a secret, but she would never expect him to keep one from his wife. Sarah kept secrets, too, but her cousin *didn't count* when she promised not to tell. She told Neil and Neil told Ash.

The thought *everyone* might know scared her, but it passed quickly. She knew better than to let what other people knew matter.

The hardest part of Jason's affair hadn't been the betrayal. It had hurt to see him with Sarah, yes, but she *loved* them. Forgiving their mistakes came quickly, naturally, if only for herself.

Fellowship at church stung more than the affair as time went on. She had known most of the people in this ward since she was eight. Her friends were all born in Coulter. Jason, Sarah, Sam, Neil… Their mothers walked through this very room while carrying them in the womb.

The ward gave her their prayers. Their outrage. Their pity when not even a year ago, Jason walked hand-in-hand with Marie one Sunday and with Sarah the very next Sunday. Their assurances that his unfaithful heart was part of their Heavenly Father's plan for her were well-meaning, but unwelcome.

Church should have been a comfort in those weeks. They tried. They truly did, but instead, every word and gesture of support reminded her that her world was tilted off its axis while killing her with kindness. She responded as expected, with smiles and thanks. God knew her ungrateful heart, though, and she could imagine no world in which He was not ashamed of her.

Nearby, a young boy delighted in making life difficult for his heavily pregnant mother. Marie shook off her thoughts and walked in their direction.

Jennifer Knutzen, her swim team co-captain in high school, balanced an infant on one hip while trying to reach the shoulder strap of the diaper bag at her feet. Her repeated pleas for her son to sit were ignored. Marie panned the room for the woman's husband but didn't see Peter anywhere.

"Jenny! You look like you could use some help." In truth, it appeared she should be in bed with her feet up, but it seemed a horrible thing to say.

In the time it took Jenny to find her in the crowd of people, the little boy had climbed onto the foyer sofa again. The woman did a double take on her.

"Marie! I heard you were home." Jenny pulled her into a hug with her free arm. "How was Phoenix?"

"Warmer than here. Christmas with cactus isn't the same, though."

"I bet." She grabbed her three-year-old by the wrist the moment he jumped. Marie started at the sight of the child hanging by his arm from his mother's fist. "Justin, I said no!"

The boy whined and kicked in his mother's grasp, but she managed to set him on the floor gently and without popping his elbow out of socket. He started climbing back onto the couch the moment she let him go.

Marie panned the people gathered in the foyer again. "Peter left you here with all this?"

"Oh, he saw Sam and..." She waved her hand dismissively toward the priesthood offices. "Men just get in the way anyhow."

Jenny's voice left a light but weary impression in her mind, so Marie slung the diaper bag over her shoulder.

"Let's get them to their classes so you can catch your breath."

Jenny exhaled gratitude. "Thank you."

Peter had returned from his mission a month after Jenny graduated high school. He proposed to her in July. They married in August. She announced she was pregnant in September.

The ward's mothers and grandmothers fawned over her and how gracefully she accepted her calling to be a wife and mother. They promised her their Heavenly Father would bless her. And each time these words were spoken in Marie's earshot, to any of the ward's young wives, they chastised her for being single and childless.

Worse, though, was listening to those same women talk about Peter when Jenny wasn't around. How would he provide for the kids while changing oil and tires? Why wasn't he in school? Why hadn't he gotten a better job?

Marie took much for granted as a rich man's daughter, but since her father hired and fired hourly employees, she understood Peter's problem. School cost money. Training cost money. Jobs earning the kind of wage he'd need to provide for his family and pay for his education required experience, and those jobs required skills learned in school or from training.

With four children still living at home, Peter's parents couldn't help. His personal contribution to his mission was paid from oil change work he'd done in the Baez dealership garage. He served the Lord for two years. He settled quickly—as his priesthood leaders advised him to do—and got his wife pregnant immediately upon marriage. Peter was already doing the job he was qualified for. It paid the bills, barely, and it kept him too busy to find a better job.

Marie's father had pushed Peter into getting a number of certifications so he could move up in the garage and take more money home. She admired her father for seeing a need and giving Peter an opportunity, but the whole situation struck her as tragic and unnecessary. If Peter and Jenny waited only two years to have a child, they could have put their wages toward a welding degree. In this county, those guys made good money.

Instead, Peter worked overtime, and the baby in his wife's belly appeared to be sucking what life the other two children hadn't already syphoned away from her.

Jenny walked in front of her, struggling to keep up with her skipping and hopping son while keeping her baby secure on her hip. Her mood seemed to have lightened a bit to Marie's ears. She enjoyed hearing Jenny's fanciful answers to the boy's questions about dragons. As mother and son giggled together, her doubts about her own long-standing goals faded.

Until a voice whispered in her ear. It was so close and so clear, she stopped to face the person who spoke them only to find no one near enough. She hugged her book of scriptures close to her heart and forced a deep breath against the sudden weight on her chest.

It's a lie.

They were unrighteous words. Selfish ones. She pushed them aside and speed-walked to catch Jenny. With the baby safe in the nursery teacher's care, and Justin with the Sunbeams class, they continued onto Relief Society.

Her testimony was weak enough for the Adversary to slip through the cracks. The harder she shoved the words away, the faster they swung around her, like a ball on a tether.

A terrible lie.

In their classroom, heavily-pregnant Jenny sat to one side of her, and a careworn woman not yet twenty rocked a newborn in the row in front of them. The voice whispered those ugly words again.

You don't want kids.

Marie clenched her hands into fists atop the book of scriptures on her lap. *Of course*, she wanted to have kids. Every woman wanted to have kids. It was their biological imperative.

Isn't it?

Except, Ash didn't. Marie was inclined to believe she'd resigned to not having children on account of being a lesbian. But the fact remained she denied any desire to be a mother.

I do.

Marie had wanted children for as long as she could remember.

The Adversary had spoken the words. It was the only explanation for the ugly thought.

Get thee behind me, Satan.

She placed her attention with Sister Rigby, who was teaching the sisters about how to manage a household while putting the gospel first. Before long, she caught herself staring at a stain on the carpet in the aisle splitting the Relief Society room left and right.

In the corner of her eye, ballet flats stepped into the aisle. She glanced up as Sarah walked to the front of the room. Sister Rigby let her disapproving glance toward her son's high school sweetheart linger, but Sarah's back was turned and didn't see it. She quietly slipped out of the doors that led to the gymnasium.

The lesson continued. The sisters discussed homemaking scenarios Marie couldn't relate to as an only child of a stay-at-home mom who, at that very moment, sat across the aisle from Marie and listened with tight lips.

Her mother had struggled with infertility after giving birth to her. She regarded fertile woman as her personal trial from the Lord and met it with outstanding grace. When talk turned to the burdens of home and children, as it did most Sundays, every word became a stick to beat her with, yet she never walked away. She chose to endure it. Every Sunday.

Marie watched the clock. Every passing minute, the suspicion something was wrong with Sarah grew stronger. She couldn't have explained if she were asked. Ten minutes passed and the voice of concern within her screamed. She apologized softly to Sister Rigby and slipped out.

The gym was pitch black and smelled of stale sweat and floor wax. She closed the Relief Society door behind her and oriented herself by the thin blades of light under the gymnasium's doors. The kitchen was to her right as she faced the room. The light under the doors in that corner was pale, cast off from daylight.

There was also a dim glow floating above the stage. The faint tickle of piano keys played a familiar melody. Pink Floyd's *High Hopes*. It was one of Jason's favorite songs to play, so she assumed it was him.

Jason skipping Elder's Quorum wouldn't have surprised her even on a normal Sunday. His activity in the Church seemed compulsory now, and if so, she guessed it was a condition of living rent-free in his parents' basement. But now, Sam was home and with two years in Brazil to rub in his disgraced friend's nose. Not intentionally, of course, but Sam embodied what Jason should have been, what he had been expected to be, but failed to become. She didn't begrudge her ex-boyfriend for hiding out in the gym.

She walked as softly as her heels would allow on the hard floor and pulled open the door into the building's back hallway. Her gut clenched. Sarah lay in a gangly heap in front of the accordion doors that concealed the baptismal font. Marie hoped the location of her head, closer to the kitchen than her feet, indicated she had been on her way back from the restroom. If not, she'd been like this for the whole ten minutes she'd been gone.

"Sarah?" She knelt next to her and found an irregular pulse in her neck. "I'll be right back."

Marie got to her feet again and pulled open the door to the stage. In the dark, she nearly tripped over the first stair before making her way carefully up the rest. She followed the melody toward the piano.

"Jason." The piano keys fell quiet. "Sarah needs a doctor."

· ❄ ·

Being a Sunday morning, the emergency room at Coulter Medical Center was quiet when she and Jason helped his semi-conscious wife walk through the doors. The nurses brought a wheelchair and whisked the ill woman into an exam room on the spot. Jason followed after them.

It was peculiar, the feeling that overcame Marie as he left her behind. This was the first time in a year she'd been alone with the two of them, and all the emotions she expected to have were conspicuously absent. There was no hurt. No bitterness in her. No jealousy. Not even awkwardness. Only a year ago, she'd been planning to spend Time and Eternity with him, and now she couldn't imagine it at all.

Concern. Helplessness. Hope. These were the sensations of a daughter of God felt for friends in need, and she had an abundance of all three.

Watching him care for Sarah in the truck did have a *strangeness*, though. Like, catching a glimpse of something sacred. It was a beautiful thing. Precious. Something she was unworthy to see and honored to be shown, even if accidentally.

She supposed it caressed the scar he'd left on her heart. Jason's affair may have been a mistake, but his marriage was serious to him. He hadn't betrayed *their* future over nothing. It made Marie...*happy* was the wrong word while Sarah was so sick, but it did give her peace. Pride, too, in seeing the boy she'd loved becoming a man.

He came out of the exam room and dropped into the chair beside her like a sack of sand. "You can go back to church. I'll have my sister come by on her way home."

Instead, she offered him an unopened can of root beer from the vending machine. He shook his head, declining while yawning.

"Fast Sunday," he said.

She cracked the can open and held it in front of his face. "Drink it. Before you pass out and they send both of you for tests."

He took the can from her with muttered thanks. As he guzzled the sugar, she mentally traced the yellow at the outer edge of the bruise left a week ago by Sam's fist.

"I'm sorry about the eye."

He shrugged. "Looks worse than it feels."

"It shouldn't have happened."

"That's true of a lot of things." He peered downward, through the hole of the can to the contents within. "It's way too late, I know, but…whatever I said, that made you…you know. I didn't mean…" His voice trailed off as her hand settled on his arm.

"You didn't, Jay. The gun had nothing to do with you."

"No?" His eyebrows arched with doubt.

"Cross my heart." She slipped her hand away. "What's wrong with Sarah?"

Leaning forward with his forearms on his knees, he exhaled long and slow. The action deflated him.

"Do you remember those fainting spells she had in high school?"

She'd never forget them. "The upper deck at the pool was stuffy."

No one else had a problem, though. They—she and Jason—assumed back then Sarah was insecure and acting out for attention. For six months of every year, Sam spent more time with Marie than with her, mostly on the pool deck. If it bothered Jason, he'd never let on, but Sarah's annoyance wasn't subtle.

Sam said yesterday he'd been in love with Marie for a long time. Could he have meant *high school*? Did his girlfriend know?

"She wasn't pretending. Heat causes her blood pressure to drop."

A chill flashed through Marie's body. "Heart defect?"

"Heart, yes. But it was a symptom."

After several seconds of excruciating silence, she prompted him. "Symptom of what, Jay?"

"Bulimia."

A sour storm of bile and guilt whirled in her chest. *I didn't know.* She spent time with Sarah every single day. How did she miss her friend's struggle? The heat of long forgotten anger bubbled to the surface and her sympathy evaporated away.

"She's purging *now*? With a newborn? Why would she do—?"

"Marie, don't."

"No, *you* don't! She's always played the victim and now she's got you—"

"Shut up!"

His snap shoved the rest of her complaint right down her throat. He'd never raised his voice to her. Not once in the whole six years they were together.

"Everyone always assumed she's faking." He crumpled the pop can as he ground out a bruising indictment. "Why does she keep messing up? Keep doing things to hurt the people around her? You, Marie. You've always been the worst. You asked why she'd cheat on Sam? Why'd she embarrass her parents? The Church? Thumb her nose at God Himself? Me? Why would she purge now when she has a baby depending on her? Why? Why? Why? You want to know why? Because no one asks what's hurt Sarah."

Marie's mouth dried as it hung open. Yes, she'd spoken them all. She'd meant them all. Gathered together in a steady spray of mean, they flayed her soul. Her throat stuck together as she swallowed, and he kept throwing razor blades.

"She was never as thin as you. Never pretty, smart, or sweet as you. No matter how hard she tried to change all of that, she could never be like you. The only thing she ever had going for her was being as close to you as Sam was ever going to get. So you can think whatever you want about me, Marie, but—"

"Mr. Swing."

He snapped his attention toward the room where a doctor was treating his wife. A nurse was now standing in the doorway, beckoning him with a hand.

"Even when she does everything right, she worries she'll never be the woman she should have been. That she'll fail her daughter. Fail me." He stood as the nurse waved at him a second time but didn't leave. Instead, he looked at Marie with moist, bloodshot eyes. "If I explain, will you promise not to put a gun to your head?"

Her shame wrestled with irritation. "I'm done with that."

"The damage to her heart is permanent."

He walked away.

· ❄ ·

Marie climbed behind the wheel of her father's truck—she always rode to Church with her parents—and shut the door. Jason's anger ricocheted about her skull. She suppressed her indignation at the things he accused her of doing to her best friend and allowed the hateful words to sting.

She'd never considered Sarah's feelings, and in the past year, Ash had assured her whatever lack of care she had for the woman was justified. But, Jason was right. Her impatience with Sarah's neediness went back years. In high school, she'd found her friend's jealousy selfish, burdensome, and even ridiculous. And she was too busy with diving, homework, and Jason to care about how she might help defuse the situation.

So many amends to make, and none conveniently located in the hospital parking lot. She turned the engine over and drove out of the parking lot.

At the church, she returned the truck to the spot she'd left an hour before. She reached across the seat for her scriptures. Jason's copy—identical to hers, but less-well cared for—laid under hers. She hadn't noticed he had them with him earlier. Putting her own aside she picked up his.

It surprised her to see bookmarks. Post-it Notes, cut into strips, marked passages through all four books of scripture, the dictionary, and the topical index. She had assumed over the past year he was steadily leaving the church, but there were *dozens* of these tabs. He'd even color-coded some of them.

What are you looking for?

Curiosity curled its finger, beckoning her. Of all the bookmarks, two were white and seven were black. She opened the first black verse. It marked 1 Nephi 3:7.

For I know that the Lord giveth no commandments unto the children of men, save he shall prepare a way for them that they may accomplish the thing which he commandeth them.

Late for Sacrament meeting, she left her scriptures in the truck and jogged through a veil of falling snow with Jason's book clutched to her chest.

At the door of the chapel, Marie froze as an elderly woman wailed how wonderful it was Jesus should care enough to die for her. The hymn had long been one of her least favorite songs to sing. Jason was the organist and, knowing she disliked the hymn, he always managed to convince the chorister to not choose it. Today, though, he was otherwise occupied.

She wasn't sure which was worse, as she listened to the ward sing it through the door: the morbid delight in death in the lyrics, or the *feeling* with which sweet, elderly Sister Jorgenson chose to sing them.

As the ward began the second verse, Marie backed away and leaned against the wall. She had time. The priests would need all three verses of the hymn to finish prepping the sacrament. One of the boys would pray over the torn bread, at which time, everyone in the chapel would have their heads bowed and eyes closed. She could enter without anyone seeing her.

She waited until the hymn fell silent.

"O God, the Eternal Father..."

As Josh Praetor gave the day's blessing over the bread, she ever so gently opened the door to the chapel and slipped inside. As she slowly, silently, closed the door, she marked the locations of people who might be concerned about her disappearance.

Her father sat beside Bishop Swing on the dais at the front of the room, facing the congregation. Her mother sat alone. Sam was between two of his sisters, sixteen-year-old Abigail and four-year-old Caroline. On the far side of the room, Jason's mother had baby Carmina and the three children who still lived at home with her and the bishop. A few rows back from Sister Swing, Neil wore a blue dress shirt next to his mother, step-father, and their three young children.

Marie tip-toed past a woman with long red hair sitting alone at the back of the room and sat a few feet away. A visitor, perhaps? She doubted she was a student. The college ward met in the Institute building next door. Her clothes were church-appropriate, stylish even. A black turtleneck sweater with a red broomstick skirt. But, her footwear...Marie eyed the woman's combat boots longingly and imagined the fit her mother would throw if she dared wear her Doc Martens out of the house on a Sunday.

At the end of the blessing over the bread, the Priests gave each of seven Deacons a tray of broken bread. The twelve-year-old at the head of the line ascended the stairs to where the bishopric sat. Her father took a piece from the boy's tray. His hand halted half-way to his mouth as he noticed her. He ate the bread and bowed his head again. She anticipated a talk later about where she disappeared to after walking out of Relief Society.

The woman with the red hair waved her hand, refusing the bread as it was offered to her.

Marie took her piece out of habit but chewed it thoughtfully. She didn't try to kill herself, but she did put a gun to her head to manipulate her parents. Her father would know it wasn't loaded; he would have told her mother, but Marie hadn't yet admitted to them she knew.

Am I worthy of Christ's flesh and blood?

Minutes later, as she took a sip of blessed water, she still wasn't sure. The gun aside, she'd resisted temptations. Sin wasn't an action, though. It was desire. She looked around the room at the people of her ward. Were *any* of them worthy of the sacrament? Could someone be truly worthy? She dropped the tiny plastic cup into the tray and the boy went on his way.

The first Sunday of the month was Fast and Testimony meeting. They abstained from eating breakfast and lunch. It wasn't a problem for her now, but as a teen, when she was burning thousands of calories diving in high school, skipping two meals had been rough. Not having to listen to prepared talks was a bonus, though. On Fast Sunday, members of the ward were prompted by the spirit to share moments that had damage or strengthened their faith. They'd be nervous. They'd tell funny stories. They'd sob uncontrollably.

Some in this room probably expected her to get up and unburden her conscience. Her mother would love to see her stand in church and bear her testimony, but Marie would disappoint her once again. She hadn't felt so inclined in…she couldn't remember when.

Her parents had always accepted reading her scriptures as a substitute for active participation, so she opened Jason's copy to the first of his black markers and read 1 Nephi 3:7 again. He'd printed a small, tidy note in the margin. *The Lord does not make impossible demands.*

The scripture verse comforted her, as it always had with the assurance her Heavenly Father was not unreasonable. Whatever trials she faced in her life, she could surmount them. Leisurely, she flipped through the pages to the next tab he'd painted black, which marked Alma 11:37. *No unclean thing can enter the kingdom of Heaven.*

She'd read the whole of *The Book of Mormon* three times, so she had seen the verse before. It seemed an obvious statement and left no impression. Combined with the previous verse, as Jason had done with these black tabs, the words struck an ominous chord.

Pushing the onion skin pages aside, Marie found the third marker in the Book of Moroni. Verse 10:32 was underlined. She stared in horror at the neatly printed words in the margin, copied mostly verbatim from the verse.

His grace is sufficient AFTER ungodliness is denied.

Urgently now, she flipped through and read the other verses, all four in the Doctrine and Covenants. Verse 1:31 told her God does not allow sin; 25:15 admonished her to keep all commandments continually; 58:43 equated "repentance" to the confession and abandonment of sin, and 82:7 promised all former sins would return to soul who sinned again.

Each verse was familiar to her and none of them had ever caused her a moment of concern. Together, they constructed a ladder to Heaven no human could climb! Surely, this could not be what the Brethren expected of her.

Jason had placed a torn scrap of paper in this spread of the book. She slid it away from the spine and turned it over. *Perfection is an achievable goal. — Spencer W. Kimball,* The Miracle of Forgiveness, *pg. 209.*

Her head floated and her stomach lurched. She closed the book. Her hands trembled as she squeezed the soft, vinyl-bound volume tight.

What put her ex-boyfriend on a mission to disassemble the scriptures as he'd done? What could he possibly have been looking for?

She eyed the two markers painted white. At the risk of finding something else shocking, she pushed the onion skin pages back to reveal the first white verse.

In an instant, the words transported her four days into the past, to Tia Sarita's kitchen island and a conversation with her aunt she'd managed to mostly forget. She closed her eyes, but she could not un-see the words. As with the other verses, she'd read this one three separate times. She'd thought nothing of it. Forgotten it. And when Tia Sarita spoke of it, Marie dismissed her accusation of racism in the doctrine as a lie.z

Elsewhere in the chapel, Jenny Knutzen testified she knew *The Book of Mormon* was true, and that the man who translated it was a true prophet of God.

More words that had given Marie peace and inspiration all her life. But not now. Not with the "black" and "white" verses fresh in her mind.

And the linchpin of her prison door was also a sentiment meant to be inspiring. . .while all of Christ's churches had a piece of His gospel, hers had *all* of it. If she believed that was true, then the saving grace of Christ's crucifixion—a promise made to all who believed in Him—became a prize to be awarded to one who managed to die without sin.

Marie fled the chapel.

The snow had been falling gently when Marie returned to church from the hospital. Now, it fell so heavily she could hardly see the houses across the street from the lobby. She pressed her head to the glass on one of the inner doors.

Did Sam pray for snow? Or had it come to burden her? It was ludicrous to think snow was sentient, but she was close to believing as it practically trapped her. Blizzard in front of her. Chapel behind. So little room to maneuver in between.

"*Mija*?"

The deep timbre of her father's voice throbbed in her bones. "Yes, Papa."

"What's bothering you?"

She shook her head with a deep exhale, hoping to release the ghosts taking an interest in her soul. "Nothing."

"You're a horrible liar."

She obeyed the command of a gentle tug and turned around. Her father regarded her with a smile. It soothed her a bit, but as his mirth faded, so did her comfort. He tapped his finger on the book of scriptures she held clasped to her chest in both arms.

"You were reading. Something upset you."

Something? Try *everything.* Including her father leaving Sacrament meeting to talk to her. She couldn't remember him ever leaving the podium before closing prayer. It would be rude to those speaking, he'd said once. She checked her watch. The meeting wouldn't let out for another fifteen minutes.

Her father knew the scriptures and the doctrine better than she did. He could explain how her impression was wrong. Set her straight.

Marie unfolded her arms and found the white tab. She opened the book and blindly turned it around. Her father took it from her hands, but before reading, he closed the pages on his thumb and looked over the front cover.

"These are Jason's." He looked at her. "Does this have something to do with you disappearing today?"

"In a way. I drove him and Sarah to the ER. He left his scriptures in the truck."

The soft-cover book bent as he twisted his wrist. The bookmarks lay flatter and nearly covered the pages. "And it didn't occur to you that maybe what he's working on here is none of your business?"

A knot tightened in her chest. "I hadn't, actually. I just saw them as scriptures."

Nodding, her father opened the book again. The verse Jason marked said the dark skin of the Lamanites became white when they joined the righteous Nephites. Her father's lip twisted hard on the left. "This is about your conversation with your *tia*."

"You know about that?" She had intended to take their middle-of-the-night conversation to her grave. Her mother would flip out if she knew what Tia Sarita said about the Church.

"She told me she crossed 'the line'." Her father made a quote gesture with his fingers. "It's all I need to know that your talk stumbled into race relations."

"I didn't believe her." A big part of her still couldn't believe her church ever taught *behavior* moderated melanin production. "It was translated from ancient text. 'White' is a metaphor, right? The word had a different connotation then?"

Her father didn't answer. "Tell me what you and your *tia* talked about."

He gestured to the nearby couch. She sat on the edge while he settled in.

She relayed the early morning talk with Tia Sarita as she remembered it, from apples to racism. He listened silently, perhaps formulating a reply. She expected him to say Tia Sarita was blaming the Church for the hurt her family inflicted. Anti-Mormon lies led her astray. People were flawed—oh, how terribly flawed—but the gospel was perfect. It was what she would say in his place.

"Do you know how the Selective Service works?"

Her brain stumbled on his question. It was unexpected, for one, but also something the daughter of a Vietnam veteran should know.

"It's okay. It's easy to miss things that don't affect us."

She cringed at the rebuke in his tone. Arguing a draft hadn't been authorized in her lifetime would likely make him angry. Ignorance was a choice, he'd often said. She had many friends required by law to register and ample time to look into how they might be called to duty. She held her tongue.

"In 1970, they drew lots for calendar dates in 1951. July 9—my birthday—drew number one. It pretty much guaranteed I'd see combat. Now, the government gave a number of deferments to churches for clergy. Your grandfather pulled some strings. I'd have served my mission in Germany had I gone, but I reported to the Army instead."

He had an out and he went?

"Why?"

"The priesthood ban your *tia* mentioned. No priesthood means no mission call, thus no deferment opportunity for black men. I thought that was horribly unfair. Un-Christ-like."

She'd long known her father had a defiant streak. He wouldn't have remained close to his sister all these years if he didn't, *but...*

"You enlisted in the Army. During the Vietnam War. Out of *spite*?"

"And I enjoyed the military. For a while. Thought I might make a career of it, but Vietnam..." His eyes unfocused and he stared at something a thousand miles past her shoulder. He blinked. His gaze sharpened again. "As my tour was ending, I counted down days until my flight back to the states. We were ambushed in the jungle. PFC Aaron Harris pulled six of us to safety only to bleed out on the helicopter."

She slapped her hands over her mouth and stared at her father with wide eyes. Why had no one told her he'd come so close to death before? She relaxed her arms and let her hands fall a bit. What would any of this have to do with Tia Sarita and Uncle Carl?

"First opportunity I had, I visited his home in Seattle. He'd worn a ring and I promised to return it to his wife. But, when I got there, a man answered the door. Late twenties. Cardigan sweater over trousers. Black. My first thought was that the man didn't belong in the home of a white soldier's widow."

"Papa!"

"Horribly racist, I know." Her father held his palms forward. "I was your age at the time and still so naïve. Your grandparents raised me to be courteous, though, so I introduced myself. Name. Rank. Whole nine yards. And I asked to speak to the misses. The man said I must have the wrong house."

Her father's gaze unfocused again, but this time, he smiled and spoke as if daydreaming. "I verified the address. And it was then that I saw the gold band the man wore. It had three stars cut into it, exactly like the one in my pocket. The way he looked at me…a man in a uniform shows up on the doorstep, hat in hand, looking for a soldier's wife." His focus sharpened on her once more. "*That* was how I met your uncle Carl."

Marie's brain turned its shiny new gear with effort. "He's…" She looked around her nervously. They were alone in the foyer. Still, she mouthed *bisexual*?

"At the time, I thought he was"—he mouthed *gay*—"so I didn't think anything of introducing him to my sister a few years later. And they fell madly in love in about ninety seconds flat. Your grandparents were so mad at me. They tried for months to break them up. They threatened to disown her if she married anyone outside of the temple, which, of course, disqualified Carl no matter what."

Marie already knew how Tia Sarita responded to the threat.

"My sister called me from the road and told me they were eloping, so I flew to Vegas."

"To stop her."

"To walk her down the aisle."

On one hand, it pleased her Tia Sarita had one member of the family who supported her. On the other…who was this man who looked like her father and what did he do with Estefan Baez?

"Why 1978?" Her dad's eyebrows arched. She proceeded cautiously. "If God reveals His will in His own time, why wait until '78 to lift the ban. Why not '68?"

Better yet, why put a ban in place at all?

"I can't speak for God, *mija*." Her father sighed. "But I can tell you those were awkward years, the '70s. BYU was in a vulnerable position with the federal government. Egyptologists attacked our scriptures. The temple in São Paulo was under construction."

"São Paulo?" That was Sam's mission. "What does the temple have to do with anything?"

"Brazil has a long history of African immigration and poor family records. Distinguishing between members with black ancestors and those without is impossible."

"Are you saying…" She looked around again and lowered her voice. "Are you saying it was a *business* decision?"

"The apostles are men, and men are products of their time. And…*sometimes*… God's will can seem awfully convenient." He leaned in closer. "But Mormons are resilient people. We hold steadfast to our principles in the face of great opposition. And, when our living prophet turns on a dime, the membership follows. Like starlings in a swarm. We adopt new world views as if the old ones never existed and some of us even get upset when we're reminded of the past."

She frowned hard in disbelief.

"Do you remember what I said a few minutes ago? About things that don't affect us?"

When he had poked his finger at her ignorance? "It's easy to miss them."

Her answer earned her a smile. "The priesthood ban existed in *your lifetime*, yet you learned of it four days ago. From an apostate. And you thought it might be an anti-Mormon lie."

Oh, yeah. He also mentioned being naïve a moment ago. It apparently ran in the family.

"We—Mormons—take for granted truth is beautiful, because ours is. But, true things are never shallow." He laid his hand on the scriptures. "There will always be dirt in the depths. And once you see it, it's on your hands, and you must make a choice. Wash or plant seeds."

"But the truth is still the truth. Tia's denying her family the chance to be together forever because of the fault of men."

"Your uncle gave me permission to share something with you. It is deeply personal to him. Only three people know now. You make four. It must go no further. Promise me."

"I'm honored to have his trust, Papa." She drew a cross over her heart with her finger. "I promise."

He stretched his arm behind her shoulder and spoke softer.

"I took Carl aside the day he married my sister. We talked about the Lord's mysterious ways, and I told him I was grateful same-sex attraction could be overcome. Because he loved my sister, I got the brother I always wanted. And you know Carl, the saint he is. He *thanked* me for what I recognize now as a bone-headed thing to say. He said I had him all wrong. He wasn't gay. Never was. The soldier who bled to death in my arms was his *girlfriend*."

She pulled away. "His—?"

Her father wasn't sarcastic with the saint comment. Growing up black in the '60s had somehow given Carl Johnson a love of people unlike Marie had ever encountered. A more open mind would require a skull with a sunroof. But what did her father mean? The Army required soldiers to go through physical exams. A woman couldn't have possibly fooled a doctor into thinking she was a man.

"I don't understand?" she said.

"Aaron had a male body and was living with a man in a one bedroom house. Homosexuals were considered *unfit* for military service until two years ago. *Unworthy* of it. Even now, they can't serve openly. Aaron had an out, but *she* didn't take it." Emotion bled through at the edge of her father's voice. "Today, the men she gave her life for are an active combat medic, a grade school principal, a fire chief, a tattoo artist..." He paused, placing a hand on his chest before continuing. "...A car salesman, and the current lieutenant governor of California. Between us, we have nineteen children and six grandchildren." He touched her nose with a gentle finger. "Including you."

Unfit. Unworthy. She. "They named Erin after...*her*?"

"Carl won't betray Aaron's memory by repenting of their time together as a sin." Commotion from inside the chapel floated into the foyer as the doors opened. Her father stood from the couch. "And your tia's washed her hands of everything, and *everyone*, who would ask that of him."

She remained seated and utterly stunned. Her aunt met her non-member husband because his girlfriend, who was born a man, saved her brother in Vietnam after he enlisted in protest of the same racist doctrine that would later prevent her from marrying her soulmate in the temple. Until God changed His mind.

Like her mother and her father's extended family before her, Marie believed there couldn't be a single reason good enough to abandon the gospel.

Could they all be wrong?

Because Tia Sarita seemed to have a good one.

She acted without a lick of shame.

And Brother Estefan A. Baez, First Counselor of the Coulter Second Ward Bishopric, respected her.

"Marie!"

She looked up sharply towards Sam's voice. She'd been staring into space and hadn't notice him approach her. He sat down next to her, moved her hair away from her shoulder and bent in close to her ear.

"Please forgive me," he said. "I couldn't know she'd say anything."

"She?"

His cheeks flushed as he cringed. He laid his hands palms upward on his knees, and she placed hers on his. That seemed to settle his nerves a bit and he curled his fingers over hers.

"Caroline. I was helping her with her testimony."

His baby sister. At four-years-old, she was the youngest of Marie's soon-to-be sisters-in-law. She liked handling the microphone and had born her testimony every first Sunday for almost a year.

"And?" she asked.

"And, now they know." Sam grimaced again. "The whole ward. Everyone knows we're engaged."

Jesus Forgive Me (For The Things I'm About to Say)

Sam had expected her to be angry and to assume he had broken his promise from the night before. If not for her father's revelations, she might have been, but as things stood, she was in shock.

He supposed his older sisters had wondered aloud about why Marie was at the farm, Caroline had taken their gossip for fact, and no one had asked her to stay quiet. With the cat out of the bag, Sam knelt on the floor in the church lobby and presented her with a modest diamond ring.

She hugged him after he put it on her finger because she wanted him to chase away the ghosts in her soul. His embrace was warm, which she welcomed, but also heavy, which she did not.

It did repel the thoughts haunting her, though. She managed to get through the wave of well-wishers and an evening with her parents as her mother revealed notebooks, plural, of wedding ideas she'd been gathering for years.

Marie went to bed early but didn't sleep a wink. Her father had put the "white" verses into a kind of historical perspective. The policy keeping the priesthood from black members existed and was lifted. She put the issue on a shelf to consider another time. From the moment her head hit the pillow, it had been Jason's "black" verses whipping up a storm in her soul, and she'd spent the better part of sixteen hours trying to shear the wind.

Work helped most of all. Applying her brain to project specifications gave her blocks of time when she thought about nothing but job parameters. She listened to

Mitchell's CDs and Cal's jokes. She laughed at one as she had never laughed before.

After her coworkers left to grab lunch, she opened the next manila envelope and found a ZIP disk inside along with a spec sheet for a poster. The client was a local credit union and they were advertising investment consulting.

She placed a line drawing of Sisyphus pushing a boulder up a hill into an image box on her document. The image bothered her. Each time, she knew, the rock he pushed would slip from his hands before making it to the top, and the condemned man would have to start all over.

She drew a parallel to the warning in the *Doctrine and Covenants* she'd read the day before. All sins returned to souls who sinned again. And from there, the rest of Jason's "black" verses came back to taunt her. They tumbled over and over in her mind, debunking her rationalizations of each in turn.

The conclusion was Christ's sacrifice was reserved for those who perfected themselves in *this* life. The words were there. In black ink on onion skin. Under her church's copyright pages.

And, as she had also done many times, she dismissed her deduction. She was misinterpreting what she read. Taking the words out of context. The scriptures couldn't be saying Jesus Christ suffered *crucifixion* to redeem the already perfect. It was heresy.

"Hey, you alright?"

Ash's voice woke her from her daze. She glanced her friend's way and back at her monitor, which was filled with flying toasters. The screen saver came on after five minutes of inactivity, so she'd been lost in thought at least that long.

"Yeah. Why?" Marie swiveled away from the workstation to face Ash, who was carrying a barstool from a nearby light table.

After sitting, Ash took her hand. Tingles brought her skin to life as Ash's palm touched hers. She curled her fingers over Ash's hand as she admired the diamond ring.

"He did a good job. This is totally you."

The ring was dainty, a small stone flanked by pink and green leaves, set in a narrow band of Black Hills gold. It was exactly the kind of ring a farm boy fresh off his mission might afford if he had the forethought in high school to put money away.

Ash's scrutiny became distant as she looked at the ring. Her lips curved downward, and her nostrils flared, as if she'd detected a whiff of something rotten. Marie sniffed but smelled nothing unusual. Ozone from the copy room mixing with ink and solvents from the press room.

"My turn. What's with the frown?"

Blinking rapidly, Ash let her hand go. "Sorry." She planted both palms firmly on the seat between her legs and leaned forward.

"Don't be sorry. Be verbal."

"Your ring put me on a weird train of thought." Ash bounced one foot on the lower rail of her stool. "Engagement. Marriage. I was mentally thumbing through a wedding album with pictures of you and Sam in front of that castle in Salt Lake City."

"With a frown on your face?"

Ash blanched. "I'm sure your photos will be stunning. I was just thinking... Can I ask you a church question?"

Marie's eyes shot open. She'd offered Ash a *Book of Mormon* once, but she'd declined it and made it clear she wanted no part of religion at all. Church things came up in conversation, of course, but only about events conflicting with plans in the making. Never ever doctrine. The nervous voice in her mind was quickly drowned out by her inner missionary. A non-member asking questions was the *best* opportunity to share the gospel.

"Sure." Marie straightened. "Fire away."

"Your prophet. The first one."

"Joseph Smith."

Ash nodded. Crossing her legs, Marie leaned back in her chair. "What do you want to know?"

"Did he really have thirty wives."

A hundred years later, and it's still about the polygamy thing.

She shoved her frustration aside. Of course it's the question Ash would ask. It's the one Marie might have asked if she didn't know better.

"Brigham Young was the one with all the wives. Joseph just had one. Emma."

"Oh." Ash shifted her attention to the desk and played with the corner of a piece of paper sticking out from under the keyboard. "I guess I assumed all of the early prophets did."

"A lot of people do." She was careful to keep her voice light. "There are a lot of rumors about the Church floating around, but our beliefs aren't that much different from other Christians."

Ash met her claim with wide eyes and high arching eyebrows. "We believe Jesus was born of a virgin mother, and He died to atone for the sins of the world. What more matters?"

Ash didn't argue. Her disbelief softened but remained. "It's just…your book. Not the Mormon one. The other."

"The *Doctrine and Covenants*. Or the *Pearl of Great Price*?"

"The first one. Doesn't it say having more than one wife was necessary for a man's salvation?"

The hair on Marie's body stood up on end. *What is she talking about?* As she adjusted her posture in her seat, she watched Ash swallow hard.

"I'm just curious…why would Joseph Smith have only one wife if God commanded him to take more?"

Marie frowned deeply. "He wasn't commanded." She'd never seen such a thing in the Church's publications. Never heard it in Sunday School.

"I'm sorry." Ash shrugged. "I was told he had thirty wives, and I just wanted to know what you thought about it."

"To be honest, I never have." Non-members were the ones obsessed with polygamy. "The Church abandoned it a hundred years ago. But…since you brought it up…the idea of sharing my husband with another woman is repulsive."

"And yet, you still believe the man with all the wives is a leader worthy of praise today?"

"Why wouldn't I?" Marie hadn't meant to sound curt. Ash's questions had knocked her off balance.

"You said it yourself. He was a polygamist."

"Brigham was a righteous man. A wise man."

"He was also a criminal."

"A crim—what?"

"Your church believes in obeying the law of the land, right?"

"Of course. It's one of our Articles of Faith."

"Well, polygamy has always been illegal in the United States." She turned her hands over in a clear request for an explanation. Fortunately, Marie had one.

"When Brigham Young led the Saints to Utah, it was beyond the US border."

Ash gaped at her. "They left the country?"

"More like they were chased out, but yeah. Utah was still part of Mexico at the time."

"Never mind that. Why did they marry all those women? I don't understand."

"The pioneer trail was rough. Men died. Survivors married widows to care for them and the orphans. Keep them safe."

Ash's frown tightened. "They required *marriage* to take care of women and orphans?"

"Why does that offend you?"

"They offered things women needed to care for their children in exchange for sex."

Marie scoffed. "That's ridicul—"

"Is it?" Ash rubbed her hands over her face before slapping them on her thighs. "Those men had the resources to provide for those women before they married, or they wouldn't have taken on the burden. Why *marry* them? Why not just take care of them?"

The question snuffed out Marie's indignation.

"And if it was about providing for widows and orphans on the pioneer trail, why did they keep up the practice once they were settled in Salt Lake?"

"To grow the population."

Ash pointed rudely at her. "Which involves sex."

"Yeah, but—" *Why does she have to be so crass?* "God commanded it."

"When? You said only a minute ago that polygamy wasn't a law God gave to Joseph Smith."

This was exhausting. "Our church has a living prophet for continuing revelation. Plural marriage must have been a commandment given to Brigham."

"If that's true, and the revelation was given to the pioneers—who were still in the US until they weren't, by the way—why was Joseph threatened by a newspaper accusing him of having more than one wife?"

What!

"I don't know where you heard this...this...totally bogus, anti-Mormon *crap*."

"People don't destroy printing presses over crap!"

Marie whipped away and flicked the mouse to wake up the monitor. When she faced her friend again, Ash stared at her with a quivering frown.

Testimony, don't fail me now.

"I don't claim to know everything about my church. And I admit I've never really researched its history. Maybe what you're saying is true, but the past doesn't matter to me. I have prayed, and the Holy Ghost has told me the *Book of Mormon* is true. I know my church is the true church of Jesus Christ, and Joseph Smith, whatever mistakes he made in his life...he was a true prophet of God."

The muscles in Ash's jaw were visibly clenched. She slipped off the stool backwards and spun around to leave.

"Wait!"

Ash stopped cold in her tracks but didn't look back.

"Did I answer your question?"

Ash's shoulders rose and settled again. "You answered more than one."

The door clicked shut.

Marie swiveled her chair back toward her workstation. The illustration of Sisyphus and his boulder taunted her. She rubbed her forehead with her fingers. The storm swirling within her regained its gale force. She laid her forehead on her arms and prayed Cal and Mitchell would take a long lunch.

Not going on a mission might be her only good decision recently. Clearly, she sucked at talking about the Church.

· ❄ ·

After finishing the tasks Mitchell had assigned to her, Marie left work and drove to the swimming pool. She didn't expect to see Sam. It was his first full day on the dealership's sales floor and her father wouldn't give him slack just because he was almost family. Sure enough, when she walked onto the pool deck in her warm-up slicks, there were swimmers warming up laps in the four outer lanes of the pool and divers stretching underneath the boards, but no Sam.

Marie was grateful for that. There were nine young men who had only weeks to prepare for their first meet, and when he came to practice on Friday, it wasn't for them. He came to see her, to challenge her to their old game, and to show off. Making matters worse, the young divers were a bit starstruck by the former state champion in their midst. For her, it was an annoyance, but for them, it was a waste of their valuable time.

About a half-hour into compulsory dives, one of the boys over-rotated a reverse somersault. She leaned away from the water splashed back onto the deck, and as she turned back toward the pool, her gaze panned over the spectator section upstairs.

Ash was sitting in an otherwise empty section of the bleachers nearest the diving boards. Her arms were stretched out along the bleacher behind her, head dipped back. If she was awake, she'd see discolored patches of peeling paint on the ceiling.

Marie offered her hand to the boy who'd almost splashed her and helped him out of the pool. After giving him a few pointers, she left the diving board area, ducked into the office, and then exited into the lobby. She took the stairs two at at time, and walked alongside the bannister, glancing down at the pool. The boy under-rotated the somersault this time and was half-untucked when he landed on his face. She smiled. Happened to everyone.

There were more people in the bleachers today than usual. High school students, most of them showing no interest in the swimmers. Marie couldn't blame them. It was three degrees below zero—a *heatwave* by comparison to the previous days. The spectator deck was warm, connected to the high school by an internal hallway, and open to the public. A lot of kids found it a good place to study, hang with friends, and wait for rides home. She knew, because she had done it on cold days at their age.

Of course, she had also done it on warm days. And the days in between. When she thought back to those days, she and Sam had been on the pool deck more often than not.

She stepped onto the bleachers and walked up until she stood one level down from Ash's feet. Her eyes were closed, and Marie's warm-up slicks swished softly as she walked, but she hadn't stirred.

Part of Marie wanted to tip-toe away. She didn't want to start another fight. It hurt to see Ash walk away, disappointed for reasons Marie hadn't been able to puzzle out after she left. She owed her friend an apology. No time like the present.

"Crazy place for a nap."

Ash's twitch didn't have the shock of sleep wearing off. She'd been relaxing. She was tense now though, pulling her limbs into her like a threatened turtle. With her hands pushed deep in her slick pockets, Marie rocked from her heels to the balls of her feet and back. As seconds passed, Ash steadily began to relax again.

"No, I was just thinking." Ash sat up and looked around the spectator deck of the pool. "Not a bad place for it."

Marie agreed. She rolled up onto the balls of her feet. Water squished between her toes inside of her aqua socks. "You were right earlier. I was bothered. Still am."

"Yeah? What about?"

Everything. But she didn't have to confess everything. There was an imagesetter sitting opposite Valkyrie's plate burner capable of irritating her to tears. In fact, she'd used Valkyrie's front door today just to avoid seeing the thing.

Marie straddled the bench next to her and slouched. "I forced Signy's hand, didn't I?"

Ash shook her head. "Forced her hand? On what?"

"The imagesetter." That machine replaced manual graphic artists and camera operators. Basically, it all but replaced her.

"Sig had money to blow at the end of the year," Ash said with a shrug. "Taxes were mentioned."

The explanation made sense, but she didn't believe it. Signy cared about her feelings, but she was a business owner first. Marie had been gone almost three months when Signy ordered the imagesetter. She couldn't count on her stripper changing her mind, if she'd been inclined to offer the position back, nor was Marie staying now a guarantee. Mitchell and Cal were solid guys, but they were unable to pick up her slack. They couldn't carry on as they had been indefinitely.

Signy needed someone who could replace Marie's quick, precise, *invisible* hand. Instead, she found some*thing*.

"What don't you like about it?"

"It's too easy." She met Ash's eyes, felt pulled by gravity and averted her gaze again. "Anyone in the shop can now click 'print separations' on a client's file and that machine will spit out film with most of what I do already done. Next will come a plate printer and then files will print directly to press. See where I'm going?"

"Prepress production as you know it goes away."

Marie nodded while biting at the cuticle on her pinky.

"But the machine can't run itself. And someone still has to strip the plates."

"For now. When an industry automates, do you know what happens to labor?"

Ash frowned. "Signy's not going to lay off her strippers because a machine made their jobs easier."

Marie wrung her hands to keep them busy. One of the divers was stalled on the edge of the board as she had been on Friday.

"All that's left is to make the ordering and delivery systems easier, and a six-color press run by two or three men could produce the student magazine at the college for less than the press in their own graphics lab. And I mean 'men' literally, Ash. Valkyrie's an odd shop. Print production is a man's world and it's getting smaller."

"How?" She covered Marie's hands as they fidgeted. "How could the ordering and delivery system be made easier?"

"The Internet." She chuckled sadly. "Once there's a system in place to take orders and transfer money direct from banks, everything we know about commerce will change. Ordering will become a digital thing. The product will get boxed and delivered, like any other package."

Conversation between them fell quiet for a while. They watched the boys practice rudimentary dives. Now certain her friend wasn't still mad about earlier, Marie took comfort in the warmth of Ash's hands. Their touch calmed her troubled heart.

"A warehouse could just as easily be here in Coulter." She brought Marie back to the present. "You have the foresight, the money, and the connections to be the high volume press of the mountain west. Why not do it?"

"I suppose it's the privilege of a rich man's daughter to whine about losing what I love when there's a potential to make a killing at the next best thing. But the dark room, the lab, the press…that's where the magic happens. That is where my heart is."

She tightened her grip as she considered the things slipping through her fingers. Jason. Stripping. Innocence. Faith. Eventually, Ash too.

"At least, it's an easier pill to swallow than the truth," Marie said.

"Which is?" When she didn't answer, Ash prodded her. "Marie?"

"I'll be a housewife in six months. None of it will matter."

The grip on her hands became stiff. "Why are you marrying him?"

Marie froze, shocked by the sudden about-face. "What choice do I have?"

"Try *not* marrying him." Ash released her and abruptly stood.

"You don't—"

"Understand? Please. Come back when you're an abomination in the eyes of God and ask me about your choices."

For the second time that afternoon, Ash was walking away from her. Marie ground her teeth together, angry at her friend's rudeness, and pushed off the bench. The metal skeleton of the bleachers protested under her footfalls.

"Ash!"

She kept walking, escaping now from Marie's wrath. *No.* Not this time.

Marie ran to catch up and grabbed Ash by the elbow as they reached the landing in the middle of the concrete stairwell. She tugged and Ash stumbled a bit as she pivoted, pulling Marie off balance.

Ash caught her as they started the fall, hitting the wall with the force of their collective weight and a sharp groan. A stray hair could have snagged in the space between their noses. Ash shifted on her feet. Marie did as well, taking on her own weight again, but the arms that had held her up now held her in place.

Marie slowly exhaled the breath she was holding. Ash's eyes fluttered closed, and her head drifted sideways, and her lips parted ever so slightly. In that moment, Marie could no longer deny herself what she'd wanted for months.

She leaned in, closing the distance.

Ash stiffened a bit as Marie's lips brushed her, but then tightened her embrace. The kiss set fire to Marie's skin. Her nerves sizzled like long fuses. The critical organs along her spine hummed, from her brain to her heart and lungs, and the sparks trailed through her sternum and diaphragm as they made their way south. And when the blaze hit payload, her entire sense of self exploded in a shower of light.

Jason's kisses hadn't felt like that. Sam's hadn't, either.

Then, Ash pushed her away sharply. With mouth agape and tears welling, she stared as if Marie had scales and claws and she held the monster away with wobbly arms.

Oh, God. Oh, Jesus. What have I done?

· ❄ ·

After grabbing her things for the shower room, Marie ran out of the pool and drove straight to Raleigh White's house. She expected Neil to be here, as he lived in the spare bedroom, but Jason's truck was an unexpected sight as she turned onto the frozen dirt lot beside the house. She thought having a newborn would mess up his band's practice schedule, but if the music permeating the walls of the house was an indication, he and Sarah had it worked out.

She parked in the hole left between a late model Nissan Sentra and Neil's rusted '83 Cadillac and slammed her door behind her. There were half-a-dozen other cars here, too, most of which she'd never seen before, so she assumed the house rules hadn't changed while she was in rehab.

Every step across the frozen dirt and gravel of the driveway delivered a painful shock to her cold feet, but she kept on pace. The wood stairs weren't much kinder as she took them two at a time. Inside, the pain would subside.

House rule number one: if the door was unlocked, walk right in.

She turned the knob and shouldered her way into the kitchen. Not a soul in sight, but rock music rose through the floor at such a volume the vibrations rumbled through the plastic soles of her wet aqua socks.

Brilliant choice of footwear, Ash would say, given the weather.

Ash.

Marie's skin recalled the kiss. Her gut became gelatin, then stone, as Ash's horrified face flashed in her brain. How could she be so weak? So selfish?

She made her way for the basement stairs, where she was reminded of house rule number two: don't be a dick.

This rule was intentionally broad and included a growing list of examples of how to be a dick. Raleigh printed the list on several sheets of dot-matrix paper, tractor holes still attached, and hung it on the wall next to the door that led downstairs. Examples included drinking the last beer in the fridge, removing beer from the fridge without first putting beer into the fridge, and using the bathroom sink as a urinal.

Additions to the list were penned at the bottom and the list had grown since the last time she'd descended these stairs. It was the inevitable result of Raleigh allowing twenty-somethings to let their friends in on rule number one.

The band—they called themselves The Basement—had potential. Their original songs had good rhythm and catchy lyrics, but the band had revolving doors at vocals and guitars. The downside of recruiting out of the music department of a two-year college was the band lost members before the tunes were ever perfect. Truth be told, though, Neil and Raleigh were messing around. And Jason—the band's pianist and songwriter—had higher priorities. If and when a better opportunity for his family came along, he'd pack up his wife and child and go. Marie was certain of it. In fact, she'd be disappointed in him if he weren't actively looking for one.

As for the *groupies*, Raleigh's basement gave them a warm place to drink and smoke. The live entertainment was a free bonus.

The Basement did play the occasional bar gig, and on those days, they played covers. Arena rock from the '70s and '80s was their bread and butter. Grunge was dessert. The originals were a Monday night indulgence to remind them they were artists.

She sat on a pile of pillows between a threadbare couch and Raleigh's high-hat stand. The potheads always passed their joints to the left, so she'd avoided being offered weed simply by always sitting as far to the right as possible. After seeing she preferred sitting there, Raleigh added "sitting in Marie's spot" on his "how to be a dick" list and ejected people off *her* pile of pillows whether she was there or not.

Raleigh had acquired a soft spot for her in seventh grade, when the boys were succumbing to the throes of puberty. It started with an incident in math class. He'd been called to the board to work a problem and couldn't exactly use his inconvenient hard-on as an excuse to decline the teacher's request. He tried to hide it, but the boys caught on and lit up like paparazzi on a rock star. She couldn't remember what Sam had said, but it had been cruel.

Heavenly Father expects better of you, Brother *Rigby,* she had scolded him.

Sam had blanched at her stiff rebuke and blushed several shades of pink and red. The other boys in the class appeared to stop breathing as they looked sharply between her and Sam. The teacher scolded her to mind her own business.

After Raleigh solved the math problem, he took his seat in the aisle across from her and whispered an apology for getting her in trouble.

Marie settled back into her fluffy cushions, surrendered her lungs to tobacco and marijuana, and embraced the noise. It occurred to her the smell would catch a ride home with her on her clothes and hair, but her parents weren't on her list of major problems right now.

No, she had a fiancé expecting to marry her in the spring, a forbidden kiss still sizzling on her lips, and a temple recommend interview in the near future. And, she couldn't forget the list of scriptures promising she'd waste her life trying to perfect herself because failure was inevitable.

She ground her teeth to push the tears back and refocused her attention on her oldest friends.

Neil sat on the arm of an old upholstered chair, with one foot in the seat between the knees of a guy who might be too stoned to notice he was in the way. Jason glanced up from his keyboard and half-smiled as he swayed to the music.

As she watched him and Raleigh play, an uncomfortable question crept into her mind. Sam had apologized to her on two occasions for things he'd done to other people. Ten years ago when he humiliated Raleigh in math class, and again on Friday, for punching Jason.

Are there others?

At the end of the song, Neil stood up from the chair and placed his bass in the stand by the wall behind him. "I think *Manita* came to vent."

Little sister. Marie felt a grin tug at her lip. She always felt a little less alone when he called her that.

Raleigh dropped his sticks into the coffee can at his feet. "And I need to piss." He stood up and stretched. "All you deadbeats. Upstairs. Get some fresh air."

"You're kicking us out?" A Goth girl's whine was followed by others.

"Your brains are starving for oxygen. Now git." Raleigh grabbed the guy in Neil's chair by the shirt and yanked him to his feet.

"Dude! What about not being a dick?"

"It's my house, *dude*." After the stoner got his feet under him, Raleigh pushed him up the stairs. The groupies and the band filed out.

Jason stayed. She wished he'd go. She was glad he didn't. She couldn't trust her heart anymore.

Neil curled his finger at her. Reluctantly, she rolled to her knees and stood up on her burning, throbbing feet. Leaving the pool in wet shoes was so stupid. Neil opened his arms. She stepped into his brotherly embrace and sniffled back a sob.

"Talk or sing?"

It was Jason who asked.

Marie had almost no musical talent. She could hit notes in two octaves, keep time, and learn songs in single listens. This allowed her to mimic the studio recordings of songs she really liked and sing with the church choir. Period. It was a source of annoyance for Jason. His day job tuning instruments at the local music store put him in contact with a half-dozen singers every semester, all good at improvising yet sorely lacking in some technical aspect they didn't care to improve upon. He'd rather have her cold precision, he said, than a lazy wanna-be rock star.

She'd rejected his pleas to join the band. She enjoyed singing, but she didn't want to be a singer. Her sojourns into Raleigh's basement were quests for music's cleansing power. When emotions built up pressure in her heart and head, singing bled her dry faster than anything else.

Jason didn't wait for her to answer his question before playing the opening of *Down in a Hole*, the song he knew she was most comfortable singing.

She pushed Neil away. "No. *Man in the Box*."

Jason pulled his hands off the keyboard. "What happened?"

"None of your business."

"Talk or you can go sing in your car."

"I can't!"

Jason's brow furrowed. "Talk?"

"Sing in my car." She squeezed her arms tighter across her chest.

Neil's head cocked a bit, giving him the appearance of a shaggy dog. Jason was now scowling at her. Their reactions were warranted, as she owned two copies of Alice in Chain's *Facelift* album, one of which hadn't left her car since 1990.

Had owned. She cursed her mother's tough love attempt to save her soul. "You said talk or sing. I don't have to talk if I sing."

"You won't have a voice left to talk." Jason huffed.

It surprised her that he still cared.

He played the *Down in a Hole* intro again. "We have a few minutes. Warm up on this."

"I'll be right back." Neil kissed her forehead and ran up the stairs two at a time.

Jason gestured with his head toward the seat behind the microphone stand. She pulled it around, so she'd be facing him instead of whichever potheads followed Neil and Raleigh back downstairs.

She sat down on the stool and lowered the mic stand. She missed her lead-ins while arguing and getting comfortable, so Jason kept repeating the intro of the song as an unspoken invitation to jump in when she wanted. And she wouldn't get to scream until she did, so she didn't waste time.

Down in a Hole came easy for her after years of singing it in her car. She knew the rhythm and every slight inflection of Layne Staley's voice as well as any of her best dives.

When her cousin Erin had offered to bring her tapes to listen to in rehab, Alice in Chains was what Marie had asked for. The music filled long, solitary hours while a lifetime of doctrine bombarded her like a shower of sand. She'd withstood it, hoping each grain would steadily wear away her unwanted feelings toward Ash.

Somehow, her life had gotten turned inside out. It made as much sense to her as a dream, her wish to fly away into a beautiful sin as God's plan crept like vines up her limbs like tar to hold her back.

She loved *Down in a Hole* because it was beautiful. And she hated it because she didn't like what it told her about herself. And she mourned it as it ended.

"Wow." The male voice was a vulgar intrusion in the quiet space. "So, um… why am I even here if you have her?"

The Basement's new singer, she assumed. So new, he didn't know when to keep his mouth shut. The twinkle in Raleigh's eyes warned her that he was about to say something filthy.

"Ral! Don't." Marie held out both hands toward him, pleading. "Whatever you're about to say, please just don't."

Raleigh winked and then shifted his eyes behind her. His eyes tracked a moving object. "We don't have her, numbnuts."

She took pity on the young man and turned toward the sound of couch springs squeaking followed by the crack of an aluminum can being opened. "I don't sing."

"Well, you coulda fooled me, chica."

She turned around on her stool. A guy with ripped jeans and a respectable haircut chugged beer on the couch. She wasn't great at faces so she dismissed the sense she'd met him before.

"Chill out, babe. I'm just being friendly."

Everything about him annoyed her, but before she could put a finger on why, a cymbal crash grabbed her attention. She turned back around.

"That little one's not worth your effort, sweetness." Raleigh sat behind the drums. He looked past her again to address the singer on the couch. "Pay attention, Rigby. *This*…is how you sing *Man in the Box*."

Rigby. It explained the familiarity. He was related to her fiancé. From Byron. Maybe Burlington. Sam had so many cousins, she crossed paths with a future in-law almost everywhere she went. Work included. Her supervisor, Mitchell, was a third cousin from the Ephraim side of the family.

"I'm here to decompress, Raleigh." She rolled her head to stretch her neck. "Not school your front man."

Raleigh gave her a wink and beat his drumheads and trash cymbal. Neil joined in on the third beat. The room was filled with the angry grit she'd been craving since Thursday.

She turned toward the sound of stomping feet on the stairs. Jason pointed two fingers back at his own eyes. *Don't worry about them. Watch me.*

Back in the day, when they'd sung this in the car as an alternative to making out, Jason sang the lead vocal and she sang back up. That was how she discovered *Man in the Box* was a cathartic beast, and she used it in the previous year to vent the rage Jason's betrayal fueled. Of course, getting to watch her cheating ex squirm while she sang for his band and he sat there was a delicious bonus, but it wasn't the pay off.

Screaming about denying her maker and having her eyes sewn shut…it calmed her down when nothing else could. Singing worked faster than diving. It strained her voice the same as crying but lasted longer. It left her as empty as long-distance swimming, without the energy to do much more than exist.

As the bridge ended, she seized onto her memory of Layne Staley grabbing a wire fence in the music video and shaking it. She grasped the microphone with both hands and wailed the first line of the last chorus.

"Yeah, girl!" Raleigh pointed one of his drumsticks at her.

She closed her eyes and finished out the song, with Jason filling in the alternating lines. The song ended abruptly. She wasn't nearly done.

"*Head Like a Hole.*"

"Yes, ma'am." Jason tapped a button on his keyboard and the room filled with static.

They played Nine Inch Nails, and Metallica, and two more Alice in Chains hits, until the effort of singing wiped out the bottled energy threatening to rip her apart. She and the band punched out the last line. A beat later, she slammed her hands on the barstool.

Her hair fell around her, hiding her from the room. Air passing through her throat hurt. Her arms shook under the burden of holding her upright.

Jason filled the silence with soft piano notes. The opening of Nutshell. She shook her head. "I'm done."

He kept playing. "Gotta cool down, M."

She pushed the hair out of her face, placed one hand on the microphone, and at her cue, she sang softly about misprinted lies and coping with life's struggles. The ending line wrapped its message around her like the arms of a demon.

Being dead is better than living a lie.

Heavenly Father, you made me what I am.

Why did he expect some souls to sacrifice more than others for Eternal Life? Could she believe in such a God?

Singing had left her too drained of *everything* to scold herself for asking such a question, so it remained in her mind as the drunks and potheads cheered for an encore.

The microphone stand was pulled away from her. Neil stepped in front of her and pushed the stray curls in her face behind her ears. "*Manita*?"

Her eyelids drifted closed, partly from exhaustion, but also from shame.

He threw the hood of his sweatshirt over his head. His forehead pressed to hers and brought her into his shadow. They were as alone as they could be. "Talk to me."

She bit her lip and swallowed against an ache in her throat. It was from singing alone. She didn't have it in her to cry right now. The words came freely, as if someone else spoke them on her behalf.

"I kissed Ash."

Neil pulled her closer and held her tight for a moment, and then took her hand and led her upstairs. Behind them, a piano played the opening of R.E.M.'s *Losing My Religion.*

He led her in his bedroom and released her hand to shove clothes and random junk to the floor. She frowned. "You bring a lot of girls here?"

"Only the ones I *really* like." He straightened his linens and comforter and swept his arm over the bed. "*Señorita*?"

Marie sat down stiffly on the corner of the bed, which made his attempt at tidying up for her benefit largely unnecessary. He leaned against the wall in front of her, crossed his legs at the ankle and his arms across his chest.

"How did Ash react?"

She cringed at the memory of the horror on Ash's face. "She pushed me away like I was a monster intending to eat her."

For a long time, he said nothing. He just looked at her, studied her, until she couldn't bear his scrutiny anymore. When she averted her eyes to the floor, his feet backed out of her field of vision. He shuffled through objects on the top of his dresser for a moment, and then he knelt at her feet.

"You need to talk to Ash about this. Tonight. Waiting is only going to make it worse." He lifted her chin gently until she met his eyes again. "If you don't, I will, and I don't wanna, so, promise me."

She was due home for supper soon. She'd need an excuse to stay in town her parents would accept.

"Promise."

He took her left hand in his while biting off the cap of a permanent marker. He shoved the back end of the pen portion into it.

"First, though," he said as he started writing on the inside of her wrist, "ask about him. Ash won't want to tell you, but it matters."

As Marie read the name upside-down, it meant nothing to her. She pulled her sleeve down and she saw he wrote high enough that she could hide the ink.

"Now, I gotta know," he said. "Why can't you sing in your car?"

· ❄ ·

Marie's explanation had made him angry, but had also confused him. Why hadn't she replaced a few of her favorites? It wasn't like she didn't have the money, the time, or a music store a block away from Valkyrie that, thanks to Jason, *always* had Alice in Chains in inventory.

Truth was, buying new CDs hadn't occurred to her.

Her mother didn't want them in her house. Her father took her forgiveness as a fair exchange for going back to work. She'd chosen last Thursday to not be mad about them and forgotten she had a right to be. Not having them became a new normal. Posed to her now, and given the circumstances—the disappointments, the gun, the stint in rehab—buying CDs seemed rebellious. *Provocative* even.

The more she had rambled, the angrier Neil had gotten. Did the Praetors' divorce give him a perspective on "parents" so much different than her own? Or was Jeannie, the home-wrecking psychologist-now-step-mother putting subversive ideas in his head? Marie couldn't imagine, but she didn't expect Neil to launch into a tirade about "property" and "rights" and her parents still treating her as a child.

Fuming, Neil retrieved the CD magazine from her car and loaded it with *necessities* from his own collection. She had Alice in Chains in her car for the first time since coming home, but no desire to listen to them. *Figures*. She had bled her well of angst while singing and was hungry now for something else.

Concrete Blonde's *Jenny I Read* filled her car. She thanked her Heavenly Father silently for Neil's rare fits of intuition. It was what she craved. Depth. Guts. Intensity married to poetry. The presence of a mature woman.

She pulled into an empty spot in front of the coffee shop and switched off her headlights. There, she sat back, and while waiting for closing time to roll around, she let Johnette Napolitano's voice caress her raw soul.

Five hours and fifty-seven minutes after their kiss on the stairwell, Ash *finally* stepped outside of the coffee shop's door. The wind caught her hair as she turned to lock the door. Marie marveled at the wildness about Ash. She'd been drawn to it from the start, in some moments to *be* her, and others, like now, to be *with* her.

Frightening urges, both of them.

Ash paused at the door far longer than it would take to lock it. Marie switched on the headlights, illuminating the whole front of the coffee shop. Ash stood taller, stiffer, and ticked her head slightly over her shoulder. Marie opened the door and stepped one foot into the snow outside.

"Going in?" Marie asked, "Or coming out?"

Ash looked at her hands, still holding the door knob and key. "Um…out." She locked the deadbolt and faced the car. Her already pale complexion became bone white in the glare of the headlights.

"Then let's go. It's frickin' cold out here."

She got back into the car and shut the door. Ash didn't move. Instead, she stared through the windshield with narrowed eyes. Marie rolled her window down and waved her inside.

Finally, Ash stepped from the curb and into the street. She opened the passenger door enough to avoid hitting a pick-up parked next to them, squeezed into the car, and dropped into the seat.

She pushed the stereo button, silencing the music. Marie pressed the dial again and Concrete Blonde filled the space between them. She needed to be somewhere solid before breaking the ice. That meant not talking now. About anything. She pulled out of the angled space in front of Blessed Beans and drove away.

Signy Swing's home was six blocks away from Main Street. A ninety-second drive in the summer if she obeyed all the traffic laws. Today, there was ice and snow. She pulled into the driveway three minutes after leaving the coffee shop and parked next to the truck their boss had bought herself for Christmas.

"It's a mess downstairs," Ash warned her.

Marie shut off the car and pulled the keys. "If housekeeping was a concern, I'd have driven to a motel." She caught Ash's gaping maw in her peripheral vision before exiting the car. Seconds later, the passenger door slam shut.

"What the fuck, M?"

Marie stopped in her tracks and dipped her head back. A wisp of frost blew up from her lips and floated away. "We need to talk."

"And we need to do that here?"

"Yes, actually."

Ash glared at her reply.

"I told my parents I'm working out an imagesetter workflow with Signy. If they call, I have to be here to go to the phone."

Ash shook her head with disgust and plodded up the stairs to the side entrance of Signy's house. She pushed open the inside door.

The mid-century home could more accurately be defined as two apartments. The door opened onto a landing. Three stairs led up to Signy's kitchen door. Marie descended the seven steps down to a short hallway with three doors. Left led into the laundry room. Right, when she was here last, hid a six-foot tall pile of storage boxes belonging to Signy's parents.

Ash passed behind her to unlock the door into the basement studio that had been her home for the past two years.

Marie entered when invited and looked around. A side from rumpled bed covers and stray bits of laundry, the room was clean. "Mess?"

After straightening the bed, which doubled as a couch, Ash picked up the laundry and a long elastic bandage off the floor and dropped it all into the hamper.

"Make yourself at home." It was a dry welcome Ash punctuated by slamming the bathroom door.

They were on Ash's territory. Why would talking here anger her so much? It was the kiss screwing things up things between them. Why would where they talked about it matter at all?

She took off her coat and hung it on the back of one of Ash's dining chairs before sitting on the edge of the bed. She pulled at the laces of her boots and slipped them off her feet. This freed her to cross her legs on the bed, the posture she found most comfortable while waiting for the world to crash.

The bathroom door opened again. Ash stepped through, pulled it shut, and leaned against it.

"This was your idea." She studied the floor at her feet. "You start."

"I—" Marie's throat betrayed her. She swallowed and tried again. "I gave Neil my word, but..."

Ash scoffed quietly. "Of course, there's a fucking 'but'."

"He gave me a name and said to ask you about it first. He insisted, actually"

Ash jarred from her funk. "Name?"

Marie glanced at her wrist and read the words penned in Neil's immaculate letters. "Brandon Teena?"

Color bled from Ash's face. She grew two inches as her step backward laid her flat against the door, forcing her posture to straighten. It wasn't shock widening her eyes this time. It was fear.

"Neil told *you*...to ask *me*...about Brandon Teena?"

Marie withered under the scrutiny but nodded. In an instant, all Ash's apprehension transformed into red-hot rage. Her fists clenched at the air and her face contorted in horrible gestures.

"That fucking…fuck!"

Ash had already been mad when they pulled into the driveway, and Neil warned her it was a sensitive subject. But if Marie had suspected the name would enrage her, she would have ignored Neil's insistence and come clean with her feelings. That ship had sailed, though. Now, she just had to hope Ash would relax enough to explain why. She pushed back on the bed and pulled her knees into her chest to wait out the storm.

And eventually, Ash did abandon pulling her own hair while pacing and cursing Neil's existence. "I'm going to kill him."

"You don't have to tell me. It doesn't have anything to do with what I came to say."

Ash's head rolled back onto her shoulders with a groan. She rubbed both hands over her face before clasping them together on her forehead, like she was offering a silent, desperate prayer.

"He gave you that name because he wants me to tell you something, and I can only assume it's because it might change what you came to say."

Marie steeled her nerves.

"*God* couldn't change it." Couldn't, or didn't want to.

"I appreciate your confidence, M. I really do." She rolled her head back again, this time knocking it on the door. Her eyelids drifted closed and she laugh a little, but it was humorless.

Marie chewed on her thumbnail as Ash opened her mouth as if to say something only to shut it again. Was she stalling? Or perhaps she wasn't considering the question at all but debating over whether to throw her unwelcome guest out. As she accepted Ash wasn't going to talk, she reached for her boots.

"Brandon was the reason I left Minnesota.

Abandoning her plan to leave, Marie settled in again. "Boyfriend?"

Ash shook her head. "No. I never met him. First time I saw his name was in a newspaper." Her face screwed up for a moment, but she relaxed again. "New Year's Eve, 1993. A pair of low life scumbags shot him in Nebraska, along with two of his friends. One was a mother. Her toddler was left alive, but alone, in the trailer."

Marie gaped at Ash in horror.

"My dad split when my mom was pregnant with me. She married our pastor when I was six. I don't know what she ever saw in the asshole. I'd wanted to run away for years, but I had nowhere to go and no money to get there anyway. I'd had a job for two weeks when they put me in gay conversion therapy, and I was fired while I was gone."

"Oh my gosh."

Ash had already moved on. "The morning he dropped that article about the Nebraska murders on the table during breakfast, and *smiled*, I knew I had to get out of there."

Who would find that funny? Ash shrugged as if she'd asked the question aloud.

"The dude abused us six ways from Sunday. I was used to it by then. That morning, though…I felt fear for my life. The moment I was alone, I stole my mom's emergency cash and left the house. Didn't stop for more than gas until I wrecked. Until I met you."

"But why would he—?"

"He doesn't like queers. Thinks we're abominations in the eyes of God."

Marie cringed at the words, remembering how Ash had spat them at her at the pool. They had been what prompted her to run after Ash. Now, she cursed her thin skin for letting the outburst get the better of her.

"So, Brandon was gay? These guys killed him…?" Ash shook her head, and Marie swallowed the rest of her question.

"He wasn't gay." Ash pursed her lips. "The name his mother had carved on his grave stone was Teena Brandon."

Marie's train of thought jumped from the horrible track Ash had laid out and careened into a ravine. His last name was Brandon. He was born Teena, but he died as Brandon. Why would Neil have her ask Ash about—

A tickle of familiarity in her brain became a tug back into the church foyer and the story her dad told her about the soldier who pulled himout of an ambush. A woman born with a man's body. *Tia Sarita and Uncle Carl named Erin after Aaron.*

While Ash maintained a piercing gaze with bloodshot eyes, mouth abandoning attempts to speak before making a sound, Marie recalled her friend in snapshot memories over the last two years. Pauses. Poses. Greetings. Laughter. She'd had gravitated towards the *boy* in Ash from the beginning. The simplicity. The near complete absence of female drama. She'd never considered her impression of Ash might be literally true.

The lighting in the room seemed to dim as a dawning settled on Marie. *Aaron. Brandon. Ash….*

"Which are you?"

Ash's eyes widen again. Apprehension, this time. Cautious hope. Embarrassment too, maybe.

"Your birth certificate," Marie said. "Male or female?"

"Female."

"But it's not right…is it?"

Ash hesitated before shaking her head. "Do you still have something to tell me?"

· ❄ ·

Marie bolted out of the side door and hurried down the stairs to the driveway. Cold rose through the soles of her feet, and when she looked down, her boots were missing. Her coat was still in Ash's room, too. Winter poked through her clothes…t-shirt first, then flannel. Her jeans held up better, but not by much.

The freezing air attacked her cheeks extra hard. When tears had fallen, she didn't know. She pushed her hands across her face, wiping the wetness away, and laid her wrists on the aftermarket grill of Signy's truck. She bent at the waist, leaned back, and let her hair hang toward the ground.

As the pose burned the muscles in her arms, back, and legs, she pictured a diving board. She visualized the sequence of one-and-a-half somersaults. Easy. Elegant.

The cold ground. The bite of ice on her skin. The sear of the freezing chrome under her wrists. These things prevented her from losing time.

As the pain became unbearable, she left the grill and tucked her hands beneath her hair to warm her wrists on her neck. The skin there was hot and the chill of her hands caused a delightful shiver down her spine as her body sought equilibrium.

The back door opened. "Thinking about how to leave when all your stuff is downstairs?"

Ash chucked her coat over the railing. Marie caught it in midair and wrapped it around her shoulders. "I just needed air."

"What you *need* is to get your dumb ass back inside."

Her body from head to toe agreed. Downstairs, Ash entered the bathroom again. The shower turned on.

"Ten degrees below zero and she walks out barefoot," Ash said from past the door, then raised her voice. "What the fuck is wrong with you?"

"It's kind of my thing, Ash." Marie hugged her arms tighter around her. A violent tremble set in. "When I screw up, I *really* screw up."

Ash whipped around in the doorway of the bathroom. "Fuck off, M. It's fucking pathetic the way you cope with failure and I'm *done* holding your fucking hand."

The scolding slapped her. Ash had always talked to her. *Reasoned* with her. She had—*he* had always been gentle. She didn't know this person yelling curses.

"No. Don't even." Ash pointed his finger at her as he took two steps back into the room. "*This* is the part where you start making this about you. Not today, princess. *You* kissed me. You drove us *here*. You dragged *this* out of me. You get to go *home* when it's done." He held up his arms to the room. "*This* is all I have, and now I have this goddamned memory to live over and over."

What have I done?

"I'm sorry. I didn't think—"

"You never do." Ash covered his face with his hands and groaned loudly. "Why did you have to kiss me?"

The words stung more than the rest. "You didn't want me to?"

"No!" Ash let her—*his*—hands fall. "Yes, but..." He found her hands and held them. "You live in a bubble, M. You have this picture in your head of the perfect life. It was planted there when you were *four years old*. By a fucking lullaby. And you cling to it like a goddamned security blanket."

He jiggled the ring on her left hand, reminding her she wasn't free.

"I want you, but I can't have you. That kiss—?" Ash looked at her—*his*—feet, arms hanging from slumped shoulders. *He* let go of her hands. "If your parents do show up, you shouldn't go to the door smelling like weed. Go."

Marie did as she was told.

The shower water was warm, but it burned her feet as she stepped inside the stall. The odor of marijuana wafted off her as she moved under the stream, reviving the contact high she'd had when she left Raleigh's.

I didn't think.

You never do.

The cold faded. So did the oregano scent of the marijuana. Marie she shut off the shower, but remained where she stood, letting the water sheet from her hair and skin. She wished it would take the whole day with her. It wouldn't, though. Couldn't.

She stepped out of the shower, and as she toweled off, she noticed a pair of straight leg sweatpants with pockets and a t-shirt folded and stacked on the toilet. Sometime while she showered, Ash brought her clean clothes.

And now, she—*he*—was out there. Waiting for her? Dreading her return?

When she opened the bathroom door, dressed in clothes that smelled like Ash, she found him pacing the kitchen floor. Four steps one way, four the other. That was how wide this basement studio was. Enough room for eating, sleeping, and bathing in peace. Cozy enough for two, until she made it uncomfortable.

She pushed her hands into the pockets of the sweatpants and took two steps into the room. "I'm sorry."

"For what?"

"I have been selfish." Marie slowly closed the distance between them. "Ash, I *always* think about you. Having you. Losing you. And...while I've been struggling so long with your effect on me, I've never thought about what affect I might have on you." She touched Ash's arm but pulled back when he flinched. "I'm sorry."

He blindly touched her neck and hooked his thumb on her earlobe. As she leaned into the hand, he pulled it away and turned toward the sink. Marie held herself in her arms and debated whether she should leave or not. She decided on not.

"I saw a boy when we met."

Ash shook his head at her claim.

"I was convinced until you walked into the ladies' room. It confused me for a long time."

"Stop."

The pain in Ash's plea hurt Marie's heart as much as any of her own trials. She wanted to wrap her arms around him, to absorb it away from him. To fill whatever space within him was hollow.

"Ash. Look at me."

"No."

Marie stiffened and pulled her hands back. "Tell me why."

"I'm scared of what I'll do."

Knowing Ash hated hugs, she resisted the urge.

"Ash—"

"Please, Marie. Just—"

"I lo—"

"No!" Both hands slammed on the counter. He hung his head so low he seemed not to have one. "Don't say that. I can't hear you say that."

Marie took one step back. "Ash…"

"Please." His arms trembled as he sniffled back a sob. "You walk those words back later, and I'll—"

So tough. So vulnerable.

"I love you, Ash."

He laughed. It was humorless. Hollow. "You are a selfish *bitch*, Marie Baez."

"I am." She accepted it. And she'd work on it, but for now, honesty was the only play she had. "And I'm in love with you."

He fisted his hands on the counter, growled, and slapped his hands again. "Fuck it." He turned on a heel, yanked her to him, and kissed her like the world was ending.

Bullet with Butterfly Wings

Marie couldn't clearly recall how they came to be under the covers of Ash's bed. They were still fully clothed—she hadn't entirely lost her head—and lying so her body half-covered his while his shoulder served as a pillow. With one hand, he held her palm flat against his sternum. The other hand twisted a long lock of her hair about his fingers.

"So," she said, breaking a long silence between them. "How should I think of you?"

He stiffened under her. "How do you mean?"

"Well…" She paused a moment to consider her word choice. "Yesterday, before *this* happened, I would think of you as 'she'. But, I don't think you'd want me to say 'he' to other people."

"No! Hell, no." Ash sighed heavily, but he did relax again. "Not in this town. But, if you think 'he'…that would mean a lot to me."

It seemed like hours before he spoke again. "Say 'Ashton'."

"Ashton?" She said it quizzically. "Are you going to change your name?"

"I've been thinking about it. I thought it might sting, like Ashley does, but I like how it sounds when you say it."

Marie smiled to herself and turned to kiss his neck. "I like Ashton."

"Please don't take this the wrong way, but I fucking hate you right now."

His tone belied the feelings his words suggested. Marie chose to take his comment as an invitation.

"Because I said I love you?"

"Because it doesn't matter, M." He hugged her tighter for a moment and kissed her head. "Because yesterday, doing this with you was a dream. I was okay with that. Here we are...first time, last time."

His kiss filled her with the sense of being in the right place, a sensation simultaneously strange and familiar. She'd felt it with Jason, and on the diving board, but never so strongly as now. And Sam's hugs...*oh, God, Sam...*

"And in the morning, you'll be my coworker again. My friend. Another man's fiancé."

"I'm giving the ring back."

"Don't be stupid." His tone was both caring and condescending. "I mean, he's a chauvinist prick and I *hate* the idea of you marrying him. But...you and me...M, what you do next has to be for you. Not me. Not *us*, because there is no us."

"I don't know if I can do it anymore." The tears tickled her nose as they slipped. "Pretend I don't want to be with you."

"Then you'll never see me again."

Marie sat up, shocked and horrified at how firm his statement was.

"It's not a threat, M. If you can't pretend, I can't stay. I won't say good-bye. I won't even pack. I'll just be gone."

"But why?"

"You're engaged to a Rigby. He's got like five hundred cousins. I'm not betting my life they're better than the assholes who killed Brandon." He combed her hair behind her ear. "Not when I know you won't choose me in the end."

"Ash—"

The kiss he interrupted her with soothed the sting. "I can't take you to the temple. I can't give you children. Much as I might want to someday, I just can't."

She burrowed her face into his neck and sniffled back tears. Suddenly Tia Sarita's anger at the Church, anger at God, made sense. Like her aunt, Marie was in love with a man she couldn't have, not without surrendering everything she'd ever wanted.

Unlike the doctrine that kept black men from holding the priesthood, though, the Church's position on marriage, gender roles, and sexuality had only been assumed until recently. The Church released a letter defining all three only months before. So, she was confident Ash would never be recognized as a man. Their relationship would always be between two women. Not only could they not marry in the temple, but it was unlikely Marie could ever show her face in a Mormon ward house again. And she had no hope that would suddenly be lifted soon, the way the priesthood ban had been a year after Tia Sarita married Uncle Carl.

No. This is the way things would be for a long time.

"M, did I ever tell you I was raised to speak in tongues?"

"What? No!" The claim yanked her right out of her headspace. "*You* spoke in tongues?"

"Yeah."

"Doesn't that require some sort of devotion? You've never seemed the type."

"Oh, I totally faked it." He voiced his admission as if it were a childhood prank. "The Holy Ghost never spoke to me, let alone through me. I was terrified of anyone finding out, so I mumbled gibberish and convulsed on the floor. It kept my step-dad off my back until—until I gave him other things to berate me about."

"Like what?"

"Like, not wearing skirts. Wearing my skirts too short. Not wearing make-up. Wearing too much make-up. Not dating boys. Dating the wrong boys. Having sex with the right boy but accusing him of something else. Kissing *girls*."

A cold dread washed through her. "Wait. Something else? You mean—"

"I understand the pressure of faith, M. I've already forgiven you." He didn't want to talk about that *something else*. Marie understood. And the pre-emptive pardon for a future hurt…that wasn't to make it easier on her, and it didn't, knowing he was protecting himself from her. "Which I hope will get me a pass on something I did."

"Oh, man, what?"

His lips pulled back in a pained, toothy smile. "I uh…I talked to Jason on Saturday night, after you left the coffee shop. I hadn't meant to, but he had me knees-deep in a conversation before I realized we were talking."

"Why do you think I'd be upset about that?"

"He cheated on you."

"And I still talk to him. Why shouldn't you?"

There had been a point when she wasn't talking to Jason or Sarah, but it was due more to them avoiding her, not the other way round. She ran into Jason last year in Raleigh's basement and they got used to each other again as she vented her anger at him while singing grunge rock. Sarah, though, had mostly succeeded in avoiding her, which was an impressive feat in a town of five thousand people.

"Jason's your friend, too."

"And you're *more*." He nuzzled her hair. "The moment I rolled my window down, that night I crashed, and I saw your face…I knew God had sent you. Whether to save me, or destroy me, I still don't know, but…I knew."

A thrill washed through her, followed by a shiver. She cuddled closer. "You two must have had a lot to say after a whole year."

"We talked about you. Mostly. What went wrong between the two of you."

That was easy. "He cheated. End of story."

The affair she'd been able to forgive quickly, but there was no future for her and Jason after the baby news broke. His child deserved a chance to grow up with her parents together. Marie wouldn't dare get between them.

"What he told me happened before I got here."

She scowled. "What does that mean?"

"He mentioned a book. I forget the title. Forgiveness something? Anyhow, he said you saw it and assumed he'd been cheating or *going solo* and you didn't care which."

Oh, yeah… She'd chosen to forget about that day, but it came back to her in vivid detail. After his father dismissed him from his mission interview with a copy of *The Miracle of Forgiveness* in his hands, Jason swore to her he hadn't cheated. She took him at his word, but it would be a few weeks before she warmed up to him again.

"It wasn't the *going solo* I was angry about. I mean, I thought it was kinda gross, but…well, Mama thought waiting for Jason to come home from his mission was a waste of my time. Jenny—she was my swim team's co-captain—married a Returned Missionary two months after graduating high school and was pregnant a month after that. And Mama talked about it constantly.

"She had a list of missionaries on their way home that she thought would make great sons-in-law. She didn't care whom I chose; she just really wants grandchildren, so she built this scenario in her head where I announced a baby for Christmas. But, obviously, that didn't happen, and she's never gotten over it."

She'd told Ash more than once about her mother's grandchild craving. The first time she'd mention it, he'd reacted with a wide-eye gape. Now, he just listened quietly.

"Anyhow," she said. "I loved Jason. I wanted to be with him forever, and I was committed to waiting for him to serve the Lord and come home to me. When the bishop told him to repent and come back 'when he was worthy', it meant at least six additional months of listening to my mother complain about wasted fertile years. It was just bad timing."

"Forgive me for asking, but…why did he punish Jason and not Sam?"

"Why would he punish Sam?"

"For…*going solo*."

"He didn't. The priesthood gives the bishop the power of discernment. The Holy Ghost would have told him if Sam lied about it."

Ash was incredulous. "Sam dated Sarah for what…three years? Four? If he wasn't jacking off, he was blowing off steam somehow."

"He does live on a farm. Lots of ways to work it out."

"Shame he didn't share his trick with Jason. If he had, Jason might not have been punished for something stupid, and the perfect life you planned with him would still be on track."

"Yeah." Marie couldn't blame Sam for Jason's behavior, though. "Is it possible Sam just has self-control? We trained together for years. The man has discipline."

"Maybe." He snuggled her closer. "I'm just worried about you. The man who walked into Valkyrie on Saturday and demanded to talk to you…he made my skin crawl."

Sam had made her uncomfortable at times, too, but it was her fault. The barrier between them was a product of time. Distance. The world the way it was rubbing against the way it should have been. Sam as a husband and father was *right* in any universe. It was her as a wife and a mother causing friction. But were her growing doubts truly about *want*, though? Or was she scared of the coming changes?

New responsibilities. New expectations. A new normal.

Sex.

Cold rolled through her body. Ash tensed under her and pulled his head back to look at her. "Something wrong?"

"I don't—" She swallowed against an ache in her throat. "I don't know where to start."

He settled again. "First thing that pops in your head. Go."

"I think I'm bisexual."

"Okay…?"

"But Neil says they're just horny and indiscriminate. That's not me."

"Hold up." His tone was doubtful. "*Neil Praetor* did not use the word 'indiscriminate'."

"No, he said, 'bleep anything that moves'."

"He's such an asshole." His chuckle sounded genuine. "He's describing himself, M. The fact he's bi is a coincidence."

"Oh." She bit her bottom lip. "So, I could be? Even if I don't really think about sex?"

"Of course. How long have you been wondering about this?"

"Um…since the Fourth of July? I think?"

"Six months?" His thumb brushed her cheek. "Why didn't you say something?"

"I didn't know how to explain. And it wasn't too hard to ignore at first. I just told myself it wasn't real. Then I told myself you were leaving. And then…"

"You tried to kill yourself."

"No! That wasn't about you. I just…can we not talk about that tonight?"

"You're right." He kissed her forehead. "Go back to the not thinking about sex part."

"So, I dated Jason for six years, right?"

"Lucky dumb fuck." Ash paused. "His piano skills are damn sexy, though."

Marie hadn't noticed, but she did love to hear him play. He was a genuine prodigy; his mother said she set her three-year-old son at a piano in the Relief

Society room while she prepared an activity. Half an hour later, he was playing Supertramp's *Give a Little Bit*, the last song they'd heard on the radio before exiting the car.

Marie and Jason had made plans to leave Coulter after they were married so he could pursue a stage career. Instead, he was buying diapers with money earned tuning pianos. The part of her that loved him as a man forgave him early on, but as a fan she wanted to strangle him for wasting the talent God gave him.

"Anyhow, we held hands." She laced her fingers with Ash's. "Hugged. Kissed, but rarely. I've done more with you tonight than with him the whole time we were together."

"You live by a law of chastity. He did, too. That's devotion to your faith, not a problem."

If only that were true. "I'm praised for the good example I set, but it's not all me. Truth is I've never been tempted."

"You were never attracted to Jason?"

"That's where it gets complicated." Marie sighed heavily. "Like…Sarah loved Sam. And not just him. She was obsessed with actors, models, athletes, rock stars…all the girls were, *except* me. When I look at people, I see what other people like about them, but they're no different to me than sculptures or paintings. Jay was the *only* person I've ever been attracted to."

He traced a line along her back with his finger. "Then what's today about, M? You're like a bomb that's been triggered."

She couldn't describe how she felt any better.

"The part of me that connected to Jay…it's awake again." Marie pressed her lips to the hollow behind his ear and was rewarded with a deep moan. "And it wants you."

Ash rolled a bit, shifting her onto her side and pinning her between himself and the pillows shielding them from the wall. He drew his knee further between her legs and pulled at her hip, bringing her flush to him. "I'm yours." His lips brushed hers as he spoke. "Until dawn."

· ❄ ·

As Marie brushed her teeth the next morning, she inventoried the contents of a shoebox on the back of Ash's toilet. First, there was a bottle of cheap vodka. Of course, she couldn't judge alcohol quality, but she did know a thing or two about packaging. She doubted the "good stuff" was bottled in plastic and labeled with stickers.

The remaining items were basic: hair brush, clean-scented gel deodorant, toothpaste, cotton swabs, tweezers and toenail clippers. A bottle of generic cough syrup and extra toothbrushes, all still factory sealed. These items were stored neatly on the left side. A handful of sanitary napkins were stored in the space on the right.

She worried about the vodka, which her friend used to separate the different sides of himself.

Can I still call him a friend after last night?

She spit the spent toothpaste into the sink and sucked water off the bristles to rinse out her mouth. As she stood straight again, a pair of arms wrapped around her from behind. A kiss placed where her shoulder met her neck made her insides wiggly.

"You okay?" Ash asked.

Am I okay? He was the one with liquor in the bathroom and a towel hanging over his mirror.

"Do you drink in here often?"

Ash snickered. "I prefer whiskey in the closet, actually."

The hair on the back of her neck stood up. "Please tell me you're joking."

He let her go to pluck the bottle from the shoebox. "This has better uses." He unscrewed the cap and held the bottle out to her. "Swish."

She eyed the booze like a spider in his hand. "I shouldn't."

He rolled his eyes. "I said 'swish', not swallow."

She paused before taking the bottle. The small, hesitant sip burned every cell it touched. She spewed it back out into the sink and cupped a handful of water, which moved like liquid ice in her mouth.

"People drink that for fun?"

He laughed and tipped the bottle for a sip. His ability to swish the liquid around his mouth astonished her.

"Why not just use mouthwash?"

He spit the vodka out. "It's expensive. It's sticky. And it's a shit glass cleaner." Standing up straight, he twisted the bottle cap closed and presented it as if he were a showcase model for the *Price is Right*. "This watered down distillate of the humble potato also deodorizes fabric and eats hard water stains."

His joke only reminded her of the one before. "You're not kidding about the closet, are you?"

The humor evaporated. He took his time putting the vodka in the shoebox and carefully rearranging the items on the left and right. "How are you with tight spaces?"

"They've never bothered me. Why?"

He laced his fingers with hers and led her out of the bathroom. He pulled the door of his closet open. "We don't have time for me to explain this another way."

The space inside was barely wider than the doorjamb and deep enough to make room for a hangar. Most of the contents inside belonged to Signy. Winter jackets. Snowsuits. Skis. Fishing poles and tackle. The bottom was covered in a haphazard pile of old shoes and boots. These were forgotten items, she supposed, rather than stored.

At his direction, she crouched and crawled into the space between the jackets above and the shoes below. He did the same on the other side. There was hardly enough room for both of them, but with her knees hugged to her chest and his legs on either side of her, they managed to close the door.

The air, which stunk of dust and old foot sweat, became thick with their breath in no time at all. In the dark, the sound of their breathing was so loud.

"Yes." Ash's voice carried softly in the dark. Though knowing his face was within her reach, they could have been in a cavern and he on the other side from her. "I drink in the closet."

"Why?"

"Can you see *Ashley* in here?"

Marie's brain halted. He never used his whole given name. In fact, she'd seen him cringe at the sound of it. He regarded the woman she saw as a separate person, she realized now. And he *hated* her?

"No, I can't."

"She's is an illusion, M. A heap of visual cues other people use to put me in a box. So, when I come home, I put *her* in a box. *This* box. I shut out the light. I take a drink—one. Shit's expensive.—and I pretend she doesn't exist. And when I get tired of smelling Signy's feet, I go to sleep."

"Oh, Ash…" A lump took hold in Marie's chest. "Why did you let us think you were female?"

"I didn't think I'd be here this long!" he cried. "And that story about the Nebraska murders was hours old in my head. I thought…just be a woman for a few more days, long enough to scrounge the money for a bus ticket out of here, but then Neil and Jeannie convinced me to stay. California's expensive, she said. Save up some money, then go. You already knew me as a woman when I decided to settle in."

When he sniffled, Marie slid her hands along his shins, wrapped her fingers behind his calves and held tight.

"I can avoid seeing her. I can cover mirrors and turn away from reflections. I can hide in the dark, but…*she* gets to live in the sun. *She's* what other people see. What *you* see. And it's killing me, M."

Marie knew the sound in the dark as intimately as any other. The hitched and ragged breathing was a sign of a soul in agony. The struggle to rise above despair. She pressed her lips to her knee to hold the heartbreak in by force. It wasn't her time to cry. Not her space. She would not let him hear.

The story about the soldier who saved her father's life took on weight. Marie wondered Sunday, as her father had years ago, why Aaron didn't dodge the draft. Why didn't she tell the Army doctor her roommate was her gay lover and stay in Seattle with the man who loved her?

Was she so principled she would not tell a lie? Or did she need the Army as much as it needed her?

Did she disobey orders to save her Army brothers? Or did she keep running back into the jungle to catch a bullet and six trips was how long it took?

Will Ash someday wish for death?

Marie leaned backwards, unfolded her legs, and placed her feet on opposite sides of him. She shoved aside shoes as she rolled forward and repositioned herself. He shifted beneath her and she straddled him but didn't give him her weight. As his hands settled on her hips, she wrapped her arms around his shoulders and kissed his head as he'd done so many times with her.

"I'm sorry." He choked out his apology between violent sobs. "You have enough shit of your own to deal with."

Clearly, the same could be said of him. He lived in a prison. He had done nothing to deserve it. He couldn't escape it. And yet, he'd been there for her. For two whole years. With all his own pain, he'd put her first.

My turn.

"Hush." She held him tighter as he lost his fight for control.

She hugged him to her as his sorrow shook him senseless from within. The rages passed through him in waves, each less powerful, each leaving him heavier in her arms than before. Quiet fell upon them slow and soft, like a silk sheet dropped from on high. Still, she held him in the silent dark, and he held her, as if there was no world waiting for them.

"Time to go."

Ash's voice was a ragged whisper, but it held conviction. She let her arms fall away and reached for the door knob, but froze as Ash's hands moved along both sides of her body. They tickled her ribs as they passed. His thumbs caught under her breasts and lingered a moment before continuing upward. He found her shoulders and neck and fanned his fingers into her hair and held her head in his hands.

"I love you, Marie."

Not that it mattered.

"I love you, Ashton."

As soft skin pressed to her lips, she opened her mouth and invited him in. He kissed her slowly. Sweetly. A sense of belonging bloomed within her chest and radiated outward. It was warm, like the first breeze of Spring, and her flesh tingled with its presence. She wished to stop time and live in this moment forever. She cursed her mere mortal weaknesses when the kiss ended, as all things must, but far too soon.

They untangled from each other and crawled out of the closet. As if a clock rolled back twenty-four hours, everything that had changed between them reverted when they passed through the threshold of darkness into light. He avoided her eyes. His touch was casual, but sparing, and the hug he gave her before leaving for work was stiff, almost awkward.

They drove to work in silence. She replayed their morning, searching for the cause of Ash's sudden cold shoulder moments after the *perfect* kiss. She came to an intersection and took advantage of the slippery roads to pause for longer than necessary. He was turned away from her, looking out the window. Dawn painted him in lovely shades of pink and gold.

Marie lifted her hand from the steering wheel, intending to hold his, but froze as a realization struck her like a punch to the gut. Ash didn't leave the closet with her. *Ashley* walked in the light of day. *She's who you see...it's killing me.* She lowered her hand and proceeded through the intersection instead.

They parted at the pressroom door. She paused while he walked toward the courtyard bisecting the block on his way to Blessed Beans for his morning cup of coffee. He stopped before turning, gave her a smile, and disappeared around the corner. She knew then but resisted knowing. When Ash kissed her in the closet, he kissed her good-bye.

· ❄ ·

Hours later, Marie completed her work for the day early and left Valkyrie by way of the pressroom door. Ash hadn't come into the Strip Club all day. She assumed he didn't wish to see her and respected him by leaving without a word. It was too early to go home, though; she had no desire to be alone in the house with her mother for hours.

She drove to the pool more out of habit than anything else. It was mid-afternoon on Tuesday. There would be a lifeguard class, but this early in the semester, they'd be in the classroom. Maybe kayak or scuba, but the college usually scheduled those as night courses. She pulled on the door, surprised to find it open, but as expected, the building was quiet inside when she entered.

After passing the building manager in the foyer, and promising him she wouldn't so much as get her feet wet, she walked out onto the pool deck. The dull roar of the dehumidifier system washed over her while a trickle of water in the drains tickled her ears. She breathed the chlorinated air deep into her lungs and exhaled. Already, she felt better than she had when she left work.

She leaned against the wall to pull off her boots and then shoved her socks inside. Her aqua socks were in her car, still damp and surely frozen, so she was thankful the floor was dry. After removing the apple she'd swiped from Valkyrie's break room, she dropped her coat on top of her boots and made her way to the low diving board.

The bite of the pumice texture was both irritating and wonderful to her. She sat on the edge of the board and let her feet dangle toward the water. The white noise cleared her mind and let her drift back into Ash's closet.

She wiped the tears from her cheeks and sniffled back a sob. It hurt. The distance between them was so sudden. So sharp. So necessary. For them both.

The apple had enticed her when she swiped it from Valkyrie's break room. Now, as she stared at it, she couldn't muster the appetite to eat. It reminded her of Tia Sarita's house. The kitchen island. A restless night spent worrying about a Star Trek lieutenant's soul after she died on an alien planet. And once that train of thought got up to steam, there was no stopping it.

The world as she knew it a week ago was gone. Her father had secrets. So did Uncle Carl, Ash, and the *Book of Mormon* too. On her finger was a diamond ring, a promise made by a man she had no feelings for. She worried once more about where the souls of space explorers would go when they died. And, in her heart, was a desire to leave the complications of her faith behind, to clutch her soulmate with both hands, and to follow him to the end of the Earth.

Because Ash could not stay with her. His sanity, if not his life, were in danger every hour he remained in Coulter. And going with him…?

No. Tia Sarita's choice ripped their family in half. Seventeen years later, she still wasn't talking to her parents. Marie's family needed her, her future husband, and her children to hold them together in this life and the next.

There, she encountered, a brand-new problem.

Worthiness to go to the temple required her to repent of *everything* she did with Ash the night before. Repentance required remorse.

Marie wasn't sorry. Not one little bit. A half-hour later, when the boys arrived for diving practice and threatened to throw her in the pool—street clothes, apple, and all—she wasn't even certain what she did with Ash was wrong.

· ❄ ·

Marie hadn't slept a wink in Ash's bed. When she finally arrived back at home, she was two steps from tears and three from collapse. And the knob on the garage door…she didn't recall it ever being so hard to turn. Inside the mud room separating the garage from the foyer, she dropped to the bench.

The air in here was cool, dry, but hard to pull into her lungs. The faint, stale smell of feet took her back to Ash's closet. The butterflies trapped in her gut took flight as a phantom kiss brushed her lips. The urge to cry simmered beneath the surface, but blood-shot eyes would not do, nor would anything else that would call her mother's attention to *something wrong.*

She had to get through supper. Maybe answer some questions about work. A bit of wedding planning was unavoidable. Denied more children, the only thing her mother prayed for was grandchildren, and after years of trying to marry Marie off to every available returned missionary in town, she finally had a future son-in-law with a name.

Oh yes, the wedding would be discussed at the table tonight. And tomorrow night. And every night until Marie was sealed to a husband. Sam or some other man—her mother couldn't care less what his name was as long as he was worthy. Tonight, Marie would talk. She'd make her mother happy. And then she'd drag her butt upstairs and let sleep take her.

She pulled off her boots and placed them alongside a pair of sneakers in the cubby with her name on it. She pushed off the bench with effort and opened the door leading into the home's foyer.

A familiar spicy aroma washed over her. Years of conditioning had her mouthwatering at the smell despite having no appetite at all. She latched the door silently before laying against it and swallowed hard. How could her heart have any further to sink?

The family tamale recipe made ten dozen and her mother chose to make them today. Alone. Was it her plan for the day? To keep her hands busy? To bide her time until Marie got home? Maybe all three. Didn't matter. The smell of supper promised trouble rolled in cornhusks.

Love is spoken here.

Those words shimmered in gold cursive with flourishes and swashing strokes, set apart from the creamy beige wall below the staircase railing with brown shadows. Seeing them started a duet she learned as a young child about her praying mother and priesthood-holding father teaching her trust and obedience.

She shut her eyes tight, blocking her view of the words and the family photos placed around them. It was in vain. The entryway of their home been burned in her memory long ago. Even blind, she sensed the warm glow of the tin star chandelier her father bought her mother on their honeymoon. The whimsical Oaxacan light fixture welcomed guests as they entered the house and cast a warm glow on paintings of Joseph Smith and Jesus Christ.

Everything in this room had a place and purpose. There were no stray objects. Not even a mote of dust. Not ever.

From deeper in the house, a hymn played on classical guitar floated on the air. *I Know That My Redeemer Lives* tickled her ears and tempted her to forget her troubles. She was so tired of rejecting desires and battling conflicting truths and pretending everything would be okay if she made the choices she was supposed to. But, she couldn't let her guard down. Not yet.

Peace in the Baez home was coated on every surface in a thin veneer brittle as eggshell. It was never a matter of if or even when it would shatter, only who would be responsible. And in recent years, it had mostly been Marie and her habit of rejecting marriage opportunities. And staying with Jason after his temple recommend was denied. And *then*, after she wasted three fertile years with him, he fathered a child with her best friend.

Marie feared she'd still be hearing about the last bit in the Celestial Kingdom. If she made it there. Which was looking less likely all the time.

"You're home." The relief in her mother's voice jarred her from the thin silver lining glittering on the underbelly of her situation. With impeccable hair and wedge high heels, her mother carried a pile of towels from the laundry room to the kitchen. "Set the table, please."

"Yes, Mama."

Marie scuffed her socks along the gleaming marble floor and followed her mother into the kitchen. It was much brighter than the foyer, almost blindingly so. As she gathered the pieces she needed to set the table, she glanced around her. The supplies for tamale-making were mostly put away already. And rather than using the towel she'd needed from the laundry room, her mother was folding the whole load to put away first. Beyond the kitchen, the carpet in the living room had marks left by the vacuum.

Marie groaned inwardly. Being a housewife who lived fifteen miles out of town, it was understandable that her mother often felt lonely and isolated. It was always worse in the winter, when her gardens slept under snow. And sometimes, she also felt unappreciated by her husband and daughter. She never admitted as much, but when she felt this way, she would engage in a storm of homemaking activities and wait for family to notice.

Not only did Marie have to talk about wedding plans, she feared she would need to be sufficiently excited or her mother might well burst into tears. That would anger her father, and the Lord knew what he would insist they do to cheer her mother up. The timing couldn't be worse. She was too tired to play this game.

"Mama. Leave the towels. I'll fold them when I'm done with the table."

Her mother continued folding with the efficiency of a robot. "Did you manage to work everything out last night?"

A cloud of starlings danced in her chest at the memory of the angry kiss Ash might now regret. The plate she was pulling from the cabinet slipped out of her hand and smashed on the counter.

She and her mother gasped together and stared at the array of broken stoneware. Snapping free of her shock, Marie jogged to the broom cupboard for the dustpan. When she returned to the mess, her mother was collecting the larger shards of stoneware with her hands. Marie brushed the smaller shards off the counter into the pan.

"What are you doing?" The shrill rebuke caused Marie to jerk away from the counter. "I use that to clean the floor. I just scrubbed that counter."

"It's okay, mama. I'll clean it again." She continued sweeping the small shards and dust. Her mother grumbled at the contents of the dustpan before Marie could dispose of them.

"I don't know where all the dirt comes from, *mija*. Your papa's gone all day. You're gone."

Marie looked at the pale dust among the plate shards and imagined the faint cloud of flour around her mother as she scooped eight cups from the big plastic bin to make masa for the tamales. When she helped, she swept the floor and wiped the counters as they worked so her mother never saw the fallout.

"I'm sorry, Mama."

"It's a plate, *mija*. We have many more." She washed her hands before resuming her towel folding. "Did you and Sandra sort out how to get her shop caught up?"

Sandra was the name Signy's mother gave her at birth and some people insisted on calling her that. Marie thought that was rude. Her mother thought it was rude Signy would abandon the name her mother gave her. Marie had long since stopped trying to talk to her about it.

"The imagesetter will speed things up, but it requires—"

"Imagesetter?" Her mom returned to her pile of towels and resumed folding. "What's that?"

"It's like a laser printer, but it prints on film. We had to establish a whole new workflow around it. The shop should be in good shape by Easter."

Her mother stared at her. "Ofelia. You're getting married in May. That doesn't give you much time to plan."

She had suspected her mother assumed her going back to work would be a temporary thing, but to hear it said out loud annoyed her.

"About that—"

"Hot tamales on a cold day."

Marie and her mother both snapped their attention to her father's voice. He walked into the kitchen and kissed her mother's cheek.

"And both of my ladies in the kitchen. What a wonderful surprise."

Her mother blushed deeply with embarrassment. "I meant to have the kitchen clean before you got home."

"There are only so many hours in a day."

Her eyes narrowed and her face tightened. The words were meant to relieve her mother of the burden of taking on too much, but Marie knew she'd taken them to mean he thought her incapable of seeing her plans through. Which was ridiculous, because her mother was an amazing woman. She juggled projects like bowling pins in the hands of a career clown. But on days like this one, when she felt unappreciated, she wanted her husband to notice what she'd done, but she didn't necessarily want him to see her doing it. Having him walk into a dirty kitchen she had intended to finish cleaning before he got home was a personal failure.

Was she always like this?

As her father assured her mother it was possible to eat a meal in the same room as dirty dishes, Marie took her pile of stoneware and utensils to the table. She placed each fork, knife, and spoon with a promise to herself. She would not let marriage change her as it had her mother.

Settled into their seats, they folded their arms and bowed their heads for her father's blessing on the food. Then, Marie spooned rice and beans onto her plate. Finally, she took one tamale, because her mother had worked so hard on them.

"I was thinking..." Marie groaned inwardly at her mother's voice. "You always loved the Mesa Temple. You and Sam don't have to wait until May."

At least it was a suggestion with a reasonable counter-argument. "Winter flights for twelve people, if they took only Sam's immediate family? They couldn't swing that kind of money any time soon."

Her mother lowered her fork and gave her a warm smile. "Your father and I would be happy to cover their travel costs, *mija*."

Her father ate his supper as if her mother hadn't spoken.

"Yeah, if they accepted the offer." There was a list of reasons they'd balk. "But they'd have to pull their kids out of school. And half of Sam's family lives in Idaho..."

"It's your wedding. We will make the plans you want."

Marie moved her fork through her rice. The sweetness of her mother's approach to marrying her off as soon as possible crawled under her skin like a whole colony of ants. She knew then they weren't getting through supper without a fight. And, suddenly, that wasn't so important to her.

"What I'd really like," she said, then paused a bit as her mother's gaze gave away her excitement, "is São Paulo."

On the other side of the table, her mother's smile tightened. It had all the warmth of a plastic doll. She scoffed. "Brazil?"

"I'd like a *spring* wedding in São Paulo." Her mother's eyes bulged.

Marie's father moaned in delight. "My love, you have outdone yourself with these tamales."

Her mother ignored his praise. "*Mija*—"

Marie interrupted her. "It was Sam's mission district. You and papa have friends in Rio you haven't seen in years."

"It's summer there now. We'd be pushing the date back to September. What about Sam's brothers and sisters?"

"We make it early September and we can take them to the Independence Day parade."

Her mother sighed. "They'll have to skip school."

"They're in school *now*." Marie gingerly unwrapped the husk on her tamale. "Admit it, Mama. This isn't about what I want. It's about what you want."

"*Estefan!* Are you listening to your daughter?"

"Yes, Isabela." Her father kept his gaze on his plate and assembled his next bite. "She's not wrong."

"She's put off marriage so long it drove her man into another woman's arms."

The words shouldn't still hurt after a year, but they did. Marie gasped at the kick to her gut. Her mother's face softened. Tears welled in her eyes as if on command.

"Your papa and I have wanted to share the temple with you since you were born. How much longer will you make us wait?"

Marie's supper remained mostly uneaten. The sight and smell of the pork filling were delightful to her senses. They dredged sweet memories of her childhood, when she'd learned to spread the *masa* on cornhusks and fold them into these savory treats. She tried to put a bite into her mouth, but every time she did, the piglet Josh Praetor raised for 4-H last year popped into her head. It was so small and precious in her hands.

"*Mija*?" Her father glared at her sharply. Playing with her food was a sure way to earn his wrath. "Is there something wrong with that tamale?"

She didn't have it in her to humor her mother, so she told the truth. "I'm vegetarian."

"Why does she do this to me!" Her mother cried.

Her father's fork hit his plate with a clatter. He sat back in his chair with his hands on his hips. "Since when?"

"February."

Her mother stood from the table and took Marie's plate. "You expect me to believe you haven't eaten meat in eleven months?"

"Mama—"

She stomped toward the trashcan. "I feed you, Ofelia. You eat—"

"I eat what I can't pick out to make you happy!"

Marie didn't realize she had spoken aloud until the plate flew off her mother's hand and hit the backsplash behind the stove. The stoneware shattered. Tamale, rice, and beans smeared across the wall. One of the hand painted tiles, brought home from their family trip to Brazil was cracked in half.

Her mother clapped her hands to her face and muffled her wail. "I don't know you anymore!"

Looking skyward, her father wadded his linen napkin and threw it down in his plate. "Go to your room."

My room? "I'm 21! You can't just send me—!"

"I don't care where you go, you ungrateful brat!" he bellowed.

Marie stared down her angry father with equal rage. Her heart banged against her chest. She held her breath until her lungs burned. When she left the table, she pushed against it as if it offended her, shaking the surface and knocking over water glasses. The legs of her chair rumbled on the tile floor. She tossed her napkin where her plate used to be and stormed out.

Brat. Ungrateful.

She pushed open the door of her room. Her father's furniture. Her mother's redecorating. Boxes with her name on them. She slammed the door.

This isn't my home anymore.

Marie took hold of her top CD drawer and yanked with a roar.

She let go of the drawer and it crashed into the row of framed pictures stacked against the pile of cardboard boxes. The frames shifted. Wood cracked and glass broke. The front frame fell face down.

Oh, man. She could pick up the mess, but she couldn't hide that.

Groaning at the thought of more trouble, she fell to her knees in a pile of church magazines and pushed her hands through her hair. She weighed her want of sleep against her need to straighten the mess before her father saw. She it cursed her thin skin.

She turned around and crawled over the now crooked row of frames to survey the damage. The wood frames of a few were weakened or cracked by the impact with the drawer. Glass was broken in several of the frames. The photos and artwork appeared okay at a glance, though.

Finally, she picked up the frame that had fallen. The one in front showed their family posed in front of a white building with a central tower and a long, lean spire against a blue sky. The glass was actually intact.

She pulled the heavy mahogany frame onto her lap. The wood was wider than her palm, stained dark and burnished in areas to glow black cherry red. The black matte had two rectangular cuts. The first for the photo, and a second for a block of calligraphy.

São Paulo, Brazil Temple
30 October - 2 November, 1978
President Spencer W. Kimball

Marie sat on her mother's hip in this photo with her father at her back. She was only four at the time and had little recollection of their trip to South America. Also in the photo was a couple her parents knew. They were from Rio de Janeiro.

She touched the glass over their dark faces and drew her finger across the date.

1978. She couldn't recall their names, but she knew her parents had met them on their honeymoon. The couple had worked so hard on the temple's construction, but only a month before this picture was taken, they'd thought they wouldn't be allowed inside.

Did Heavenly Father answer their prayers? Or did the Church decide it was easier to let them in than weed them out?

She returned the frame to the row with the others, sat back, and wrapped her arms around her legs and rested her chin on her knees. She wouldn't mind getting married in São Paulo, if she was to marry at all.

Why wouldn't her Heavenly Father answer her? She'd done everything she was supposed to. Read her scriptures. Accepted her callings. Obeyed her priesthood leaders without question. Performed baptisms for the dead. Bore her testimony and tried her best to be a good example to her friends. She firmly denied Jason's every request to make out, even on those rare occasions when she actually wanted to.

What did it get her?

Betrayed. Cheated on. A crush on someone the Church would never allow her to be with. And when as she prayed for relief from grief and temptation, she fell in love with Ash while the Holy Spirit suntanned on a beach somewhere. *Thanks so frickin' much!*

As she calmed again, her eyelids became heavy. She shook off the urge to fall asleep. On her way to the bathroom to wash her face, she saw the cover of one of the magazines and stopped.

The *Ensign's* October 1995 issue was half-buried under another, but it stood out to her. Her bottom lip trembled as she plucked it from the floor. She flipped through the pages, searching for the article she remembered.

The purpose of life on Earth was to marry in the temple and to keep the covenants made there. Marie's thoughts and feelings for Ash, the authoring apostle said, were the temptations of Satan, and unless she resisted them, and repented them, they would make her unworthy to enter the Lord's temple, to be sealed to a husband, and be with her family forever.

She had seen this article the day her father brought it home from the post office. As she read it, she had felt like she was eavesdropping on a conversation she wasn't meant to hear. The writer wasn't talking to her, but to someone else in the room *about* her, as if she wasn't there at all. The words on the page transformed her, right there on the couch, from a woman with daydreams into a patient with an affliction dangerous as alcoholism or compulsion to murder.

For a long while that day, she had sat with the magazine in her hands, becoming more worried with every tick of the grandfather clock down the hall, *why* the writer had to remind faithful subscribers of an *LDS* magazine of their duty to love friends and family. She began to wish she could speed up time or disappear until Ash had moved along. Then, life could go back to the way it was before she developed her strange attraction to another woman.

And then, she realized, she could disappear. Her mother would fight her going to Tia Sarita's for an extended visit, but she wouldn't win if her father decided to check her into rehab. She didn't need to harm herself; she just needed to get caught. It was a shameful thing to do, and it didn't even work.

A knock at her door startled her.

"Come in."

The door opened, and her father walked inside. She dropped her gaze a bit. "I'm sorry, Papa."

He pocketed his hands. "As am I."

She had expected anger but he gave her shared guilt, and she wasn't sure what to do with it.

"Where's Mama?"

"Downstairs. Washing dishes."

Perfect. One more thing I'm supposed to do but didn't.

Marie sat down where she stood and pulled her knees into her chest again, trapping the magazine she held between her legs and chest.

Her father sat on the foot of the bed and laced his fingers in his lap. "What's on your mind?"

Oh, so many things, but could she talk about them with him? She looked at at him for a moment, seeing genuine concern in his eye.

Growing up, her mother had been the fixer. When Marie had a problem, Mama was there with a solution ready to make everything better. Her father preferred to listen and share anecdotes he thought would help her solve her own problems.

Her mother couldn't fix what bothered Marie now, and her father was right here. She preferred his approach to hers now anyway. "If I tell you, will you promise to not get mad?"

"I can promise to do my very best."

Here goes. "I don't think I can marry Sam."

His head tilted and studied her. She twisted her fingers around each other, waiting for him to respond. She expected rage, especially after what happened at supper.

"May I ask why not?"

The skin around his eyes and mouth were relaxed. He wasn't mad.

Still, she answered him cautiously. "I don't really want to."

"That goes without saying." He regarded her with the same confusion blooming in her own mind. "The look on your face, when you saw him in my office…you were not happy to see him."

"You saw that?" She frowned as he nodded.

"It was hard to miss. I expected your reunion to be much happier."

"He wrote me a letter last year. Asked me to think about marrying him. It makes sense. I mean…it's *Sam*, Papa. He's the *perfect* man."

"You know there's no such thing, right?" When she didn't reply, her father dovetailed his fingers. "Relationships are hard work, mija. Perfect parts are not as important as interconnecting ones. You and Sam fit as well as any two pieces can."

"No, we don't." She couldn't believe she was about to try to explain to her father. "His kisses are like…wet cotton balls on my lips."

His eyebrows arched high, demanding details.

"I'm supposed to have babies with him? My skin crawls when he touches me."

"Well, this wasn't the conversation I came upstairs to have."

He slid from the bed and sat on the floor in front of her. He rested his forearms on his knees and turned his hands palms upward. She placed her hands on his. This was how he'd once given her pep talks before diving meets and advice after rough days at school. This was how she told him about Jason and Sarah, and right about the same spot on this floor. Only now, the old carpet was gone. Hardwood had taken its place.

"Your mother will punch me for telling you this story, so keep it zipped."

"I will."

"Our wedding day…worst day of my life."

She frowned. "You've been shot at in a jungle on the other side of the world."

"Yes, I have."

"You've lost seven unborn children."

"At least."

Seven were detected by ultrasound. How many more may have passed through her mother without notice? Her father refused to speculate. Her mother couldn't help it.

"I'm serious. Wedding day takes the cake." He paused for a long moment. "Your mama and I, we had modesty and purity and worthiness drilled into us too, and we had big plans for after the sealing."

Marie whined. "Papa."

"No, you brought it up. Now you get to hear all about your mom and me."

"Fine."

"We got into the honeymoon suite. We were alone, and…your mama shut down. Locked herself in the bathroom. Wouldn't come out."

Her jaw fell agape.

"Two hours later, I called her papa, my brand new *father-in-law*, for help coaxing her out."

"Oh, no!"

"Oh, yes! And *then*, I got to stand there and watch him give *my wife* a priesthood blessing to help get her through *her* wedding night."

There was still bitterness there. That seemed odd after twenty-three years.

"It helped her, though, right? The blessing?"

"We really should have waited. But, she was afraid it would stretch out the awkwardness, so we fumbled through. I was clumsy. She felt dirty afterward. We slept in separate rooms." He gave her a thumbs up. "Real romantic."

"I'm sorry, but this is supposed to *encourage* me?"

"Yes." He smiled brightly. "A week later, we were in Oaxaca. Saw some ruins. Met lifelong friends. Bought the chandelier downstairs. Fed each other breakfast in bed every morning. Came home with you. Our miracle."

It did comfort her to know the bedroom didn't remain an awkward, scary place for her mother.

"Whatever your feeling, it's normal, *mija*. I'm sure, when you talk to Sam, he's feeling it too."

Was focusing on *her* right now too much to ask?

"I'm not afraid. I don't want to have sex with Sam."

He regarded her with caring condescension. She knew in her bones the next words out of his mouth would be along the lines of "don't knock it 'til you try it." Like it was something she could choose but didn't.

"You say that now, but how can you know? You've never done it."

"I'm not nervous, Papa." She hugged her knees into her chest tighter and laid her chin on her knees. "I'm not curious. I'm not interested."

Her father stared at her. "That can't be true."

"It *can* be, because it is!" With Sam, it was. With Ash, totally different story, but she was not sharing that right now. "There's no place in Heavenly Father's kingdom for a woman who doesn't want children."

"There's a place for everyone who does all they can, *mija*."

All they can. He meant to reassure her, but only reminded her of one of Jason's black verses. *For we know it is by grace we are saved, after all we can do.*

He kissed her head and left. The door clicked shut behind him.

Marie scrambled across her bed and grabbed her cordless handset. She started dialing Blessed Beans, but hung up before finishing the number. Another number popped into her head. While pressing the digits, she wondered if it was right to call. So much time had passed.

Before it even rang on the other end, a familiar voice answered. "Marie?"

Hearing Sarah's hushed voice hurt more than she anticipated. "I'm sorry. I know it's late, but…"

· ❄ ·

Marie parked her car in the alley lot the Swing family had created for their kids and entered the back yard by a tall wood gate. As she walked down the concrete path that bisected the bishop's back yard, Jason barged out of the door of the basement apartment and bounded up the stairs to meet her.

"Why did you call Sarah?"

His anger stunned Marie. Jason had never raised his voice with her in the whole six years they'd dated, and he'd done it twice in three days. It wasn't uncalled for, but it shocked her.

She fought the tightness in her chest to breathe. She had a reason, moments ago. "Does it matter?"

"Yes!" He crossed his arms and widened his stance, blocking the stairwell to his apartment like a guard dog. "Our home is the one place in this town she isn't judged. You're not dragging heartbreak into—"

She slapped her hands to her face at the realization she had done it again. "I'm sorry!"

Her problems tonight didn't involve Jason and Sarah, but they didn't know that. Far as they knew, she'd come to hash out their affair in *their* house. She let her hands fall and looked on the scowling face of her ex-boyfriend.

"I didn't think. It's been brought to my attention I never do."

Those words softened him a tiny bit.

"I need to talk to her, Jason."

"About?"

"Tamales." The word tumbled out of her mouth, surprising her as well as him, but as it hung in the air between them, she warmed to the simplicity of it. It precisely fit why she'd called Sarah.

He looked at her bag and back at her with hope. "Oh, please tell me you brought your mama's tamales?"

Marie shook her head and he frowned. "Sorry. I left home in a hurry."

She had left home with her oversized purse and called out to her parents that she was going out as she made her way to the mudroom. Her mother ran to stop her. Her father ran to stop her mother. She ignored them both. She shoved her feet into her boots, grabbed her coat, and pulled her keys out of her pocket as she navigated the garage. Her parents followed, bickering all the way. As the garage door opened, her sobbing mother begged Marie not to leave while simultaneously berating her father for not doing anything to help with their daughter.

She's an adult, Isabela.

"So, if you didn't bring tamales…" Jason prodded her

Marie crossed her own arms to block the chill boring its way through her coat. "Making them takes a certain amount of space in the kitchen. We clear the counters first, so that we'll have room to work."

Jason's head cocked.

"Do you find solving problems can be like that? You get to a point where you run out of room in your head to process everything thrown your way. You have to let things go before you can work on what matters?"

Sarah emerged from the apartment wrapped in a crocheted afghan. With the porch light behind her, Marie couldn't see her face, but her approach seemed timid.

"It doesn't matter anymore. You and her. To me. It doesn't matter." She spoke the words so Sarah could hear them. It pleased her to see the puff of frost from both of her friend's mouths, evidence of the collective breath rushing from both of their lungs. "I need you, Sarah. More than I was ever hurt. I miss you both."

Sarah took hold of his arm. "I told you."

He pulled his wife into a hug. A spark ignited on his cheek as a tear caught the porch light. He sniffled and pinched his nose. Marie recognized the gesture as him unsticking his frozen nasal passages.

When he finally spoke, his voice was breathy. Vulnerable. "She never gave up hope you'd forgive us. I doubted, but she—"

Marie closed the distance between them and wrapped her arms about them both. "You know I can't hold a grudge to save my life."

With his free arm, he circled her waist as if she were made of glass. It was Sarah who replied. "You were so angry, for so long, and then you—"

As she suspected her suicide attempt was about to come up, she pulled away. "It's really cold out here."

Jason chuckled. Wiping the tears from his eyes, he nodded, and Sarah led the way back to the house.

Inside, Sarah rounded the open door and grabbed for the teakettle as it began to whistle. Their kitchen contained a fridge, a stove, and a sink. The microwave was on top of the fridge. They had butcher block on wheels that they kept between the stove and the door when not in use. Cabinets had been mounted above the sink and the butcher block's storage space. Their pantry and their cooking supplies were stored in commercial shelving on the other side of the door.

Jason slipped off his sneakers and Marie followed his lead, pulling off her boots and placing them in the line of footwear by the door. When he pointed toward the couch, she tiptoed across the floor.

Her hosts performed in well-practiced harmony, placing a respectable tea service on the coffee table almost without making a sound. It was as if Jason and Sarah did this every day. Is this what their lives had become? Were they, at the ripe age of twenty-one, mute slaves of an infant master?

Her concern was banished by an adoring smile on Sarah's face as she peeked into the crib, which was sandwiched between the couch and the wall. She turned away from the baby and sat in the chair opposite the couch.

From prior visits, back when Jason's older brother had lived here, Marie had climbed over a queen-size bed to get to the bathroom on the other side. There was another door to the basement's small bath and laundry, but at the time, there was a bookcase in front of it.

That corner was really the only spot in the tiny home a crib would fit.

"I'm sorry," Sarah whispered. "I really thought Neil would keep Jay out later."

Jason sat on the arm of her chair. "Ash came by the pool hall to talk to him, so I left."

"Is Ash okay?" The question sounded too eager to her own ears. Jason and Sarah cocked their heads to the right in almost perfect unison. Marie added, "It's just a question."

"She was out of sorts, actually." Jason eyed her with suspicion. "I mean, we haven't hung out in a while, but I remember her cutthroat game being a lot better."

Marie dropped her head into her hands. *What should I do?*

"I can't tell you how happy it made me to hear your voice on the phone." Sarah's spoke quietly, barely whispered. "But I know you didn't call to catch up. You're not okay, are you?"

Sarah was right. She and Jason knew her, maybe as well as she knew herself. It was why she had shoved her pride on a shelf and drove over here. She needed people who would *listen* to her instead of reminding her giving birth to some man's children was the point of her existing at all.

And she wanted to tell them everything, but she couldn't speak. Not without crying. Not without waking their sleeping child. Instead, she opened the bag she'd brought with her and pulled out the October issue of *Ensign* magazine. She walked her fingers across the upper corner, pulling back the pages, until she found the article that made her want to die. Pressing the spread to her chest, she said a small prayer for their mercy on her and passed it across the table.

Sarah took the magazine. Her eyebrows pinched together as she read the first page. She glanced at Marie, back at the article, and read some more. Her lips twisted more and more as time passed.

Jason gave the page a bare glance over his wife's shoulder, perhaps long enough to catch the headline, and smiled. He released a soft sound, part huff, part snicker, and shook his head with closed eyes.

The article concerned Sarah, though. "Are you trying to say you like girls?"

"No!" Marie cringed and looked over at the sleeping baby for signs of stirring. "I mean I—I *do*, but—" Shaking her head, she deflated. "It's complicated."

Sarah's eyebrows knitted together and Jason's lifted. Marie had surprised him. Twice in one night was a new record.

"The gun thing." She tipped her head at the magazine. "It was the day *that* showed up at my house."

That visibly piqued Jason's interest. "May I?"

Sarah put the magazine in his hand. As he thumbed through the article, his eyes flicked rapidly back and forth. The frown on his face deepened and twisted.

"Ugh, reading this makes me want to off myself," he said.

Jason's sarcasm riled her a bit. Back in October, the fear of anyone suspecting she had feelings for a *girl* chilled her skin while raising her blood pressure. She had quit Valkyrie and fretting about her attraction to Ash occupied a lot of her time. That article pushed her to do something disgraceful. She'd carry the shame of it all her life.

"The gun might have been my worst idea ever."

"*Might*?" Sarah's voice stirred the baby and the three of them froze until Carmina settled back into sleep.

"I'd take it back if I could, but…anyway, I just delayed facing my problem. I've been back five days and I've gone from *thinking* about Ash, to—" She cut herself off, remembering her promise to pretend nothing had changed.

"Explains her sucking at pool." Jason flipped to the next page. "She got a taste of you and now she's jonesing."

Marie frowned at ambivalence. "You aren't surprised? I just told I like women, and—"

"No, you don't." Jason spoke distractedly with most of his attention still on the article. "Or men, either. That's where you're confused? You're attracted to both. And yet…*neither*."

Sarah glowered at him. "You're not making sense."

Jason closed the magazine and turned to his wife. "Do you remember how much it bothered you when Sam became the girl's swim team manager?"

Sarah stiffened and her lips pursed. She leaned away from him. "He did it to be with her. You know that."

"But she didn't," Jason said.

What?

He shrugged. "No matter how much time Sam spent with you, or how obvious he was, you looked at him like he was a poster on a wall."

"Sam was obvious?" Marie asked.

This time it was Sarah who scoffed.

"You don't respond to sexual cues. And you don't give off any of your own." He continued reading the article. "Once, when we were fifteen, I saw something in your eyes and thought you *might* be receptive to fooling around a little, but…"

With an evil glare, Sarah pinched a bit of leg hair between his pants leg and his sock.

"Ow!"

Carmina wailed in her crib.

Sarah frowned at Jason and pushed out of her chair. She returned a few moments later with their fussy daughter clutched to her breast.

Jason caressed the baby's head with a gentle hand. "Sweetheart, I'm so sorry."

Three feet away, Marie's ex-boyfriend adored a child he'd made with another woman. And she was oddly content at the sight. There was no bitterness in her heart. No stirring within her to have one of her own.

When Carmina was settled again, nursing happily, Jason lifted his hand away. "Anyhow, because I am also a gentleman, I spent the next several years looking for your tell. Waiting for it. It happened now and then, but never when making out might have been possible."

"Hold up." She snapped herself free of awareness she *really* didn't want to be a mother. "What does any of that have to do with who I'm attracted to?"

"I know you only agreed to marry Sam because that's what you're supposed to do. Get married. Have kids. Grow the Church. But you're indifferent toward him, M. Always have been. Maybe always will be. You could make it work if sex was something you were into, but..."

She swallowed back the bile rising in her throat.

"You're so rarely turned on, it might actually scare you when it happens."

The words rumbled through her like a pile of log collapsing. Her hands clenched at the couch. Her back teeth ground together as her toes curled hard in her floor.

"How much babymaking do think you can take if reading this..." Jason said, holding up the magazine, "made you want to die?"

Her entire body recoiled at the thought. Sarah watched her with sharp, haunted eyes. "Sam will expect quite a bit."

The comment shocked Marie out of her nausea. "What?"

Sarah caressed her suckling daughter's fuzzy head with her thumb the same way Jason had and said nothing.

He closed the magazine. "If it's a second opinion you need, the article has nothing to do with you."

She ripped her attention away from Sarah. "How doesn't it?"

"It's about ministering to homosexuals, M. You're *not* gay." He shrugged a bit. "You're not straight either. You're something else…like, you were *Jay*-sexual, and now you're…*Ash*-sexual."

She forced her next question past her burning throat and tight vocal chords. "How do I square that with the gospel?"

Jason tossed the magazine past Sarah. It fell with a thump into the diaper pail. "You can't."

Don't Speak

A cry coaxed Marie from a nightmare into a strange place. By the time she'd placed herself on Jason and Sarah's couch, she'd forgotten what the dream was about, but the foreboding remained with her. She pulled the crocheted afghan covering her tight as a list of her circumstances scrolled in her head. Her fiancé was bound to take issue with her sleeping at her ex-boyfriend's house. She didn't know what time it was but assumed it was after midnight. Her parents were undoubtedly worried and most likely angry she'd hadn't come home.

She had to be at Valkyrie at eight in the morning. The clothes she had on were the same she'd worn to work two days ago, and she hadn't thought to bring a pair of clean underwear when she left home.

The wail that woke her became louder. A door closed, and Jason walked through the living room. He pulled open the fridge, retrieved a bottle, and after a deft maneuver to remove the top while holding his child in one arm, he popped it into the microwave for exactly seven seconds.

Marie watched him in the dim light as he put the bottle back together and squirted some of the contents onto his tongue. Satisfied, he situated the baby in his left arm and gave her the nipple. Carmina's cries suddenly stopped.

He sat in the chair across from her. Pretending to sleep while her ex-boyfriend fed his daughter seemed voyeuristic, so she sat up.

"I'm sorry," Jason said. "I didn't mean to wake you."

She rested her head against the arm of the couch. "I'm the one imposing."

"You're no trouble." He jiggled the bottle a bit. "You will always be welcome in our home."

It was a relief to hear, but impractical for her hosts.

"Isn't Sarah nursing?" *I sound judgmental.* "I mean, I just heard that mothers do one or the other."

"It's breastmilk. We have a pump so I can take the midnight stuff." He smiled at his daughter. "I like this time, just me and her."

"I'm supposed to envy you." Everything she'd been taught from childhood told her she should want a baby. "What does it say about me that I don't?"

"What does it say?" He seemed to be talking to himself rather than her. "In the hospital, the nurses really pushed nursing. Said it was best for the baby. One even said any woman who says she couldn't make it work didn't try hard enough. Never say stuff like that to a new mom, by the way. You can't know what kind of guilt she's already living with."

His frown was clear, even in the dark, and his gaze fell somewhere to his right. Whatever distracted him passed, though. He looked at her. "And it's baloney, anyway. Babies need vitamins and minerals and calories. Where it comes from doesn't matter."

"I don't understand."

"How it answers your question?"

She nodded.

"What a baby needs most is a *happy* mom."

It made sense to her but cracked open a more important question she hadn't yet considered. If she didn't want to be a mom, could she be happy? And how would it affect her children if she wasn't?

"Mormon girls are taught to be selfless." He put the bottle aside and lifted Carmina onto his chest to pat her on the back. "To always put the needs of other people before your own. But sometimes, Marie, what you're *supposed* to do is exactly what you *shouldn't* do. If you don't want to have a baby, for whatever reason, no matter how selfish someone else says it is, *don't...have...a baby.*"

A baby might be all that could salvage her relationship with her mother.

She groaned. "Mama must be having a cow right now."

"Maybe, but I called your dad after you fell asleep. They know you're here."

It was a relief to hear, but only a little. Her parents didn't like Jason, so she could add him to the list of things she'd be hearing about later. "Thank you."

"That's what friends are for, M." He stood to return to the bedroom. "Hey, come by Raleigh's tonight. The rock star refuses to sing *chick* songs and I'm itching to play some Tori.'"

Marie suspected by the end of the day, she'd need to sing for her sanity, but she didn't want to seem too eager. "I'll think about it."

Jason disappeared with Carmina into the bedroom.

She laid down again and pulled the afghan around her. As sleep eluded her and every minute took five to pass, she anticipated the worst day of her life.

· ❄ ·

Dawn finally oozed into the basement apartment like lava, an unstoppable force in no particular hurry to get anywhere. Marie left a thank you note on the living room table and braved the frozen morning. Outside, she found the block heater for her engine plugged into an extension cord. Tracks in the snow suggested Sarah had done it when she left for work a few hours earlier.

The Camry's engine struggled to turn over, but succeeded with a few pumps of gas, and Marie sent a quick prayer asking the Lord to bless her friend. Had Sarah always been this thoughtful? Or was she working to make amends now?

Maybe Marie's father was right when he called her ungrateful, because she couldn't say for sure.

She pulled into the rear lot at work and entered Valkyrie by the press room door. Signy's old Heidelberg chugged along like a train, which told Marie her boss was nearby. She turned sharply away from the direction of the press and passed through the loading dock to get to the Strip Club. There she found Mitchell hunched over a light table, cutting windows in sheets of orange vinyl mask. Judging by the number of sheets he kept at hand, there was only one job it could be.

"The annual report?"

Mitchell hummed. "I saved you the color signature."

"Thanks." She cringed at her unintended sarcasm.

"That's what you get for being faster than me."

She laughed, again without meaning to. *Get a hold of yourself, girl.*

Mitchell stood from his work and glanced over at her. "Seriously, though…" He eyed her with concern. "Um, if you can strip the color plates for that, I can knock out the rest."

She shrugged off her coat and laid it over her stool. "It's what I do."

Frowning, he laid his pen knife on his light table and approached her. He looked into her eyes as if trying to see what was behind them.

"If I didn't know better…" Mitchell crossed his arms. "Are you hungover?"

"Of course, I'm not." He suspected her of *drinking*? "Why would you—"

"Because you look it."

She slumped on her stool. "I haven't been sleeping well."

He pulled his seat closer to her and leaned against it. "You're only good to me sharp. Go home."

"I can't, Mitchell." She hoped her desperation achieved puppy-dog eyes. "I need to work right now. Please."

He frowned. "Okay. But I will order you to nap if you start crashing. Understood?"

"I'll be fine."

Mitchell returned to his work reluctantly. As the morning progressed, his fears bore out. Marie's hands shook. She held her tools tighter than usual to compensate. She made progress on the color signature of the booklet, but only from intense concentration.

When she broke her fifth razor blade in ten minutes, she saw Mitchell move in her peripheral vision. He walked into the copy shop and returned a minute later with a shadow.

"Cal. Let's get tacos."

Her other coworker dropped his paintbrush into a cup of water. "Yes, sir."

Ash stopped beside her light table and crossed his arms on the metal frame surrounding the glowing white glass. Marie did not look up. Panic squeezed her heart. They'd be alone when Mitchell and Cal left. She wanted to be. It was the last thing either of them needed, though.

Marie measured a precise cut across an orange vinyl sheet, focusing her attention there. Not on Ash.

"You guys want us to bring lunch back?"

"No thanks." She curled her toes toward the floor at the sound of her own voice. The strain in her throat was audible. *They know.* She carefully placed her knife point into the vinyl next to her ruler. At her left, she saw Ash's head shake, and her coworkers left out of the side door.

The moment the door latched behind them, she pressed into the vinyl. The knife point broke with an audible snap. She shoved the tool away from her. The broken blade scratched the emulsion of a loose piece of film. Ash pulled his arms back and watched the knife fall.

When it stopped rolling, he retrieved it from the floor. "Mitchell was right."

"About?"

"You look like trampled shit."

Marie wilted and hung her head. They couldn't send her home. She wouldn't go home.

"Fuck." He took hold of her arm. "Come with me."

She didn't budge from her stool. "I've leaned on you way too much."

"Let me decide when I've had enough."

This time, she obeyed when he tugged on her arm. He led her into the dim, red-lit dark room and instructed her to sit on the busted couch between the sink and the film storage cabinet. He swung around and behind her and wrapped his arms around her shoulders. She let him pull her into him as he lay back into the corner.

"You want to tell me what's wrong?"

"Me." She fought to keep the waiting sobs in her chest. "I'm wrong."

"You are not." She flinched at the hard edge in his voice.

"Then why does my Heavenly Father hate me?"

"Why would you think He does?" His question had a note of sadness.

She opened her mouth and her troubles gushed out. Commandments she'd vowed to obey and promises her heart was compelled to break. Scriptures taunting her with divine riches while demanding perfection. A mother who wanted her grandchildren *now* and a sin Marie couldn't repent.

"Why did He do this to me?"

His lips touched the crown of her head as she confessed what she now knew as the truth.

"Why would He put you in my path and then tell me no? Any worthy Mormon man is fine with Him, but if I choose *you*, He takes my family from me? Because he *loves* me?"

Ash sighed heavily. For a long time, he said nothing and held her tight with his arms wrapped around her and his legs laced through hers. And she wished they could stay there forever. In his embrace, she felt safe.

"There were three crosses on Calvary. Remember?"

She nodded. Every Christian knew how their Savior died.

"One of the thieves asked Jesus to remember him in heaven. And Jesus said, 'You will be with me in paradise'."

She sobbed at those words.

He kissed her forehead. "Jesus does not expect more of you than of the sinners he lived and died with."

Those words filled her chest with warmth as if her heart had burst. The heat washed through her body like a flood. They were so simple. So *beautiful*. They felt true. She wanted them to be.

Clutching his sleeve, she sniffled back a sob on his shoulder. "What do I do now?"

"Walk away."

"I can't!"

"I know the torment you're feeling." He spoke softly, but she could hear his patience wearing thin. "I've lived with it all my life. There's a perfect version of you painted in your head by someone else and trying to be her is killing you. Let her go."

"*The Book of Morm—*"

"Forget *The Book of Mormon* right now." He caressed her cheek with gentle fingers. "Is your *church* a safe place?"

Yes! No. "What?"

Of course, it was. *I'm what's wrong.*

"If it doesn't bring you peace, what's the fucking point of staying?"

She felt a snap within her. Ash caught her as she fell, pulling her closer to him as her body became dead weight. He always caught her.

"I don't have much, M. God knows my life is less than perfect, but...I have space in it just for you. Say the word and we'll leave this town right now."

· ❄ ·

Marie had woken up in the dark room alone sometime later. When she emerged, Cal was burning plates and Mitchell was stripping the magenta plate from the signature he'd assigned to her. She'd completed the yellow early and had been about half-way through stripping the magenta layer when Mitchell pulled Ash out of the copy shop to talk to her.

Because she needed the yellow plate film to continue working, and Mitchell had it to align the remaining magenta films to it, she couldn't continue until he was done. She promised him she'd be back and committed to staying late to finishing the other two colors. He waved her off and she left.

The high school swim coach was in the pool office doing paperwork. The room had a glass wall, giving him clear view of the length of the pool, so he gave her permission to dive if she wanted. She retrieved her swim suit from the back seat of the car.

Soon, she stood at the back of the high diving board. While going in through the motions of a forward dive with two somersaults, it occurred to her she was holding a gun in her hands once again. Unlike the real one she put to her head, this one was loaded. Ash gave it to her and let her hold onto it, because pain would follow any choice she made.

Finger off the trigger.

Know what's behind your target.

Don't point at anything you don't want dead.

His offer to run away radiated power she'd never before experienced. It warmed her flesh and electrified her skin. As it ebbed and flowed in her veins, it calmed her. Gave her space to breathe.

But it also asked questions demanding answers, beginning with Ash's. *What's the point?*

What was the point of reading scriptures promising peace while threatening her soul? Of praying for unhelpful answers she already knew? Of worshipping a God who expected absolute obedience from her while He played terrible games at her expense?

For so long, she blamed herself for the Holy Ghost not speaking to her. Was she wrong? Was her faith failing *her* and not the other way around?

It was a sin to consider such things.

She threw dives that punished arrogance with pain and bruises. She launched into them propelled by fury and landed them with all the grace of a rampant bull. The adrenaline of the fall, the burn of chlorine in her sinuses, and the sting of failure on the water's surface fueled a pursuit of relief. It hovered past her grasp, though. At last, diving left her panting in the gutter, physically spent yet still unsatisfied.

Diving used to help her put life into perspective. Better than talking through her problems. Better than prayer. And she didn't know when it failed her, or when wailing grunge rock took its place as the best way to bleed her stress.

She left the pool deck before the high school let the boys out of class. She stood under the hot shower and turned the loaded gun over and over in her mind. Her heart resisted the whispers—*what if the Church isn't true?*—but it couldn't dismiss what Ash said in Valkyrie's darkroom. Her faith required unfailing devotion and unquestioning obedience. Her fertility was a down-payment on a great reward for which she must die before claiming. In the meanwhile, the Church promised hope and comfort but delivered neither. Not to her. Not for a long time.

Leaving town tempted her. Oh, how nice it would be to let go of the ledge she was hanging onto by her fingernails. Grab Ash and drive. Escape the walls pushing in around them both.

I can't.

Her mother believed Marie was extraordinary. Most mothers did of their children, of course, but hers had the notion her daughter was foreordained by the Lord for a great purpose. What other reason could He have for taking her ability to have more children if the one he entrusted to her wasn't special to Him? She clutched nothing closer to her breast than that belief, not even her daughter.

The diving board was the only place Marie had ever failed on her own. Her mother had always shared the blame, true or not, or whether Marie wanted her to or not. No, she couldn't leave town with Ash right now. She wasn't ready, but even if she was, she feared the weight of her mother's failure to guide her safely along the Lord's path might kill the woman where she stood.

And there lay the heart of the decision she could not put off. Break her mother's heart? Or live out her mortal years with her own in pieces, holding out hope death would fix her?

First things first.

She couldn't resolve anything with the storm cloud hovering over her head. It was time to give Sam his ring back.

· ❄ ·

Marie returned to work, as promised, and stripped the two remaining plates of the color signature Mitchell assigned her that morning. Their press was small; it only ran one color at a time. Looking over at the press, currently churning out pages, the ink on the blanket cylinder was pink, and the output on the page appeared orange. Sometimes Signy pulled all-nighters, so Marie burned the cyan and black plates so her boss would have them.

She had planned to go home for supper, a shower, and a change of clothes. Then, she'd excuse herself to go to the church to meet up with Sam. The youth gathered at church on Wednesday nights, and it was a safe assumption he would go after work.

However, burning the plates kept her at work until seven. She could miss Sam if she went home first, so she called home from Signy's office phone. And her mother was already unhappy.

Mudbug, as her father referred to his Army medic friend from Louisiana, was fond of dropping in unannounced while passing through on his way from the bayou to Fort Lewis. He had appeared in her father's office doorway right about the time she was leaving the swimming pool. *Stevie*—as the man called her father–owed him a beer in perpetuity and he'd come to collect. There were only a few evenings per year her father was both in town and not at his own table for supper. This was going to be one of them.

Marie couldn't know this when she called. Nor could she know her mother would make an effort to accommodate her vegetarian diet with a pan of eggplant parmesan. Which her mother had driven thirty miles to get the ingredients for, and would now eat alone, because her family made other plans.

After the wailing and gnashing of teeth subsided, Marie told her she was going to church to see Sam. That was enough to cheer her mother. She dropped in a hint about grandchildren before Marie managed to gracefully hang up the phone.

Would the punches never end?

She opened the first of the two sets of doors. The foyer beyond the glass was empty, but the sounds indicated the building was occupied. Dribbling. Pounding feet and squeaks of sneakers on a wood floor. Shouts. In high school, they had all spent Wednesday nights in the cultural hall. Sarah and Marie would sit on either side of Jason at the piano while Sam played basketball.

Floor polish and fresh sweat washed over her as she pulled open the door of the gym. She unzipped her coat but kept it on. She didn't plan on staying long.

Panning the floor, she found Sam guarding a young black man she recognized from the local paper. The college recruited him from Wisconsin and gave him a full scholarship to play basketball. Sam did his best, but the kid had him by at least four inches when he was on the ground, which was not as often as Sam probably would have liked.

Marie walked along the wall to the edge of the stage and leaned against it. She might have watched them play for a while, but Sam looked over at her and called for a time out. He gestured at another man to take his spot and walked off the court. She glimpsed his white temple garment as he used his t-shirt to wipe the sweat from his face.

"Hey. What's up?" he asked.

She ticked her head in the direction of the door and turned from the stage. He jogged ahead to open the door for her. The foyer seemed dimmer than before. The air felt heavier.

"We need to talk."

"Can it wait until you want to?" He sat on the arm of a nearby couch. She cocked her head, feigning confusion. He frowned a bit. "Knock on a few doors and you pick up on body language. This…" He gestured vaguely to her entire body. "This says you'd rather be anywhere but here."

Behind her back, Marie played with the ring on her finger, pulling it to her knuckle before pushing it back. "I'm afraid that won't change."

His frown tightened into a scowl. Doubt clawed at her decision. Was she really going to do this? End an engagement to worthy, priesthood-holding man who wanted to take her to the temple?

"Eternity is a long time to be with someone who doesn't love you, Sam."

"M." He smiled and spoke in a hushed, reassuring tone. He unwrapped himself and took her arms in his hands. "Take a moment. Look back on the years we've been friends. How could you think I don't love you?"

His question hardened her resolve. She raised her hands between them and pushed his arms away. "I'm talking about *me*. I don't love you."

His hands settled on his hips. "You might if you made an effort."

She crossed her arms over her chest. "I thought by accepting your proposal I could fix another problem, but I've only made it worse. I'm sorry, Sam. I never should have said yes. Either way, it's not fair to you, but I can't—"

"Fair? You asked me for space and time. I gave it to you." He chuckled sourly. "My mother has told family in nine states I'm getting married. They're planning a family reunion for the week of the open house."

Open house? They were already planning a reception? "We haven't set a date yet, Sam! What open house?"

At least he had the decency to look apologetic. "Mom was talking to grandma. They found a convenient date in July when most of the family can get together and—"

How could they—? She straightened her posture and eyed him with contempt. "I'm happy for them. I hope they have fun."

He sighed. "Ash isn't just a friend, is she?"

"What?" The question knocked her sideways. It was unexpected from him, but the last thing she wanted to be asked right now by anyone.

"Here's what I'm thinking. Last year was rough on you. She was there when you were vulnerable. You got close. A little curious. You've done some things with her that you shouldn't have, and now you don't know what to tell the bishop. Am I close?"

She swallowed hard. She bristled at his casual tone and the way his words undressed her. Worse, she detected amusement in his voice and the slight pull of his lip.

"It's okay," he said. Marie refrained from shivering as he grasped her shoulders again. "It can be your secret."

He had guessed, correctly, she'd *done some things* with another woman. "It doesn't bother you?"

Sam leaned in close. "It's hot as heck, if I'm honest." He placed his hand under her jaw and closed her mouth for her. "Just tell the bishop what he expects to hear. I promise everything will be fine."

A puzzle piece, sitting askew in her head, snapped into place. The night before, when Jason had wondered aloud how much "baby-making" she could stand, Sarah had made an unsettling remark. *Sam will expect quite a bit.* The words had been under her skin since. They clung to her skin all night. The specter of this particular aspect of marriage was largely responsible for her breakdown at work.

Marie and Jason had daydreamed about the family they'd have together someday, and she'd always assumed Sam and Sarah did the same. As much as she had dwelled in the past twenty-four hours on her future husband's expectations, she had never made the jump to any other way his ex-girlfriend might know about them. It was impossible not to now.

"You lied."

He stiffened in an instant. "Pardon me?"

"Your Temple Recommend." His lips pursed and twisted. "When the bishop asked if you were keeping the Law of Chastity...you lied. Didn't you?"

She took the deer-in-headlights gape as a confession.

The Holy Ghost guided the bishop. How could he not tell Sam was lying?

Unless...

The ground beneath her feet crumbled. She put her hands on the insides of his arms and wiggled out of his hold on her.

"Marie—"

She turned away from him. "No. No, no, no…."

"Please, M—"

"This conversation is over."

He grabbed her arm as she pushed past him. "It'll be over when you stop being a brat."

Marie yanked her arm out of his grasp and stumbled backward. She landed awkwardly on the couch.

"I'm sorry." He pulled her off the couch and pressed her hand to his heart. Before she had her composure back, he'd moved in close and wrapped his other arm behind her waist. They stood there, frozen in a dance. "I didn't mean it."

"Which part?"

"I served my mission. I've brought souls to the Church. The past doesn't matter. I swear to you, I'm worthy now." He leaned in toward her and nuzzled her nose with his. "Please. Don't go."

"I have to."

His body tightened and became rigid. "Give me a chance to explain before you call this quits. Is that too much to ask?"

"Yes."

He didn't understand. She could see it. Indignation at her refusal to give him what he wanted. Blame for taking back her promise. Anger for rejecting him. Even if everything else was perfect, *this moment* would be her cue to walk away.

But nothing at all in her world was right. There was nothing he could say now to fix it.

"Let me go." She pushed as his chest, trying to get away from him, but he held her too tight.

"Marie—"

"Now!"

He pulled his hands away and held them up as if she were arresting him.

She took several steps backward, keeping eye contact with him until a metal bar hit her in the back. When she was in the empty space between the inner and outer sets of glass doors, she turned and shoved her way outside. In the freezing dark, she ran.

· ❄ ·

Marie stepped between limbs and across extension cords snaking across Raleigh's basement floor and plopped onto *her* pile of pillows by the drum kit. She leaned back against the couch, propped her elbows on her knees, and rested her head in her hands.

Sam lied.

The bishop interviewed him *twice* before he left on his mission. A General Authority did as well, followed by a mission president. None of them saw through his deception?

It isn't just me. Was the Holy Ghost talking to anyone?

Did Heavenly Father abandon us all?

No. That's not true.

She didn't believe it. Couldn't.

The metal ring on Neil's thumb ran across the fat string of his bass, sending a long, bone-numbing scratch through his amp. She looked up from her hands. From her angle, the outline of the Raleigh's hair glowed in the sharp light of a naked bulb hanging behind his head. His face was hard to see, but his grin was clear enough.

"Didn't expect you back so soon." Raleigh looked at his singer and ticked his head toward the couch. The young man repositioned his microphone stand between his stool and Raleigh's drum kit, where she had placed it on Monday night, before slipping out of her vision.

Raleigh twirled a stick between the fingers of his right hand. "What will you have us play for you tonight, madam?"

Remembering her ex-boyfriend's midnight invitation, she marveled at how well he knew her. "Tori."

The stoners lounging on the couches cheered and offered suggestions.

"Tori?" The freshman guitarist looked between his band members with concern on his face.

Jason laced his fingers together, flipped his hands, and pushed his arms out straight. "Take a seat, kid. This one's all mine."

He launched into the demanding opening of the rapid, high-pitched intro of *Precious Things.* Marie settled onto the singer's stool with her back to the room. The Basement's fans might like hearing her sing, but she never felt the same way about watching them watch her as she prayed for all her precious things to bleed away.

Holding the microphone in both hands, she wailed her frustrations and lamented her shadows. She declared her desire to find her place among good girls with dark secrets. So engrossed in finally grasping the peace that had eluded her at the pool, she failed to notice when Jason stopped playing. It was his awestruck eyes while she crowed the words "fascist panties" that told her the music had stopped. She trailed off the rest of the line.

"What's wrong?"

"You," Raleigh sighed. The word punched her in the gut. "Wasting your God-given talent."

She glanced over at Neil, who sat on the back of a threadbare lounger with his foot between the legs of a man who looked considerably less stoned than he had on Monday. *Boyfriend?*

"It's a shame, really," Neil said.

Jason threw a crumpled soda can at Neil's head and looked at her. "Nine Inch Nails?"

Yes! "Wish."

He pressed a button on his keyboard and the air was filled with static. The drunks and stoners whistled and cheered. The guitarist stepped on a pedal near his foot, and this time when he joined in, his chords were heavily distorted.

She slipped into a comfortable rhythm, setting a scene of having climbed to a soaring height and falling. She mourned throwing away the last thing belonging to her by putting her faith in God and her trust in men.

The lyrics slid off her tongue, and unlike every other time she'd sung this song, she didn't drop the dirty words. She allowed herself to embrace the profane, to project her rage through it, and she worked her way through a line with difficult phrasing that always tripped her up. She powered through. By the end she was swaying with the sound. Screaming. Dancing. Laughing.

Oh, how she missed music. She cursed her mother for throwing out her CDs.

"Guns N' Roses?"

Raleigh looked at the guitarist. "Tommy. *You Could Be Mine?*" The kid shook his head with a cringe. "The song from *Terminator 2*?"

"I know the song, but…" Tommy shrugged. "Sorry."

"Learn it." Jason got out from behind the keyboard. Raleigh circled around the high hat stand and held out his hand for the guitar as Jason sat at the drum kit. "We got this covered."

The benched singer—Raleigh had said his last name was Rigby—scoffed behind her. "Aren't you supposed to be a good little Mormon girl?"

Not so much. Marie looked at the floor joists above her. "It's called 'free agency', dude."

"Whatever you say, sweetheart."

She fisted her hands on her thigh.

Jason raised an eyebrow. "He's only here because you aren't."

"Tell him he's fired."

Jason smiled from ear to ear, exposing teeth. Behind her, Sam's distant cousin grumbled about being done with the losers anyhow. Heavy footfalls stomped up the stairs.

As the boys played the intro of *You Could Be Mine*, Marie rolled her head on her shoulders and breathed in the smell of tobacco and pot. Drums weren't Jason's favorite, but he knew this song. The band played it in high school. He played xylophone and chimes with the percussion section, mostly. Back up on drum kit, sometimes, but not often.

Raleigh played drums at school, guitar at home, and was good as Tommy seemed to be.

When her lead in came, she crowed about ripping a lover's heart in two and leaving their bed before dawn. Horrible, horrible lyrics, but so much fun to sing.

The band played Bon Jovi, Metallica, Garbage, and Soul Asylum. Marie sang long after her feelings were bled dry, until she forgot everything but lyrics and notes and cadence. Until she recognized the foreign feeling in her body.

Happiness.

How long had it been since she'd felt joy? How had she lived without it?

"No Doubt?" Jason gave her a cautious glance. "Have you heard them yet?"

"Um...just the one single. My cousin put it on a mix tape for me." It was the only song she'd listened to in rehab not by Alice in Chains.

"Just a Girl? You know the words?"

"Every one."

Raleigh snapped his fingers. "Kick it."

"Hey." Tommy seemed a little shy. It was the first time he'd spoken to her. "Give us some attitude."

Oh, that's why I'm here, kid.

He played a funky descending melody. Raleigh joined in with his drums, followed by Neil a few bars later. When her time came, Marie sang about the annoyances of being just a girl.

As she charged into a line near the end about how a girl is all anyone would let her be, Raleigh stood up from his drum kit. A hand clamped around her arm and yanked her backward off her stool. She cried out in shock and whipped her head around. Clutching her arm, Sam hauled her across the floor. She stumbled over legs the stoners couldn't move fast enough.

"Sam!" Raleigh's growl was followed by snare drum snaps, symbol crashes, and hard bangs. "You fuck-ass. Let her go!"

The drunks and stoners protested Sam's abuse with a chorus of curses and insults, but none of them rose from the couch.

"Sam!" She followed him up the stairs, but only because she didn't want to fall down them. "What do you think you're doing?"

"You judge me for my sins while you hang out with potheads and sing trashy music with apostates?"

"Jesus loved whores!" One of the groupies yelled after them.

"Shut up." Sam slammed the basement door behind them as Raleigh made it to the bottom of the stairs.

She pulled her arm, but he held her too tightly. "You're hurting me!"

"Hurting?" He wrenched open the kitchen door. "I'm *saving* you, Marie."

Saving? Dragging her out into the cold without a coat. Yeah. He clearly cared.

He pushed her in front of him now. Again, she walked on her own, afraid they'd both fall down the deck stairs if she fought. "I should walk away now. I was willing to overlook the thing with you and that dyke, but—"

"*You* should?"

"—if this is your idea of fun, you're not the right woman to raise my kids."

"As if!"

The moment her feet touched the driveway's gravel, Marie dropped to a squat and twisted as hard as she could. His grip on her arm slipped. She pulled her arm out of her sleeve, ducked her head, and fell backward. The move freed her of the flannel, exactly as her father once told her it would. It also sent her careening into a slushy mud puddle right as Raleigh flew out of the kitchen door with Neil and Jason on his heels.

Her eyes met Neil's. She almost saw the stupid thought form in his head. Before she could yell at him not to, he pushed past Raleigh and jumped over the stairs. He landed awkwardly in the gravel. Crying out, he stumbled forward and pushed both of his hands into Sam. With a grunt, Sam flew backwards. Neil rocked on the ground, holding his leg while screaming through his clenched teeth.

She pushed up to her feet as Sam rolled across the hood of her car and onto the ground. She threw herself at Raleigh and Jason, her arms spread wide to stop them both.

Raleigh seethed. "I see your mission didn't change you much!"

"Don't. Please." She looked over her shoulder. Sam stood up and brushed himself off. She faced her would-be heroes. "Thanks, guys. I've got this".

"I know." Jason pointed his chin past her. "But Neil needs help."

She dropped her arm to let him pass. He knelt at Neil's side and called him a dumbass.

Marie said, "He's my problem, Raleigh."

"If he touches you again—"

"I'll have a whole lot of witnesses." As he stared at her intently, she pleaded, "Let me handle this."

Raleigh raised his hands and blindly backed up three stairs. He was prevented from going further to the house by a deck full of musicians and groupies. Like it or not, she had an audience.

Marie turned her back to the house, yanking off her diamond engagement ring. Pinching the ring between her thumb and forefinger, she held it out to Sam. The temperature had risen enough that afternoon to melt thin ice, and when she fell to the ground, she landed in a puddle. Her t-shirt and jeans were wet and the freezing fabric hung against her skin. "I told you…I won't…marry…a violent man—"

"I'm not, Marie. You know I'm not. You just—"

"Shut up!" she cried. Shivering from head to toe, she couldn't hold her arm still. She fought her seizing jaw and chattering teeth. "You're wearing garments, Sam!"

He stared at her as if she were crazy. She pulled in her arms but hugging herself only pressed the cold to her skin.

"You lied and…"

Jason was watching her now.

"You're not worthy." She spoke to Sam, but looked at Jason. She knew now his father didn't punish him for masturbating. He punished him for being honest about it. And she wanted him to know that she knew. "You only got your temple recommend because you lied."

Jason's eyelids drifted closed as if he were finally relieved of a heavy burden.

"You're freezing, M." Sam took a few steps toward her. "It's warm in the truck. Let's talk—"

She thrust the ring at him again. "You can *take*…this out of my hand!" She gasped for air. "Or you can *fish* it out the snow."

Sam blanched. "You wouldn't—"

"You…know…me…better."

He reached in and covered her hand with his. She wanted to crawl into his warmth. The way his posture melted a bit told her he saw her falter.

"When I let go, that's it." His warning was punctuated by a slight squeeze of his hand. "I won't take you back."

"I won't ask."

He pulled his hand away along with the ring.

"I hope you're happy." His voice cracked a little.

Marie held herself together with sheer will against cold and adrenaline as Sam retreat to his truck to the cheers of the people on the deck. She met her ex-fiancée's eyes once more before he got in and followed the red glow of his taillights until they disappeared down the street.

When he was gone from her sight, her body succumbed to cold. Her muscles quaked. Her teeth chattered. The sudden emptiness in her chest made room for a battle royal as her heart beat like a bass drum against her ribcage, and her lungs sucked breath like a straw with a hole in it. She welcomed the blanket Raleigh wrapped around her. He said something about the emergency room as he guided her to the passenger side of her car.

· ❄ ·

Neil was given a wheelchair when they arrived at the medical center and a nurse rolled him into the exam room. The ER had only one with two bays separated by curtains on tracks. He was the only patient at that time, so the nurses allowed Marie and Jason into the exam room to keep him company while the doctors and nurses did their jobs.

Marie sat on the bed first so that Neil could use her lap has a pillow. Jason pulled back the curtain that separated bay one from bay two and took a seat on the other bed.

It was right about then that Sarah entered the exam room and rounded the emergency's room bed with a bag slung over her shoulder.

"What happened?" she demanded.

Neil groaned at his cousin's bristling tone. "I jumped over the steps at Raleigh's."

Jason had said he was going to call his wife, but he hadn't done that yet, making Marie wonder how she knew to come.

"He mentioned that on the phone." She paused with the bag resting on her cocked hip, eyebrows furrowed. "Front door or kitchen?"

"Kitchen."

The answer, spoken by Marie, Jason, and Neil all at once, turned Sarah's alarm to disbelief. "Dude, that's like...you're lucky you didn't break your neck!"

"I'm sorry, *Mom*."

"You wish I was your mom." She quipped before turning her focus to Marie. "Raleigh said you could use some clothes."

Marie was deeply touched. "Thank you."

Sarah smiled and then rolled her eyes at Neil, who was preventing Marie from moving to change clothes. She smacked her cousin in the head, drawing a yelp from him.

"Move, you lazy sack."

When Marie was free, Sarah passed her the bag, pulled Jason off the bay two bed, and pulled the privacy curtain, all in one smooth motion.

As Marie stripped out of her dirty clothes, Jason explained Neil's situation to his wife.

"He was running at the time."

"Uh-huh." Sarah didn't sound convinced, possibly because she knew her cousin too well to accept a mishap at face value.

As Marie dressed, the men explained to Sarah what had happened at Raleigh's house. Firing the singer. Having a good time. Sam coming in and dragging Marie out of the house, convinced he was doing her a favor.

"Of *course*, he was." Marie was hurt her friend would agree with him. "He's never, ever wrong about anything."

Oh. Marie felt lost. They'd been friends since they were eight. She should know why her *best friend* was readily sarcastic about her high school sweetheart.

Jason's *Little Earthquakes* shirt was in the bag. He had a thing for Tori Amos. Had it been on top of his drawer, ready to grab? Or was his wife trying to get rid of it? Sarah also brought her once-favorite pair of jeans. That made Marie feel special. She shoved her own damp clothing into the bag, particularly thankful for the warmth of the heavy socks Sarah had also brought.

Neil sat up the moment Marie pulled back the partition and patted the mattress next to him. She hopped back onto the bed, in the spot she'd been before, and weaved her fingers into his hair as he laid his head on her leg.

A nurse walked through the door as Neil got comfortable again. "Let's go x-ray your ankle."

"Ugh. Can you do it in here?"

"I would if I could." The nurse took his hand to pull him up again. "The machine's right next door."

Marie steadied him from behind. Sarah took over when he reached the floor and settled him into the wheelchair. When his injured leg was elevated and propped upon pillows, the nurse took him out of the room. Marie pulled her stocking feet onto the bed's metal frame and hugged her shins. She rested her chin in the dip between her knees.

"So…" Sarah, now sitting on the exam room's other bed, leaned forward. "You broke up with Sam?"

"Twice." Walking out of the church still wearing his ring had been an oversight. If the Spirit had said anything to Marie, at all, in her entire life, it was while talking to Sam. It screamed at her to run.

"And he just let you go?"

Marie frowned. "I wouldn't say *just*."

Jason covered Sarah's clasped and twisting hands. She sucked her bottom lip under her teeth and shook her head.

"It doesn't feel right to me." Sarah stared off to her right, toward the bottom of the exam room doorway. "What did he say? Exactly?"

"Um…he said if I returned the ring, he'd never take me back. He was willing to overlook my unworthiness and marry me any—"

"Unworthy?" Sarah frowned. "I'm sorry. It's none of my business, but unworthy how?"

"He has ideas about Ash and me…that aren't far off the mark." Though she hated the way he'd made it sound dirty. "He said he was trying to save me."

"Save you." Sarah's repeat was soft. Thoughtful.

"I think it shocked him to see me in Raleigh's basement. You know, surrounded by stoners and jamming to trashy music with my ex-boyfriend."

Sarah freed her hands from Jason's grasp and rubbed her face. "I don't like it. She hurt him. He won't let that go." She groaned loudly. "I should have told your dad everything, Jay."

"Sare." Jason dragged out her nickname warningly.

She cried into her hands. "Whatever he does is my fault. You know—"

"No. *You* know…"

Sarah turned on the bed, putting her back to him.

He wrapped his arms around her from behind and rested his chin on her shoulder. "I'm sorry. Sam is the master of his own chaos. You protected yourself when you had no one else."

Those words, spoken tenderly, squeezed Marie's stomach and twisted. "Protected yourself? From what?"

Sarah's eyes reddened with each passing second. She bit down on her bottom lip as it trembled and looked away again to meet Jason's eyes.

"It's yours. To tell or to keep." He caressed her face. She blinked tears and completed her turn. Face to face, he cupped both of her cheeks in his hands and kissed her lips as he thumbed her tears away. "I have your back. I always will. No matter what."

Sarah shuddered. She grabbed onto her husband's hands with white knuckles and turned toward Marie again. She opened her mouth, then closed it again.

"I—"

The nurse wheeled Neil back through the door of the exam room. Sarah clammed up again. He pushed out of the wheelchair while the nurse steadied his leg. Wincing and moaning, he hobbled back onto the bed and resumed his former position, lying on his side with his head on Marie's thigh.

"The doctor will be in after he sees the x-rays. I'll get you something stronger for the pain."

Neil whimpered. "You…are a goddess among nurses."

She gave him a wink and a smile before exiting the room.

Marie combed her fingers through Neil's unruly black locks. "I'm so sorry."

"Eh." He waived aimlessly in the air above his head, almost batting her in the face. "Not like you pushed me off the porch."

"I know, but maybe if I hadn't…"

Sarah chewed on her thumbnail, one leg shaking nervously while she stared into space. What had she almost confessed a minute ago, before the nurse interrupted?

Neil groaned, but this time in annoyance. "I was supposed to pick up Ash ten minutes ago."

"Oh," Sarah brightened for a minute. "I forgot. Sorry. Raleigh's picking up Ash. He said to tell you…"

She trailed off as a flurry of dark blue and loud voices's came through the ambulance bay doors. A nurse ran into the exam room.

"Up!"

Jason and Sarah scrambled to Neil's side as the nurse dropped the far handrail of the bed they vacated. Voices outside barked questions and responses in abbreviations. Numbers. Code. It was English, but none of it registered in Marie's vocabulary.

The nurse's tone, she understood though. Neil's emergency had been of little concern to her. A mishap with a minor, albeit painful, ending. What was coming in now gave commands and didn't wait for obedience. It crashed into their quiet corner of the hospital, driven by two EMTs and two ER nurses, all working on the run.

Before Neil's nurse pulled the curtain partition, the bodies cleared and gave Marie one fleeting look at the patient's bleeding face. A large shard of glass stuck up from one of the wounds.

No! "Ash!"

Neil sat up. Free of his weight, she jumped from the bed, but Jason stepped between her and the curtain and wrapped her in both of his arms.

"What happened?" Marie yelled at the shadows beyond the curtain.

Jason held her tight. Shushed her. Pushed her back against Neil's bed. The curtain hanging between her and the man she loved was a thousand miles away if only a yard.

"Ash!"

A male bellowed from beyond the curtain, "Get her out of here!"

Jason nudged her. She ignored him. He hefted her by the waist and made way for the nurse's station.

Neil grabbed Sarah by her arm. "Call the Shrink! Now!" At the command, Sarah pushed her way around Jason, grabbed the phone on the nurse's desk, and dialed furiously.

"Put me down!" Marie screamed at Jason while kicking her way free.

"Stop!" He trapped her in both arms again, physically keeping from re-entering the exam room. "You can't help, M!"

As she accepted how true it was, Marie's legs became spaghetti.

Ash has to live, Heavenly Father. Please let him live.

River of Deceit

In her Graphic Arts classes, Marie's teachers taught the physics and psychology of color. Restaurants often painted their walls in warm tones...reds, oranges, browns...to increase the diners' appetites. Classrooms and prison cells were painted in cool tones...greens, blues, and grays...to keep minds calm.

The waiting room of Coulter Medical Center was a pale shade of blue-gray Marie would call Cautious Optimism if she worked for a paint company.

Above, the subdued walls met a drop-tile ceiling with one thousand acoustic tiles measuring 24x48 inches, placed east to west. It cleared Raleigh's head by at least three-feet when he came by to check on Ash and Neil, so nine-foot clearance. Below, the floor was thirteen paces by six, which she'd counted as Jason walked the floor with his hands on his hips. It was covered in a mottled Berber carpet reflecting "sand" when she unfocused her eyes.

The room had seven windows. Between the waiting area and the hallway outside, there were eight photos of Wyoming scenery matted and framed on the walls. There were fifteen lounge chairs and seven couches, in a complimentary shade of brown. All of them stained.

Call the Shrink!

Two hours and twenty-two minutes passed between Neil shouting that order at Sarah and the moment Jeannie Praetor *finally* walked into the waiting room. Marie was ready to jump out of her skin, but she was pinned to a couch cushion by a snoring blockhead with a broken ankle. Her hands fisting in his hair didn't disturb him at all. The painkillers had him knocked out cold.

Sarah remained at Marie's side, her arm stretched behind her on the back of the couch.

Jason was on his feet a moment later. "How is she?"

Jeannie held up a hand. Like a Jedi mind trick, Jason's body language shifted and relaxed a bit. She sat in the chair opposite Marie's couch and frowned at her sleeping stepson. "Dumbass. Still thinks he's twelve."

"The doctor said it's a clean break." Marie combed her hands through Neil's unruly black locks again.

Jeannie acknowledged her with a nod.

"What about Ash?" Marie asked.

Marie had always taken for granted her parents would handle her emergencies. All her friends had family too. Except Ash, but even when he had once asked her to call Jeannie if anything ever happened to him, she hadn't understood why. Until last night, when Ash couldn't speak for himself and had no one else to speak for him.

She hadn't been in a state of mind to carry out his wish, but despite his pain, Neil had been. Sarah had been. Jeannie had walked through the emergency room minutes after Sarah had called her, with the poise of the medical professional she used to be and a power of attorney letter in her hand.

All Marie had to do was play with Neil's hair—to comfort herself more than him—and wait. And pray. She hated it was all she could do. How could she even consider having a baby right now? She couldn't hold herself together long enough to make a phone call!

Several seconds passed and Jeannie still hadn't answered her question. The pause made her anxious. "Will Ash be okay?"

"*She's*...stable." Jeannie's answer came across as overly cautious. "The doctors are keeping her under and watching the swelling in her brain."

Marie let go of the air held hostage in her lungs. "Can I see...her?"

Jeannie turned to Jason and Sarah. "Go home, you two. I'm sure you'll need to be awake for something tomorrow."

Jason sat on the coffee table between her and Jeannie. He covered Marie's hands with his and looked her in the eyes. "Ash is a tough cookie. She'll be okay."

Marie leaned into the hug Sarah gave her from the side. "Thank you."

Sarah smiled. "Anytime, M."

She let go of Marie, took her husband's hand, and they left together.

"There are some things we need to talk about." Jeannie's voice pushed aside the bubble of hope rising in Marie's chest. "Starting with where Sam Rigby might have gotten the idea Ash is a bad influence on you."

Marie swallowed hard. *Sam didn't do this.*

"I, uh...I broke off our engagement."

"I know that. Doesn't answer my question."

You hurt him. He won't let that go. Sarah had been concerned Sam wasn't done. *No. Not this. He didn't do this.*

"What happened to Ash?" Marie recalled the blood covering his face. "Where did the glass come from?"

Jeannie paused. "When Raleigh showed up at the coffee shop, he found a foot-wide hole in the front window and glass all over the sidewalk. Inside, your dad was on the phone with 911 and an Army medic hovered over Ash. Raleigh told the police he'd come to pick up Ash because you and Neil were at the hospital, which naturally concerned your dad. He was assured you're fine."

Marie groaned, this time while imagining the lecture she was going to get when she got home.

"Raleigh also told them Sam walked into his basement and pulled you out of his house. Neil broke his leg on the patio stairs while trying to intervene. Correct?"

Marie confirmed with a nod.

"Sam is in custody, charged with two counts of battery."

The words churned the fluid in Marie's stomach. What have I done?

"He blames Ash. Said she seduced you away from everything you know to be true. He seems to think if Ash weren't in the picture, you never would have broken up with him and everything would be the way it should be."

Marie covered her mouth with her hand and shut her eyes tight to hide from the accusation in Jeannie's eyes. She shook her head. "It's my fault. I did this."

Jeannie sighed heavily. "Don't blame yourself for the actions of other people."

"I thought I would get comfortable with the idea of marrying him, but the dread in my chest got worse every day." Marie fought back her tears. She had no right to them. "But, to him, I'm throwing away a temple marriage… everything I've said I've wanted since we were kids. And, I guess…Sam lashed out at something that explained why."

Jeannie's lips tightened with concern. "Why do you think he'd blame Ash?"

Marie shrugged. "He just got back from Brazil. Ash is the new thing in my life."

"New question." Jeannie sat back in her chair. With her elbows resting on the arms, she laced her fingers together. "How do you feel about Ash?"

"I love Ash."

"He came by the house yesterday."

He? Marie swallowed hard as Jeannie stared.

"He confided in you."

Ash gave her power of attorney. *Of course, she knows.*

"Yes."

"And you believed him?" Jeannie seemed pleasantly surprised.

"Why would he lie about that?" Her father's story about the soldier who saved him primed her for a revelation, but she might have believed him anyway. He was afraid to tell her. Why lie? "He doesn't even like men."

"I admire your perspective, Marie. Your church, however, doesn't share it. It won't condone a relationship between you."

Marie slouched low. "No. It won't."

"You will have to let one go." There was judgment in Jeannie's stare, now. Sadness too. "Ash is my first priority right now. If you want into his room, make your choice."

"You want me to decide right now?" Marie couldn't believe the woman would set such a condition at a time like this.

"There's no wrong answer, Marie. I won't fault you for choosing the Church. I know, and Ash does too, that is a very hard tie to cut." Jeannie leaned forward. "But, he has been fighting hope you'd ever see him as more than a friend for two years. He's vulnerable. He's fragile. And you have the power to destroy him. Not on my watch, girl. I will know where you stand before you walk through his door."

It was one thing to put off marriage and children. Leaving the Church behind *entirely*?

"Something you learn while working with at-risk kids." Jeannie stood from the chair. "Sometimes, what is best is not kind."

· ❄ ·

Brown sugar and rum wafted past Marie's nose as she stood on the edge of the three-meter diving board. She savored it and swallowed as the tiny hairs on the back of her neck stood on end.

She stepped away from the edge and sought out the source of the smell. Down, on her left, Sam was handcuffed to the rail of the lower diving board. He looked at her with utter contempt. On her right, Ash slept in a hospital bed with a bandaged and bruised face. And she saw herself, sitting in a chair, slouched forward. Her head lay on the bed next to his arm.

A sound, like a candy wrapper, snatched her attention.

Sarah stood on the opposite end of the diving board. The plate in her hand was piled high with grilled slices of bread glistening in a brown sauce.

Marie blinked hard. When she opened her eyes again, the room around her was dim. Blurry. The smell remained, though, even as every blink sharpened the features on the wall opposite her. She was still in the hospital's waiting room. The clock on the wall read 7:20.

She sat up with a gasp. She'd only closed her eyes to relieve the burn crying had caused. Six hours ago. Neil was still there, but he laid out on another couch.

"Good morning." Sarah wore her waitress uniform and was peeling off the cellophane from plastic utensils. "I told Uncle Marty you had a rough night, so he made your favorite."

Uncle Marty. Sarah. The diner. Brown sugar and…Marie's mouth watered. *Super-secret, not-on-the-menu, Bananas Foster French Toast.*

"When was the last time you ate?" Sarah asked.

Marie started to answer and cut herself short. She missed supper yesterday and had been too anxious to eat breakfast or lunch. Tuesday night, her supper smeared the kitchen wall after her mother threw her plate. And Monday…Marie honestly couldn't remember the last meal she'd finished.

"That's what I thought." A bite of fried Texas toast dripped syrup as Sarah held it out to her. "Open up."

Once Marie had food on her tongue, her body's need to eat overcame her lack of appetite. She took the fork from Sarah and scarfed the rest of the meal with a beggar's desperation.

"Have you heard what happened to her?" Sarah asked.

Marie closed the clamshell plate and moved it aside on the table between her and Sarah. "Yeah, you?"

Sarah's head bobbed slowly.

In the hours Marie had waited to learn if Ash would even live, Jeannie had been busy finding out how he ended up in the ER with a face full of glass. Sam had taped the latch on the coffee shop's rear door to enter after closing time. Once inside, he cornered Ash and shoved him head first into a cabinet of pewter dragons. One of those had been found on the sidewalk outside and the police deducted it had been what made the hole in the picture window.

Despite the blood Marie had seen, all but one of the cuts were superficial. Most of the wounds were now closed with tape. The doctors were concerned with the other side of his head. Under a three-inch knot, his brain was swelling.

Sam might blame Ash, but it wasn't why he snapped. He was mad at her. He had a right to be. But *this*? How could he beat a person unconscious and walk away and wait for his consequences to find him?

"Every time I think Sam is behind me, he does something else I can blame myself for," Sarah's whispered, drawing Marie out of the film playing in her head.

She wanted to demand an explanation for why Sarah would blame herself, but she didn't want her to clam up again. Or worse, leave her there alone.

"You were going to tell me something last night. What was it?"

With her elbows propped on her knees, Sarah laid her head in her hands and grabbed at her hair. Locks came loose of her sloppy bun as she flexed her hands into fists.

"I wanted to say something years ago. Needed to, really, but…" She stopped grabbing at her hair. "I believed in the bishop. I expected him to know Sam wasn't worthy, and I waited to be disciplined for my part in that. But, Sam got his mission call. He had to have lied. And I said nothing. And neither did the Holy Ghost."

The pit in Marie's chest grew colder. Emptier. It was one thing to know the Holy Ghost wasn't speaking to her. But to have confirmation it wasn't speaking to the bishop? Or the General Authority who interviewed Sam at the MTC? There were layers upon layers of priesthood members Sam answered to, and not one of them could see through him?

"You're not surprised." Sarah's observation carried mild shock. "What I just said…I really thought you'd call me a liar."

"He as much as admitted it yesterday." *Right before I walked out on him.*

Sarah huffed. "His humility is truly inspiring."

"Why didn't you say anything? After Sam got his call, why didn't you go to the bishop?"

"I was scared. The Sam you met yesterday, the guy who did *that* to Ash. He's the same guy who pushed me by inches over months into sex. Then he blamed his sins on *my* low standards. And *then* he got mad whenever I'd say no, because we'd already gone all the way, so what was I holding out for?"

"That's gross."

"*That* was Homecoming senior year." Sarah sat back in her chair and crossed her arms over her chest. "On prom night, we were on the dance floor, and he told me the baby I was carrying couldn't be his. And if I told anyone it was, he'd drag me so far in the mud, I'd be an archeological study in five hundred years."

Red hot rage washed through Marie's flesh like a river. *That jerk!* "A blood test would have proved he was the father."

Sarah scoffed. "*After* I got to walk around pregnant for *months* while he claimed it wasn't his kid. And then, when I proved he was lying, our parents would have forced us to get married. Sam would be pitied to be tied down to the tramp who ruined his life. He would have been praised for 'doing the right thing' and taking responsibility for his kid. I didn't want an—but…"

She sniffled back a sob and wiped her face. "I couldn't win, M! I hated him, but I was too scared to leave. Toward the end, I just prayed for the strength to hold on until he left town."

Marie had never notice a problem between Sarah and Sam. *Am I that self-absorbed?*

Diving. Grades. Jason. Her growing problems at home. Of course, she was.

"I'm so sorry. I was a horrible friend."

"I screwed your boyfriend." Sarah spoke the words dispassionately, as a fact she couldn't change.

"Technically, you could argue that Jason did the screwing part."

Sarah's jaw dropped, but her eyes brightened in a way Marie remembered from their childhood. A devilish grin pulled at her lips.

"But only *technically*."

This time it was Marie's turn to gape at her friend's boldness. She snickered. Laughing with Sarah felt good. And as she enjoyed the moment, the guilt for having fun while Ash was hurt on account of her added weight to Marie's burdened soul.

"Why are you still out here? Instead of with Ash?"

As Marie explained Jeannie Praetor's ultimatum, Sarah's mouth fell open in shock.

"What a witch!"

"She's putting Ash first. I get that, but…"

Sarah leaned forward in the same chair Jeannie had occupied hours ago. "What if I can make the decision easier?"

"I don't think it's possible." The man she loved or her parents, because if she left the Church, she was sure she'd be dead to them.

"What if I can, though?" Sarah pressed. "It would mean explaining how Jason and I…you know, but…what if?"

Marie had rejected their attempts at explaining last year, because their reasons didn't matter. Sarah was pregnant. Jason was the father. And nothing they could say would change either fact. In the end, even a reasonable excuse would amount to that…an excuse for betraying her.

Still, they'd managed to mend the bridge between them. Jason and Sarah were supporting her. She couldn't count on her own family right now.

"Tell me."

"We wanted to save you."

That was not what Marie wanted to hear, and Sarah clearly knew it. She held up her hands between them, pleading for peace.

"I know it's the wrong thing to say, but…it's where it started. Sam's mission call stunned me. But for Jay, the betrayal had much deeper roots. He believed in his dad, and his dad let him down."

Sarah clasped her hands together and wrung them. "Our faith in the priesthood fell apart at the same time, and I guess we kind of bonded over shared emptiness."

It made sense to Marie, but it didn't satisfy her curiosity. "But how does Jay sleeping with you *save* me?"

Sarah shook her head furiously. "It doesn't. It was something that happened later. Much later. M, we wanted to show you the Church isn't true. We were looking for proof you'd accept. And…we think we found it."

· ❄ ·

Marie parked in her driveway beside an old blue pickup. A symbol was stenciled on the back. The logo mark of the Manasseh homestead. She stared at it while as Sarah parked and joined her.

"You know...I've turned myself inside-out this week worrying over having to sleep with Sam. I've never considered the daily reality of being awake with him."

"What do you mean?"

"Manasseh." Marie touched the spray-painted brand. "The Rigby's *burn* this on their livestock."

Sarah acknowledged with a protracted, "Yeah."

"I understand its purpose, but…could I do it? Or stand by while he did it? Or teach my children how?"

The answer was far simpler than any other Marie struggled with in previous days: No.

"I've done it." With crossed arms, Sarah kicked at a black clod of snow that had fallen from the truck and lied on a patch of exposed concrete. "Who do you think is here?"

"Probably Regina." And after what Sam did, Marie couldn't imagine his mother would be here for a friendly visit.

"You want me to stay?"

As much as Marie would love to not face Sam's mother alone right now, there was distress in Sarah's question. Regina might have been her mother-in-law under different circumstances.

"No. Thanks, but you should go on back to work or wherever I'm keeping you from."

"You sure?"

"Thanks for coming this far, but…" Marie glanced at the front door of her home with trepidation. "I've got this."

Sarah hugged her. "If things get bad, call. I'll send the cavalry."

Marie watched her friend, her *sister*, navigate the sweeping driveway and turn onto the highway to return to Coulter. Part of her wished she'd accepted Sarah's offer to stay, but she knew whatever waited for her inside was hers to face alone.

Fueled on carbs and sugar, and armed with blasphemous words, Marie pushed open the front door of her home. She followed faint voices through the foyer and in the direction of the kitchen. One was male, but not deep enough to be Marie's father. Her second guessing about sending Sarah home vanished as she realized the visitor wasn't Regina.

Physically, Sam might as well be a clone of his father. Sam Sr. had a thirty-year head start and was graying around the edges, but the sight of him always triggered Marie's memories of Sam. Bad memories, she braced for now, as well as good. How would being in close quarters with him make Sarah feel?

Marie imagined the worst as she neared the kitchen and slowed to eavesdrop. They were discussing Sam. Mr. Rigby couldn't have been there long. He was still explaining how the police had knocked on his door at a late hour to arrest his son. *Ridiculous* accusations, said the man certain no son of his would ever harm a woman.

She ground her teeth to keep from scoffing aloud and exposing her presence. She couldn't fault his disbelief. Twelve hours ago, she wouldn't have imagined Sam was capable either. She would have gone about ending things entirely different.

"My son is a good boy, Isabela," he said, as if pleading to a judge.

"Truly, I can't believe he could do such a thing," her mother replied as a caring neighbor.

"You know my family. We value hard work and meeting our own needs is a matter of pride. But this…the bail…. We have the money we've budgeted for the wedding, but not right now. We'd have to borrow it from the bank."

Marie snagged on Sam, Sr.'s mention of money and barely heard his reasons. Of course, he'd want to get his son out of jail. And the judge setting the bail higher than the farm's cash on hand was believable. What she didn't get was why he would look to her mother for help?

"It would set us back and fall's no good for a temple trip. The harvest."

Wedding? She turned around the corner and stepped into the kitchen. "What wedding?"

Sam, Sr., her mother, and Sam's sister Abigail, whipped their heads in her direction at once.

"Your wedding, of course."

"Called off yesterday. Wasn't that why Sam lost his head?"

Marie's mother blushed with rage. Abigail's jaw dropped in shock. Sam, Sr. had no reaction whatsoever.

"Why are you here, Brother Rigby?" Marie asked.

"Cleaning up your mess." He rose from his chair. Marie stepped back as he halved the distance between them. "The judge is making an example of my son. We can't pay the bail, but it's pocket change for your parents. They can write a check and have him home by noon. And considering how he got into this mess to begin with…"

"We're happy to help, Sam." Her mother stepped between them and touched his arm before casting a glare Marie's way. "Sometimes, my daughter doesn't think things through."

She had expected her mother to agree she must have triggered Sam, but it still hurt to hear.

"You live ten miles out on the east side of town." Marie halved the distance again and looked the man in the eyes. "We live fifteen from the north. Add in two for the drive through town…that's twenty-seven miles."

Sam, Sr. crossed his arms. His eyes narrowed. "Your point?"

"*Mid*-point. Would you like to guess at what lies about half-way between here and Manasseh?" No one answered. "Baez Ford-Chrysler-Toyota."

"Well, we were already in town for the hearing." Abigail joined them near the kitchen threshold, wringing her hands nervously. "So it was only fifteen miles."

"And dealership is three blocks from the courthouse. Why drive fifteen miles when my father was around the corner?"

Her mother turned a skeptical face on Sam, Sr., who leveled a blazing glare on Marie.

"Yeah. I'm the one who doesn't think things through?"

"Bite your tongue, Ofelia."

Not today, Mama.

"You went to the dealership first," Marie assumed, raising her eyebrows at Mr. Rigby. "My papa told you no."

"My son is a good boy. Your *papa* is too wrapped around your finger to see the disgrace he raised."

"*Disgrace*?" Marie unzipped her heavy winter coat. She shrugged out of one sleeve and bared her left arm. Her mother gasped at the bruises Sam left behind when he yanked her off the stool at Raleigh's, but Marie kept her gaze locked with Sam, Sr., and ground out through clenched teeth. "How about your… *good*…boy…now?"

She hated the tears for making her look weak and the face looking back at her for reminding her of Sam. Did the marks on her arm not bother him at all?

Marie turned away from her mother and her *guests* and went upstairs before she could overhear what came next.

The door on her room no longer had a lock. An annoying, but reasonable, choice considering this was where she put a gun to her head. *Whatever*. She was tired. Tired of shaking. Tired of shame. Tired of worrying over how her parents would react to her choices.

She pulled the disc changer magazine from her car out of an inner pocket of her coat. Neil was kind enough to loan her his Morphine *Cure for Pain* CD, so she could finally take the bubble bath she'd started a week ago. When the first deep, bluesy riff played, she let her coat fall from her, onto the pile of magazines she'd left on the floor on Tuesday night.

Before going into the bathroom, she located the *History of the Church* series among the thousand books her father had temporarily stored in her room. *You want to solve puzzles?* he'd asked her last week. *Try church history.* She trailed her fingers across the colorful spines of the paperbacks. Glancing at the palm of her hand, she double-checked the note Sarah wrote there and pulled Volume VI from the shelf.

This was why she came home. Sarah said she and Jason found what they were looking for when they started the search that led to their shotgun wedding. She had the option of staying at Sarah's and looking at Jason's copy, but Marie's dad had the book. *His* copy, to her, would be unimpeachable.

After drawing the bath, she slipped into the waters and submerged. She stayed under until her lungs burned before surfacing again, and then laid motionless until the warmth had penetrated her flesh and bones and banished the cold.

Uncertainty loomed. Uncomfortable conversations. Tears. Her mother's, certainly, if not her own. But without marriage to Sam hanging over her head like a cloud, the world felt less tight around her. She had Morphine and bubbles and a book Sarah promised would make her life better, if she dared to look at it.

Marie dried her hands on a nearby towel and pulled the book off of the toilet lid. She settled into the bath and turned to the page had Sarah referenced. Her brain seized upon the passages her father had underlined. She jumped backward in time, to Valkyrie on Monday afternoon, when Ash asked her about polygamy. He said Joseph Smith destroyed a printing press after a newspaper accused him of having more than one wife. She had dismissed Ash's questions as anti-Mormon lies.

Yet, here it was. An account in her Church's early history about 300 men destroying a printing press at the order of the prophet, which was bad enough, but Joseph Smith was also the mayor of Nauvoo at the time so the order was also sillegal. She flipped to the front of the book and read the copyright page. The Deseret Book Company; Second edition. 1978.

Marie turned the pages backward and forward around the press incident, jumping from underline to underline, skimming for clues as to what could have truly prompted the order, but she found nothing else. Furthermore, Smith protested his innocence of the polygamy rumors from the pulpit. He was accused of having seven wives but he insisted he had only one.

The Church would be practicing polygamy openly a few years later under Brigham Young. It didn't make sense to her that he would fight rumors so vehemently when all he had to do was have them produce the six wives he was denying.

Unless, of course, his accusers could, but that would mean….

Oh no, no, no.

Marie could accept Joseph Smith as almost anything. A braggart, a bully, a polygamist—God chooses his disciples at His own discretion—but the man who claimed to have seen God the Father and Jesus Christ, His Son, *in the flesh,* could not be a *liar.*

She dropped the book on the floor by the tub, grabbed her towel, and wrapped it around her as she walked back into her bedroom. She stood before the book cases half-naked and shivering, a product of cool air on wet skin and a renewed sense of having been betrayed by men she trusted.

Many men. Layers upon layers of priesthood authorities to whom she was subject as a member of the Church. The prophets and apostles, past and present. Her father and her bishop today. Her husband and sons tomorrow. Because as a woman, she would never be ordained. One chromosome made her unworthy of the priesthood, no matter what she would ever do.

Like Uncle Carl. Like Ash.

Her father had chosen to renovate his office in the middle of winter. He chose to relocate his office in her room. And while they talked in the snow about her returning to Valkyrie, he suggested church history if she wanted to solve puzzles. She had all of his books. He had said she would be surprised.

She had blown it off as small talk. The presence of his office stuff in her room made her angry. She slept, bathed, and hid from her mother in there since coming home from Phoenix, but she had ignored the books completely.

They filled her three bookcases, each six feet high and three feet wide, which her father moved to line the wall between the door and the bathroom. Her own books were either packed away or lost in her mother's purge of all things worldly. Her father's bookcases, similar to hers, were slipped in where space was available. One was squeezed in between her bed and the bathroom door, blocking one of two entrances to her walk-in closet. Another two were placed on either side of the dresser where she'd once stored CDs. Finally, the credenza on his desk had software manuals and phone books. His computer was packed on top of the desk like a losing game of Tetris.

She had space to walk from the door to the window seats and bathroom, at least she did before she got angry and evicted the magazines from her CD drawer. Turning in place to take in all the books, the task of finding something useful overwhelmed her.

At a glance, she could see no rhyme or reason to the order. The books had been shelved alphabetically and by subject matter in his office, but here...they were put up randomly. She wasn't surprised. He enjoyed order, but obsessive-compulsive Estefan Baez was not.

It frustrated her, though. She only needed the Church related ones but they'd been shelved among military histories, car books, and two complete sets of—

Why did he do that?

The *Encyclopedia Britannica* was *scattered* across all six bookcases. The volumes were taken off their shelf together, but he'd arranged them here so none of the books sat next to another in the series. And it had to have been him. If her mother was inclined to put effort into shelving, the books would be together, not apart.

And it wasn't only the Britannica series. The *World Book Encyclopedia* was separated too.

Marie looked for patterns among the book spines. Her father had three more large series... Time-Life's *The Old West* and *World War II* series, and the *Journals of Discourses*, all distributed among six cases and unrelated books. A few volumes of the *Journals* were shelved together, but the others were separated. Altogether, there were more than two-hundred books in this room that she would have shelved in neat sets on two book cases. Temporary storage or not, it made sense to keep them together for when it came time to move them back to where they belonged.

Marie crossed her arms, and as she considered what her father had done, her vision blurred. The bookshelves became mottled spaces. Visual noise. The only thing that stood out was a line of brightly colored spines, broken by a rust bar tilted toward a blue one.

Focusing again, she saw the series of books she'd come home to look at in the first place. Her father kept the books of *History of the Church* together. There was a dark spot where Volume Six had been removed. Volume Seven had fallen into the space left behind.

After retrieving salmon orange Volume Six from the bathroom floor, she replaced it on the shelf.

"Ok, Papa. What do you want me to see?"

The books were on the middle shelf of the middle bookcase between the bath and the door, bookended by bound compilations of Tolkien on the left and Grimm's fairy tales on the right. There were books on either side of the series, all church-related. Biographies of prophets. Books written by prophets. She found books on the restoration of the gospel, the years in Missouri, Nauvoo, and the pioneer trek west. The volumes of *Journals of Discourses* he'd shelved together were on this shelf. Three editions of Mormon Doctrine were shelved side by side, which she found conspicuous, as well as a gold-bound copy of the Book of Mormon. It was the version missionaries gave away in the '70s, and an odd thing to find on the shelves of a man who owned nicer copies of every edition ever released. Her father placed a few magazines with yellowed newsprint bookmarks here, all published in the '70s as well.

A gear in Marie's brain engaged and slipped. The 1970s had become a common denominator over the week. Whatever bothered her father hadn't broken his faith, but it had remained on his shelves for twenty years.

On a hunch, she pulled Jason's scriptures out from under her pillow and the gold-cover Book of Mormon from the shelf. She looked up his "white" verses first and her heart fell to see her father underlined them both. Three of the "black" verses were marked as well.

Her father told her truth had dirt in its depths. Tia Sarita had washed her hands. He had planted seeds. Because he had a wife and a child?

Did I trap him?

Marie pulled all the books he'd shelved between the fantasies and fairy tales and dropped them onto her bed. Inside, she found bookmarks in spreads containing disgusting words spoken by prophets. Statements by Egyptologists put her into a tailspin. A timeline of the events leading to the policy change regarding black members holding the priesthood showed more convenience for men than will of God. And, contrary to the artwork hanging in her own house, Joseph Smith "translated" the Book of Mormon by putting a stone in his hat?

The "anti-Mormon lies" she had been dismissing from her nonmember friends since high school…many were right here, in black and white, some of it published by the Church itself.

Discarding one xeroxed sheet, she picked up the next. She read the highlighted sections of sworn testimony before the US Congress. *Continuing revelation is a lie*, her father had penned in the margin. She climbed over his research and ran to the bathroom with the paper clutched in her fist.

Uncle Marty's super-secret, not-on-the-menu, Bananas Foster French Toast was ruined forever.

· ❄ ·

"What on Earth?

If her mother knocked, Marie hadn't heard it. The screech was impossible to miss, though.

"Not now, Mama. Please." She couldn't bear whatever the woman had brought upstairs to dump on her shoulders.

Her mother stood in the bathroom doorway with crossed arms, tight lips, and severely pinched eyebrows. "What's going on with you?"

A soft chuckle escaped Marie. "I don't know where to start."

"How about why you're sitting on the bathroom floor half-naked?"

Marie looked down and saw she was still wrapped in a towel. All the time she was puzzling over the books and stepping on her father's landmines, putting on clothes hadn't occurred to her.

"I got distracted."

"Must have been *fascinating*."

After vomiting breakfast, Marie had sat on the floor trying to put the things her father had said and done into context. Twice he'd told her not to share things they'd talked about with her mother. The books…the randomization…it was his way of leaving it where she would find it while hiding it in plain sight from her mother.

She didn't know any of it. He didn't want her to, and Marie wouldn't tell her.

Her mother dropped the lid on the toilet and sat. "What did you do?"

Marie assumed she meant to make Sam lose hold of his mental faculties long enough to beat a woman unconscious, but in case she came upstairs to talk about something else, she decided to ask for clarification.

"What do you mean?"

"We've known Sam since you were eight years old!"

Marie cringed. They had. And yet, after speaking to Sarah, it was clear no one knew him at all. "Have you ever wanted something so much…and you get it, and you make plans around it, and then lose it?"

Her mother didn't reply. Tears welled and fell before either of them spoke again, but they both knew she had. Seven miscarriages before her parents stopped trying to give Marie a younger sibling.

"I didn't know Sam loved me, Mama. Not the way he does." Marie looked aside, to a corner of the floor the broom kept missing. "I would have ended things differently."

Leaning forward, her mother brushed her bruised arm with a gentle hand. "I can't help but think, though, if he'd have done this if you weren't at Raleigh White's house. With his drug-using friends and that music. Marie…the Holy Spirt doesn't go into places like that."

The mention of the Holy Spirit grated on her nerves. "I'm wondering how he knew I was there."

"His cousin told him. Said you got him thrown out of his band. And since when do you sing?"

The urge to vomit was rising again. It was her fault. All of it.

"*Mija*, whatever's going on with you, it has to stop. You're keeping company with apostates and sinners. You haven't been home in two days. You've called off your wedding."

"Sam pushed my friend into a glass wall!" The heat in her boiled away her nausea, replacing it with agitation. "Because he was mad at me. Is that the kind of man you think I should marry?"

"To be fair, it—"

"Don't defend him!"

Her mother raised her hands, open palms toward her in a surrendering gesture. "But, that happened after you broke things off. You can't use his violence as an excuse before he actually was violent."

"You know I was at Raleigh's house, but you don't know he dragged me out of it?"

Her mother shrugged. "Yes."

"This!" Marie held up her arm. "He *yanked* me off a chair and pulled me up one flight of stairs and pushed me down another."

Surprise flashed across her mother's face. She blushed with anger. "I thought when they said *dragged*...I didn't think...."

"Yeah, well...*that* was after I told him I had doubts about marrying him and he called me a brat. After he told me to lie to the bishop. *After* he punched Jason in the eye. A *week* ago. I am *done* talking about Sam!"

"Okay!" Her mother sighed heavily. "Okay. Fair enough. But you're drifting, *mija*, and you have so many options you haven't looked at yet."

Marie watched with mild dread as her mother's fingers tapped on her leg. She was *thinking*. Mission or marriage. Those were the options she'd consider, and Marie had already made it clear the mission was not going to happen.

"There are three wonderful young men in the student ward. The bishop says there are two scheduled returns—"

"No."

"—next month. I'm sure—"

"No!"

"This is your salvation, *Ofelia*. Our *family*, together forever. Have you once thought of what your resistance is putting us all through?"

"More than anything else. But have *you* considered *me*?"

Her mother's brow furrowed in a mix of confusion and offense. "Your papa and I have always put you first."

"You just listed five nameless, faceless men as possible husbands." Marie sucked in the sob building in her chest. "The idea of sharing a bed with Sam made me cringe, and I've known him for years."

"Honey." Her mother looked at her lovingly. "I understand how you feel. I've been there. And I can say, you'll be ready when the time comes."

You weren't ready. Marie held her tongue. She promised her father she wouldn't tell.

"When the time comes? He'll be expecting me to uncross my legs four months from now!" She didn't mean to yell, but the unfairness of her situation burst out of her, and she couldn't stop. "What am I supposed to say? Sorry...I know we just went through the temple and you've been looking forward to sex since the bishop told you what it was ten years ago, but...you just don't do it for me?"

"You are upset, Ofelia, but you will speak to me respectfully."

Respect? Marie wiped angrily at her cheeks and glowered at her mother. "What if I'm not ready? Huh? What if I hate it? What will you tell me then, Mama? I'll get used to it. That it's my duty to meet my husband's needs? Think of the children? At what point will my feelings matter?"

Her mother exhaled strained patience. "You have to trust Heavenly Father to guide you through these things."

Marie dropped her face onto her knees. Her Heavenly Father hadn't been so helpful to her in years.

"Why did Sam tell you to lie to the bishop?" Marie looked up to find her mother attempting to bore through her skull with laser vision. "There are only two things you'd need to lie to the bishop about, Ofelia. Again, I ask you, what did you do?"

Marie flinched. "I kissed Ash."

Her mother swore under her breath. "No wonder Sam wanted to kill her."

"Mama!"

"Just once?" She answered with a shake of her head, and bit the inside of her cheek, knowing what her mother would ask next. "When you stayed at Signy's, did you sleep upstairs or downstairs?"

"Down."

Her mother slapped her across the face. "I gave birth to you. I cared for you! You do these things with other *girls* and tell me you're unwilling to marry a man?"

She shouldn't have been shocked at her mother's outburst, but the Marie couldn't have anticipated the physical hit. Neither of her parents had spanked her since she was five.

"I have *one* child and you do this to me?"

After shaking off the stupor, she cast a pleading look at her mother for mercy, but the woman had none.

"If that's the life that makes you happy, you will live it somewhere else!"

"Mama?"

"Don't! I am *done* with your nonsense, Ofelia! You will marry, in the temple as you're supposed to, or you will get out of my house." Without a second look back, her mother grabbed the door on her way out and slammed it on Marie's heart.

For a long while, Marie sat on her bathroom floor and cried, remembering when she was close to her mother and their time together was full of joy.

When she was young, she would on a chair to watch her mother cook the heirloom meals passed down from their ancestors. As she grew, watching became "helping", and later she became actually helpful.

In the summers, they had tended flowers in one garden and vegetables in another. Marie enjoyed sneaking strawberries. She was playfully scolded when she was caught, which made swiping them more fun. Her mother always knew, she later admitted, and pretended she hadn't seen.

They had taken *mama-mija* trips to Billings, Montana, for special shopping trips. Marie had modeled baptism dresses, homecoming dresses, and prom dresses, for her mother's approval and fawning praise. In her later teens, they had window shopped for wedding dresses and daydreamed aloud together.

When the weather was nice, they had often taken day trips into the Beartooth Mountains for picnic lunches. Her mother had helped her find good angles and light for photographs. They had also fished, sometimes. Her mother would always bait her hook for her so she wouldn't have to hurt the worm herself.

They had hung ornaments on Christmas trees and prepared meals for ill members of their ward. They decorated sugar cookies and watched game shows eating ice cream. Her mother cuddled her through period cramps and disappointments and deaths in the family.

Yes, she was closer to her father now, but that had not always been so. Marie couldn't remember when that had changed, but she missed her mother. She wanted her back. But, could she pay the price? Marry a man she didn't love, give him her body and soul, bear him children, all while knowing her feelings about him may never change?

When the wracking sobs finally settled, and Marie could breathe without bursting into tears all over, she picked herself up from the bathroom floor. She didn't know what to do next, but she knew she couldn't figure that out in her parents house. She walked into her bedroom and called Marty's Diner.

A half-hour later, *Westminster Quarters* rang downstairs. She shouldered the backpack she had shoved a week's worth of clothes into and gave her room a final once over. She had put her father's books back on the shelf. The information he had compiled might end their marriage if her mother saw it. Marie wouldn't be the one to out him as an apostate, if he was.

She had expected to see Sarah at the door and prepared to step between them when her mother made the inevitable comment about her friend's morality. She needn't have worried, because Sarah couldn't come out herself. Uncle Marty was a nice man, but nothing short of a medical emergency got an employee out of their shift. But Sarah followed through with her promise and sent "the cavalry" instead.

Signy stood in the foyer, a full head and shoulders taller in heeled boots than her mother. The soft, warm glow of the tin star chandelier showered Signy in gold, ramping up the Norse warrior-goddess look she preferred. By comparison, her mother was stiff, agitated by the presence of a guest rumored to hold court in bars among grizzled bikers passing through town. Still, she spoke confidently about how her daughter had seen the error of her recent ways and would be quitting the print shop again soon.

"Perhaps." Signy held her hand out as Marie arrived on the ground floor. "For now, my stripper is coming with me."

Her mother stared at her in shock as she took Signy's hand. "You're choosing sin over your family?"

"No." Marie paused as she started to leave. The look on her mother's anguished face broke her. Through tears, she said, "You're choosing the daughter you want over the daughter you have."

Alive

A bell pulled Marie from the tattered remains of a disintegrating dream. The simple, melodic *ding-dong*, told her clearly as the Pepto pink paint on the wall she wasn't at home.

She clutched a paisley comforter to her chest and scanned the room for clues. An old Singer sewing machine buried under old magazines. A dresser with cut-glass knobs and a herringbone-pattern inlaid into the fronts of the drawers. A gold frame with a drawing of a winged woman, scantily clad in armor and brandishing a sword.

A Valkyrie.

Oh yeah...

She collapsed onto Signy's guest room pillows as yesterday crashed down on her with unfair ultimatums and unwanted information.

After leaving her parent's home, she spent most of the rest of the day on Signy's couch, huddled under a blanket, while her boss treated her like glass. Jeannie came by, this time insisting she not make a decision regarding Ash yet. Her mother was hurting, Jeannie said. She owed it to her, and to herself, to let the dust settle before she made course-altering choices.

Dust? More like nuclear fall-out.

A male voice penetrated the walls of the guest room. It wasn't deep enough to be her father, but it was all too familiar to Marie. She suspected today would be no better than yesterday.

The bishop was going to press her for a meeting until she agreed to one. Might as well get it over with now.

She pushed back the covers. She was wearing Signy's clothes. A motorcycle rally t-shirt from Sturgis and sweatpants. During the night, she must have kicked off her socks. Rather than look for them, she padded out to the kitchen barefoot.

The voices became clearer.

Bishop Swing had come to visit his sister. Knowing it was him didn't soften the blow to her stomach when she saw him leaning on the counter, ankles crossed, next to the stove. His suit jacket hung over the back of a kitchen chair. Marie's focus naturally gravitated to the line created in his shirt sleeve by his temple garment, making the shoulder whiter than the rest of his arm.

During the week, the bishop managed shift workers at the sugar plant west of town. He wore overalls there, so a suit on Friday made no sense unless he wanted to impress someone. She suspected that someone was *her*.

His conversation with his sister appeared to be casual, but his presence sucked the air out of the room. Marie held to the doorframe, half-hiding, forcing her lungs to work.

"Isabela was willing at first, but she deferred to Estefan after she saw the bruises." The bishop spoke softly. "And let me tell you, he was not happy."

"Jason should have pressed charges." Signy stirred something in a skillet. "He'd have been arrested before she came home and none of this might have happened."

"Well, you know what they say about hindsight." The bishop tapped his fingers on his arm. "Have you seen them? The bruises?"

"It wasn't an accident, if that's what you're hoping." She switched her spatula from one hand to the other and grasped her brother's arm. "He yanked hard enough to leave fingerprints."

The bishop covered the spot on his arm where her hand had been and rubbed the inside with his thumb. He hung his head and sighed. Marie imagined he was thinking about his daughters, about how he'd feel if a man had been rough with one of them. What would he do?

Signy glanced over her shoulder and met eyes with Marie. She ticked her head toward the kitchen table and pulled a plate out of the cabinet to the left of the stove. The bishop followed her gaze, straightened and dropped his hands into his pockets.

"Eat up and take a shower." She placed a platter with scrambled eggs and sausage on the table. "Big job came in yesterday. We've got to move on the work in progress."

Obediently, Marie took the chair as far from the bishop she could get. Signy sat at her right with a fresh mug of coffee.

One edge of the table butted up against a wall. The only remaining chair was across from her with Signy in the middle. The bishop sat with a heavy frown.

"May I speak with Marie alone, please?"

Signy shook her head. "No."

The bishop's eyes widened. He watched Signy spoon eggs onto her own plate. His lips moved as if he meant to speak until he closed them. Finally, he managed to respond. "You're right. It can wait until after she eats."

"You're not peeking under her skirt."

Marie straightened in her chair and crossed one leg over the other, fearing with no cause whatsoever that he'd do such a thing.

"Sandra!"

"Don't *Sandra* me, *Leland*." Signy spread butter on a slice of toast. "You're looking for what she did to turn a Boy Scout into a jealous psychopath. I'm telling you 'no'. You will not sit at *my* kitchen table and harass *my* guest about whatever sex she might be having."

The words stripped Marie bare. She hugged herself, covering her body in a way she couldn't shield her soul. Averting her eyes, she focused on the pendulum of the clock on the wall behind the bishop's head. Left. Right. Left. Right. She counted the seconds her secrets and her fears hung in the air between the three of them.

Her boss and her bishop were too focused on each other to notice, though, and she silently thanked the Lord for that tiny mercy.

"I don't *harass* my ward members. I—"

"You poke and prod them for the dirty details of—"

He glowed with rage. "How dare you!"

Signy calmly took a sip of her coffee. "You shamed your son for touching his own body, Lee. How dare you?"

Marie winced at the sight of the bishop's hand tightening into a fist. He relaxed again, wiggled his fingers, and pressed his palm flat to the table. "Worthiness interviews, Sig. They're part of my calling."

"That's your defense?" Her lips pursed. "You don't have a choice?"

"I have *responsibilities*."

"No." Signy looked at the bishop with the eyes of a little girl disappointed in the brother she admired. "You have *marching orders*. And your balls dropped thirty years ago, honey. I had hoped you'd find them before now."

He glared at his sister with a face of stone but didn't respond.

"You can invade people's privacy as much as they let you in your office. Not in my house."

"I came here because I know you'd stop her from meeting me in my office."

"I would never tell an adult women what she can't do." She shifted her gaze to Marie. "Would you like me to leave?"

She should say yes. The bishop came to talk to her. But the part of her conditioned to consent to his request butt heads with a part his presence now frightened. Signy, though. She was strong. Confident. She met the man's flinty eyes with fire, his words with wit, and his church calling with scorn. She pulled his strings and made him dance.

Marie shook her head. "Please stay."

Signy casually shifted her attention back to her brother and stabbed one of the sausages on the serving platter. She pointed the link in his direction. "If you say the word 'modesty', I swear to God you'll wear my coffee out the door."

"This isn't how these things are done, Signy."

Marie looked between the two of them. She imagined Leland Swing as a little boy whining to his mom when his sister didn't play by the rules.

"I have faith in you to persevere and endure to the end." Signy bit the end of her sausage link.

He closed his eyes. Maybe counted to ten. Marie's scrambled eggs turned cold on her fork and Signy finished her coffee before he opened his eyes again.

"May I say an opening prayer?"

"Can't have you going too far off-script. Might trip you up." She laid her fork in her plate, crossed her arms over her chest, and eyed her brother with bored expectation.

They bowed their heads together and the bishop thanked the Lord for the opportunity they'd been given to meet. He thanked the Lord for the many blessings they enjoyed, for the food on the table, and for the passing of the storms that had so recently made life difficult in their corner of Wyoming. He asked for the Lord's blessing on his sister for her support during this trying time in Marie's life, and a healing blessing on their friend in the hospital. And he asked for the Lord's guidance and for the presence of the Holy Ghost to help Marie make the right choices among those He had placed in front of her. He closed, as all their prayers did, in the name of Jesus Christ.

Marie said *amen* out of habit.

"Short. Sweet." Signy picked up her coffee again. "Passive-aggressive."

The bishop turned toward his sister with clear annoyance. "How about this, Sig. I won't ask her worthiness question if you don't talk at all."

"Uh-uh. If you ask, I will talk. Until then, I'll keep quiet."

The bishop looked aside. "How's that different?"

"Again? It's *my* house, Leland. I set the concessions here."

"Conceding is unlike you." He narrowed his eyes at her. "So is keeping your mouth shut."

Signy grasped Marie's hand on the table top and squeezed. Her smile was almost vicious. "I have every confidence my stripper can handle you all by herself."

The bishop's eyes reminded Marie of the joke glasses at the drug store downtown. Certainly, if they opened any wider, his eyeballs would pop right out of his head.

Her breath shot from her lungs as if from a pressurized air hose. The snicker sputtered past her lips as she tried hard to keep them shut. When Signy chuckled, Marie stopped holding back.

She had nothing to laugh about. Ash was in a medically-induced coma. Sam might still be in jail; the conversation between Signy and the bishop didn't make the matter clear. She was homeless, orphaned, and now possibly facing discipline from the Church for behavior unbecoming of a daughter of God.

The bishop's shock quickly became annoyance.

"I'm sorry!" She blurted her apology between forced gasps for air. "It's just—"

She sucked in as much air as she could and held it in her chest, fighting her rebelling diaphragm. When the muscles in her chest relaxed again, she exhaled slowly.

"It's an industry term, Bishop," Marie said. "Strippers create printing plates."

The bishop's frown relaxed, conveying more disappointment now than anger. "My sister's vulgar humor has rubbed off on you, I see."

Signy's hands fisted into balls. She chuckled behind tight lips and eyes shut tight. Marie assumed her boss had a comeback, but her promise not to talk prohibited her from speaking it aloud. For the bishop's part, he ignored her.

He turned his attention to Marie. "How are you?"

She caught the reflex to say *fine* on her tongue. She wasn't. She hadn't been in days, not since coming out to Ash about her sexual confusion.

"I feel—" *No, not me.* "The *world*...feels broken."

"It can feel that way when our testimonies are weak."

A few days earlier, she would have heard wisdom in the words. They didn't satisfy her now.

"It's more than that." She glanced at Bishop Swing's arm and paused on the sharp line where the garment underneath ended. The temple garment was the Church's endorsement of trustworthy men. She'd taken it for granted all her life. "It's more than me."

"How do you mean?"

"Safe people have let me down. Risky ones have caught me. Over and over again."

"Are you sure its safety that has failed you?" The bishop slouched in his chair with his hands clasped in his lap. "Or perhaps you have put yourself too far out of the Lord's reach?"

She rubbed at the goosebumps his words raised. God was all-powerful, was he not? "Do you believe such a place exists?"

"I believe if we keep the Lord's commandments, he will bless us, Sister Baez."

Again, his reply neither answered her questions nor gave her comfort. She had a hard choice to make. She wanted information she could do more with than pretend the gaping hole in her faith wasn't there.

There was so much about the Church and the gospel bothering her now. As she struggled with what to mention first, she saw a bowl of fruit on the counter. Oranges. Bananas. *Apples.*

"Can I ask you something, Bishop?"

"Of course."

She hesitated. It was her last chance to back away and rebuild her life as an active Mormon. A life without Ash in it. His body in the ER flashed in her mind. The glass. The blood. She steeled herself against her doubts.

"We believe that our Heavenly Father was once a mortal man. His righteousness in life earned him the right to create his own world."

The bishop nodded.

"My cousin Erin and I were watching Star Trek. The Enterprise crew sent a team to a planet and an officer—Tasha Yar—died." Because the fruit wasn't on the table, she lifted the salt shaker. "Would she go to our Heavenly Father's heaven?" She raised the pepper shaker. "Or to that planet's heaven?"

The question earned her blank stares from the bishop and his sister. As silence hung in the air between them, she regretted asking.

"What exactly is your concern?" The bishop asked.

"Well…" Not expecting a question, she placed the spices on the table and paused to assemble all of the pieces. "If our Heavenly Father expects of us what His Father expected of His children, then it stands to reason the One True Church would be revealed to all sentient beings on all worlds. No matter where they may be in the universe. So…let's say one of my descendants meets a non-human member of the church on Ceti Alpha V. Where will their sealed family live together forever? With our family, in our Heavenly Father's Celestial Kingdom? Or her husband's family in his?"

Signy put her coffee on the table and reclined in her chair. She crossed her arms over her chest, making a show of waiting for her brother's answer. Pride bloomed in Marie. Whatever awe the woman once had for her technical skill had long ago become expectation. It had been a while since Signy had shown signs of being impressed with her.

The bishop, though, didn't like the question. "I think *Star Wars* is more in line with the doctrine of the Church than *Star Trek*."

"That's not an answer, Bishop."

He regarded her as he would a petulant child. "I don't know what would happen in that situation. But I have faith in the Lord to sort such things out."

"Why?" Her tone was more indignant than she meant but less than she felt. "If Joseph Smith restored the full gospel of Jesus Christ, why should I accept uncertainty over details of a core principle?"

"Because God is certain, Sister Baez. What do we know about God?"

She replied dutifully. "He is all-powerful, all-knowing, and always present. He is eternal. Unchanging."

"He is."

"May I may ask another question?"

He cringed. "About *Star Trek*?" When she shook her head and the bishop relaxed again. "Go ahead."

"Why did the Brethren lift the ban on giving black members the priesthood?"

The bishop stared at her. It was shock at first, once again melting into irritation as the words settled between them.

"The Lord reveals His will on His own timetable, Sister Baez. It is not ours to question."

Years of conditioning tugged at her, like old friends pulling her away from something she shouldn't get involved in. She glanced at Signy and received a slight nod that encouraged her.

Marie asked, "How does he reveal his will?"

"You know the answer to that."

"Tell me. Please."

"Through His living prophet."

Bits of scripture and quotes from prophets tumbled in her head. She could settle her questions about the Church. All the pieces were right there, if she could get him to help her sort them out.

"When I was watching *Star Trek*, and Tasha died, I remembered what I was told about Lorenzo Snow...that a heavenly being appeared to him in the temple and told him God was once like us, and we could become like Him."

The bishop nodded.

"But, I read a statement yesterday made by Joseph F. Smith." His nod became approving, and she assumed it was because she was seeking answers in appropriate places. "At the time, he said he never received revelation from God. No one had in the twenty-one years prior. That would have included Snow."

"Smith never said such a thing." The bishop crossed his arms over his chest. "There are many anti-Mormon lies. We are advised to disregard those things contradicting what we know to be true."

Marie met his eyes and held his gaze. "It was testimony he gave under oath before the US Congress."

The bishop's brow knitted. He ticked his head ever so slightly, as if listening for a faint noise.

"Did he lie to Congress, Bishop? Or do the prophets not talk face to face with God?

Signy straightened in her chair as Marie noticed a distinct change in the bishop's body language. The held breath. The flushed skin. The tremor in his hands. He remained quiet, but his patience with her questions was fraying.

She ignored her instinct to drop the subject.

"The First Presidency *and* the Quorum of the Twelve Apostles...fifteen men, Bishop Swing. *Fifteen* men *heard* God's voice instructing them to give priesthood to black members." Her voice broke over an acute burn in her throat. She swallowed against it. "When did our unchanging God start talking to his prophets again?"

"You are fixated on the policy change." The bishop's tone was cold. Suspicious. "Does black men having the priesthood offend you?"

A flame burst in Marie's chest. "That policy ripped my papa's family in half before God said 'nevermind'!"

The bishop recoiled a bit, but he composed himself quickly. "I'm certain your parents taught you to respect your elders."

They had, of course, but her anger at him corrupted the programming. "You came here to tell me my *salvation* rides on the words of prophets who talk to God and the priesthood power of the men around me. But if God doesn't actually talk to the prophets, and the men around me don't actually have power—"

"You are treading in dangerous waters. When you question the prophets of the Lord, you make it very difficult for me to help you."

The man sitting across from Marie was called of God to discern the worthiness of the ward. He could deny her entrance from the Lord's house on Earth and cut her off from His kingdom in Heaven. And getting back into either…that was his discretion, too.

As she stared at him, seeing him for the first time in her life not as a father figure, but as a man wearing a cheap suit, the fraying tether within her snapped.

"Jason told you the truth, Bishop." His stony front faltered again. "And you punished him."

The bishop snapped. "He didn't get a Temple Recommend because he wasn't worthy of one. That's on him, not me."

"Sam—!" *Not my story.* "He sat in your office and he lied. And the Holy Ghost told you nothing. I almost married that a-hole!"

"Lied? About what?"

As much as she wanted to see the silver dollar eyeballs burst, she resisted to tell him. "Sorry. Not my story."

"Please." The bishop leaned forward. "If you know something, it is your duty to tell me so that I can help him atone for what he's done."

My duty? Humiliate Sarah all over again to *help* Sam? *No way.*

"No."

With nothing left to say, Marie ate her breakfast cold. Signy made her a cup of hot chocolate with marshmallows. So much time passed in silence, Marie lost count of the pendulum swings. She'd begun to hope the bishop would simply leave.

"I can see the various ways you feel you have been let down, Marie." There was remorse in his voice, but she bristled at the emphasis on her feelings. "I ask you to remember men are imperfect beings, but the gospel is perfect. I don't wish to see you fall away from the truth because of mistakes made by men."

Mistakes she could forgive. Live with. Maybe even forget in time.

"I lost Jason because of *lies* told by men. I won't lose Ash to them, too."

The bishop placed his hand over hers, as Signy had done to encourage her earlier. "Think about your mother—"

She yanked her hand away. "My *mother* kicked me out!" The ache in her throat was too harsh to deny this time. She wouldn't cry in front of him, so she pushed away from the table. "Excuse me. I have a phone call to make."

· ❄ ·

Marie spilled her rage over the phone. Jeannie had given her a choice between the Church and Ash with entrance to Ash's hospital room as hostage, and Marie had been angry about that. She understood, but it still made her mad. But now, she knew the choice she had to make wasn't between her religion and Ash.

She didn't want to hurt her mother, but she had been struggling with doing what she knew to be right just to keep her family together. Now, with her belief in the power of priesthood gone, she would have to live a lie every remaining day of her life, bear children she didn't want, for a man she might never love, all to make her mother happy.

"Do I break my mothers's heart?" She cried. "Or my own?"

"I can't tell you what to do, Marie." Jeannie's voice was sad but warm. "But, I will say this, you may lose your mother either way."

Sobbing, Marie said, "I don't understand."

"If you leave, she may cut herself off from you. That is her choice to make. But…"

Jeannie paused for a bit, and while the line was quiet, Marie she remembered the sting of her mother's slap and how it felt to be kicked out of the only home she knew.

"But, if you choose her, and you do everything she expects you to do, and it makes you more and more miserable day by day, you may grow to hate her."

That, Marie decided, she could not bear. She thanked Jeannie. She hung up the phone. Then, she stood for a long time under a hot shower until all the tears remaining in her body had been cried.

Soon as she was dressed, Signy ushered her out of the front door of her mid-century home. The naked trees were helpless to filter the defiant sun rising in the cloudless blue sky. The light hurt her raw eyes. After a week in the basin, the cold front finally pushed its way east overnight. Steam rose from the moist street as snow dyed black from soot melted, telling her the asphalt had broken the freezing point.

The air felt different on her skin. She stopped in the middle of the yard, snow rising half-way to her knees, and inhaled the change of atmosphere. It was heavy, but in a wonderful way. Melting snow smelled different than rain. It didn't have the same sweetness. It was dirty and clean at the same time.

She wanted to stand there all day. The warmth of the sun on her skin reminded her of Phoenix. But, she couldn't. Her feet would freeze and ruin the illusion. And she had work to do.

The stripping was done on the annual report job, but still needed to be printed folded, collated, bound, trimmed, packaged, and driven to Cody. And the new job Signy had mentioned at breakfast would require a full day of work to get on plate. Both jobs were due for delivery in a week. Tight timeframes, even when everything went exactly right. Marie couldn't count on perfect.

Signy had given her so much. Opportunity. Lenience. Support. *Love.* While Marie would much rather go to the hospital and wait for Ash to wake up, she owed it to her boss to put her work first right now. So, when the woman called her name, she shoved her thoughts of sun and Ash aside and climbed into the truck.

Everything was exactly as it should be in the Strip Club. Mitchell played Pearl Jam. Cal told a cringe-worthy story about a spider in his girlfriend's bathroom. When he revealed it was a hairball, Marie laughed until her stomach hurt. She was starting the second color plate of a miscellaneous job when Signy called Cal and Mitchell to help her in the press room.

The three strippers looked at the boss woman with concern. Everyone but Ash reported to work today, so why call her strippers off critical work when...

Oh.

Because she didn't actually need help in the press room.

Marie's father walked through the copy shop doorway. He wore a red polo with the dealership's logo on the left breast. He usually wore suits and expected professional attire of his office employees as well. It reminded her it was Friday.

She looked at Signy. "You couldn't tell him I was in the dark room?"

"He came to talk. I think you should hear him out."

Signy took Mitchell and Cal with her through the thick vinyl curtain, leaving Marie alone with her father. She exhaled heavily as he followed the safety path around to her light table. So much for a good day.

No. She wouldn't wither. If he wanted to talk, she would let him talk. She had work to do. This project was keeping her from being at Ash's bedside when he awoke, so her father could talk to the top of her head for all she cared.

To her surprise, he didn't ask her to stop. He didn't say anything at all.

Peering through a loupe, she aligned the cross hairs of two pieces of film. The heat of her father's eyes was on her shoulders as she taped the loose film to the sheet of clear acetate separating the photos.

If he expected her to start a conversation, he would be waiting wait a long time.

She lifted the acetate sheet from the metal keys keeping it in register with the orange vinyl, rubylith, and film layers below, and replaced it with a bare sheet of acetate.

"Why yellow?"

Marie placed the loupe on top of the crosshairs and aligned the next piece of film over the one below. "Pardon?"

"I get what you're doing…using the yellow layer to position the others. Was it just the first one you grabbed? Or…?"

"It's the first color Signy will run through the press."

It wasn't strictly necessary, but it was standard procedure in the Strip Club to assemble the plates in the order her boss preferred to send her runs through. Yellow. Magenta. Cyan. Black. Pantone spot color. Varnish. Embosses. Die cuts. In a pinch, Signy could burn the yellow plate and they could continue stripping the other layers as the press ran. That was not standard procedure but falling behind happened.

"I see now why this appeals to you. The precision of it."

The words should have made her proud. Instead, they reminded her of an old argument. "You still think a man could do it better?"

"I've never thought you incapable, *mija*. It's just…you have chosen to work when you don't need to. In doing so, you are taking opportunities from those who do."

It had been part of the logic he'd used in September to get her to quit. She should be honing her homemaking skills. Preparing for marriage and children. Not taking jobs from men with families.

"So, I should birth more hungry mouths. Become a burden to men like Peter Knutzen who follow the Church's instruction to get married when they have no money, no education, no training…"

Her father shook his head. "I didn't come here to rehash the marriage talk."

"No, you came here because of Mama. Or the bishop." Marie squared her shoulders and met his eyes with determination. "I'm not apologizing."

"You're not the one who needs to."

The words brought her defenses crashing down. Alongside selfless service and submission to God's Plan, accepting responsibility for the sins she provoked in others and forgiving the slights toward herself were duties of every daughter of God. She fully expected her priesthood-holding father to correct her.

"What your mother said to you is wrong. You were right to leave." Her father touched her head and smoothed her hair with a gentle hand. "And whatever you said to the bishop, I'm sure you were right about that, too."

As she stared at him in shock, he ticked his head toward the back wall and sniffed. "I smell coffee."

"Break room." She pointed vaguely behind him. "For Mitchell and Signy, mostly."

"Do you think they'll mind if I have some?"

If you…what? She shook her head. "No, but…whatever's left has been sitting for *hours*."

"Let's have a seat. Talk a bit."

She left her light table and sat in the break room. When her father placed a steaming mug opposite her and wrapped his hands around it, she could no longer stand the curiosity.

"When did you start drinking coffee?"

"Vietnam." He drank the coffee black and piping hot as Marie counted twenty-five years. "Ah, that has been sitting. I stopped after my discharge from the Army, but…do you know the story behind the Word of Wisdom?"

"Beyond what's in the scriptures?" She'd always believed the prohibition on caffeine was revealed by God to Joseph Smith. Everything she'd ever been told was up for question now.

"Back in the early days of the church, it was common for men to smoke and chew tobacco while they talked about important things. Hitting a spittoon may be harder than it seems it should be, and Emma got tired of cleaning up the mess. She asked Joseph for a revelation to forbid tobacco. He gave her one."

It explained tobacco, *but…* "What's that have to do with coffee?"

"Well, if the men couldn't have their favorite vice…"

Her jaw dropped. "You're saying a marital spat…160 years ago, about *dip*, stands between the whole church and a cup of coffee?"

Her father raised his cup and toasted her with a smile. "Not all of us."

"What does Mama say?"

He swallowed his sip and placed the cup silently on the table. "Your mama… doesn't know."

"How do you keep it from her?"

"I don't drink it around her."

"Obviously, but Papa…" She leaned forward. "You're lying to your wife."

"I've killed people, Marie." Her father's voice was soft, almost shallow. "In the service of my country, I've pointed guns at people, pulled triggers, and walked away to point more guns and pull more triggers. If God is petty enough to care about a lie about coffee, what hope do I have in salvation with the blood of His children on my hands? And if God is not petty…He will know I lie to keep peace."

He stared into the black pool in his cup as if it spoke to him. "And what is a guilty pleasure compared to bigger secrets? I live with many, *mija*. I'm here to come out, as it were."

"Come out?" She clasped her hands in her lap. "Are you gay?"

"No." His chuckle was jovial and familiar but had a note of sorrow to it. "*That* I'm sure you'd understand."

His eyes pleaded with her for compassion. She extended her arm across the table and he put his hand in hers.

"I hate going to the temple," he confessed.

As raw as she still was over the things she found in his books, her father's confession upended her. The temples were beautiful buildings. How could anyone hate going?

"Why?"

"I can't explain without breaking oaths I've made, but…I left the Celestial Room after my Endowment feeling like I must have missed *something*. Then, the ceremony that sealed me to your mother was disappointing. And I already told you how our wedding night went."

"Did Mama hate it, too?"

"No. At least, I don't think so, but again, we've never talked about it. In the temple, they tell you not to. She finds purpose in performing proxy ordinances now, so…when we can go, we go."

"But how do you keep your Temple Recommend? When the bishop asks if you're keeping the Word of Wisdom, what do you say?"

Her father gazed at her with a patient, almost exasperated, look. "What he expects to hear."

"You lie?" Marie pulled her hand away from her father. "To the bishop?"

"About coffee, yes."

Marie stood from her chair and paced the break room. Was Jason the only person who bothered telling the bishop the truth?

"So, you *are* an apostate." She said this as a statement of fact.

He nodded, not looking the least bit offended.

"You raised me to believe the gospel is true. You tried to get me to go on a mission. You encouraged me to marry Sam after I told you how I felt about him!"

"I also told you to look into the church's history."

"Because you didn't want me to work here."

"No, because I wanted you to look where the Church doesn't want you to. To make you choose…plant seeds or wash your hands."

"I was so mad they were in *my* room I never looked at them until yesterday!

What if I never did?"

Her father grasped her hand as she passed behind him. "Please sit down."

She plopped into the chair beside him this time and slouched.

"When I lost my faith, I was a newlywed with a baby on the way. The last thing I wanted was to upset your mother. Then I had a baby I was afraid to lose in a custody battle should my marriage turn sour. Then your mother miscarried time and again, and I had to wonder…and she began to suspect my testimony was weak and God was punishing us for it."

This time, the exasperation was hers. "I don't believe that, Papa."

"But do you see the position I was in? If I had told her I lost my faith, she'd have left me and taken you with her. My family was still angry about my sister. They would have sided with your mama."

Marie scooted her chair closer and hugged her father. "I'm sorry."

"There's no reason." He rubbed her back and kissed her cheek, the way he had when he tucked her into bed as a child. "Now, things are different. Your mama and I have a routine. Our daughter has grown into a beautiful, talented, intelligent woman. And I have opportunities, every day, to help others. I don't need *The Book of Mormon*, or anything else about the Church to be true to appreciate what being LDS brings to my life."

"But, what if it's not enough for me?"

Her father shrugged. "Then it's not."

"And if I choose to leave?"

"I hope you'll remember where your home is and come back to it now and then."

"Mama doesn't want me there."

Her father deflated. "Her heart is bleeding now, *mija*. I am hopeful she will regret her words to you soon enough."

"And if she doesn't?"

"Let's worry about that in the future, shall we?" Her father stood from his chair and pulled her to her feet and into another warm embrace.

"I love you," she said, very grateful to have not lost both of her parents.

"I love you, too, *mija*." He released her and gestured toward the door. "I won't keep you from your work any longer."

Marie returned to her light table, sad their time together was over as she watched him leave. It surprised her again as he doubled back.

"Just so you know, I offered him money to walk away."

Him? "Who? Jason?"

Her dad grinned. "When Mudbug was checking for pupil dilation, Ash was semi-conscious. Said some things I don't think he meant to."

A cold hand grasped Marie's heart. *Oh, no. He knows.*

He pulled his hand out of his trouser pocket and placed a pile of torn paper beside the film she was aligning. "He turned me down once before, but…talk is one thing. Check in hand is something else."

He winked at her and left the Strip Club.

She sorted through the paper pieces and puzzled them back together. Reassembled, she found a check for an obscene amount of money made out to Ashton Clarke.

· ❄ ·

The atmosphere in the Strip Club was light and snarky for most of the day. Then, near the end of their shift, Signy pulled Mitchell out of the room for a phone call. He returned a few minutes later, with Signy on his heels and a perturbed look on his face.

He stopped next to the plate burner, where Marie was arranging layers of masks and sheets of acetate onto small metal pins keeping them in register. For a moment, he looked at the wall behind the plate burner to avoid meeting her gaze. When he did meet her eyes, his expression was grave.

"It's been a pleasure working with you, Marie," he said.

"Um…" That sounded awfully like good-bye. "Thank you?"

She closed the glass door on the plate burner, flipped the platter into the machine, and pressed the start button. Inside, UV light was burning the images and words they'd stripped onto the press plate. She loved this process, and she finally had her father's support. She wasn't going anywhere.

"My mom just called." He and Signy exchanged a tense glance. "She's family gossip hub and she said the Rigby grapevine is on fire. The whole family—I'm talking right down to second cousins of married relations—everyone is in shock. Sam wouldn't do something like this, they say. They're fixating on what made him do it."

"On me, then." As she blamed herself, she didn't see the emergency. *Unless...* "Or do they think Ash did something?"

"Nah, thanks to that pissant cousin you got kicked out of Raleigh's band, everyone's blaming the...the girl who almost tricked him into marrying him."

'Girl' wasn't what he was going to say. "What are they calling me?"

He shook his head.

"Mitchell."

"No. I won't repeat it." He took her by the arms and leveled an intense stare on her. "Marie. Sam's been a favorite of the whole damn clan since forever. *You* got him arrested two weeks after coming home from his mission."

As the gravity of the situation settled on Marie, Signy finally spoke. "Call your aunt in Phoenix. Now."

Tia Sarita shared Mitchell's concern, and she made him promise to watch after Marie until she could arrange to get her out of town. He took his word seriously. He drove Marie to the hospital and escorted her into the building. Even then, he didn't leave her side.

His attention filled her with apprehension, and she saw recognition in the eyes of everyone she passed in the hallways. Were they talking about her? Was Mitchell the buffer between them, and if he left, would they jump on her? Or was she imagining scorn where there was none?

She pulled her arms in closer and resisted the urge to count floor tiles. Instead, she looked straight ahead. Would everything be okay if she pretended it was?

It's a hospital. Safe place. She wanted to wring Mitchell's neck for getting her brain going like this.

Outside Ash's room, she slowed. Stopped. She leaned in the doorway and listened. A girl cried out for *Auntie Em.* Marie smiled as she visualized the scene in the *Wizard of Oz.* Dorothy trapped in the Wicked Witch's castle, watching her aunt in a crystal ball.

She turned to Mitchell. "You don't have to stay."

"I'll be in the waiting room."

He was going to do what he was going to do. She gave him a smile and stepped through the doorway.

Past the curtains separating the room's two beds, Ash lay sleeping. It pleased her. Most of the cuts were superficial, as she had been told before, but they had made his face enflamed and swollen. The shallow cuts always hurt the worst, didn't they?

She paused her hand before touching his cheek and fisted it to stop it from shaking. *I was going to marry the man who did this to you.*

Mitchell was right to keep close to her, if not for her safety, for Sam's. She had never wanted a person to die before, but… *How terrible am I?* How could her regard for a person she'd loved half her life slip?

"What did I miss?" Ash's question rumbled through gravel. It was the most wonderful sound she'd ever heard.

"Nothing important." She took his hand in both of hers and sat. She pressed her lips to his fingers. "I got kicked out of my house, moved in with Signy, and quit my church."

"Have I been asleep for 30 hours? Or 30 years?"

"Feels like years." She laid her head on the bed. "I need to tell you something. I'm afraid you'll hate me when I'm done."

"I promise I won't walk away before you can explain." He tried to sit, but the effort was stifled by pain. "Fucking gorilla."

"I'm so sorry, Ash." She sniffled back tears. "It's my fault. I—"

"Shush. What's so important you have to confess while I want to kill people?"

"The gun." She bit her bottom lip as he opened the eye not swollen shut to look at her. "It wasn't loaded."

"You faked it?" Was the harsh sound from his throat or his heart? "Why would you ever do that?"

"I needed to get out of town. Because…" She stood from her chair to make it easier for him to look at her, though he didn't appear to want to. "I was afraid I would do something I'd regret."

"Like?"

She placed the softest of kisses on his mouth.

"It *was* me?" The words trembled from his lips and across hers. "You left to get away from me?"

She pulled back abruptly to keep her tears from falling on his raw skin.

"I was scared of how you'd react. I thought if you didn't want me to—or if you did…and there was this article in my church magazine about people like us! I—"

"Stop."

She dropped into the chair and buried her face in his bedsheets. "Please don't be mad."

He had to forgive her. He had to.

A hand settled on her head and gently scratched. "M. Look at me."

Marie rolled her head and relished the touch of his palm on her cheek. He inhaled sharply and whimpered at the movement it forced on his body.

"I have a confession, too."

"Whatever it is, I promise it won't matter." After the week she'd had, there was nothing left she couldn't bear to hear. Nothing he could possibly say to upset her now.

"Jason and I talked about more than why you broke up. A lot more."

"He's your friend. You can talk about whatever."

"He said we had to get you away from Sam. That you were in danger. And the only way might be to get you out of the church entirely."

Her quiet astonishment didn't reach him with his one good eye closed.

"He wanted my help."

"Why you?"

"He said you'd dig in your heels if he told you about Joseph Smith's wives. A nonmember, though…"

"I'd be obligated to be a missionary." And she had been. She had answered his questions the best she knew how. Defended the early prophets. Bore her testimony.

"I told him no. It wasn't my place to ruin the Church if it made you happy.

But Jason told me things I couldn't believe. Said I could see it myself if I sat in one testimony meeting. So, I did."

Marie had missed half of church last Sunday, but she was there for most of Sacrament meeting. "I don't remember seeing you."

"I wasn't there. *Ashley* was."

He regarded his body and his soul as two separate people, and Ashley was the person she saw every day. The body lying in the bed. She would have recognized him, even in a dress.

He chuckled softly, winced, and cursed Sam's name again. "I was sitting about six feet away from you."

She stared at him in shock. The woman with the red hair and combat boots? "That was you?"

He didn't answer. "Sam's little sister took the microphone, and she repeated the words he spoke to her. And that made me think you don't have a testimony any more than she does. You have words, passed from an adult's lips to a child's ears. I told Jason I was in."

"That...son of a..." Was her father in on it, too? Did he point her ex-boyfriend in the right direction? Absolutely the first thing she was going to ask Jason when she saw him again.

"I'm sorry. I should have told you. I—"

Marie silenced him with a kiss. "I will."

"You will...*what*?"

"I'll leave town with you. If you still want me to."

With effort, he raised his right arm and touched her face, hissing as the movement caused him pain. "Think about what you're saying, M. I still can't—"

She pressed her finger lightly to his lips and smiled with hope for the future. "I choose you."

Iris

Two weeks before, Marie had flown out of Sky Harbor International with her father, bound for Wyoming with a blizzard threatening. She descending onto the very same runway now, with Ash at her side this time, and the pilot announced the temperature on the ground was 65 degrees Fahrenheit.

Ash squeezed her hand as the plane jostled a bit. This was his first flight anywhere, and the adjustments of the plane scared him. But that was only part of his nerves. Finally free of Coulter, he had wanted to go straight to California. That was his plan before he crashed in her town. He'd worked two jobs for two years and saved nearly every penny to start over there.

But Ash's plans after getting to California were bigger than living comfortably. He wanted to free himself from Ashley. He wanted to be a man and live his life. The money he had saved would have allowed him to do one or the other on his own, but now he had her, too. Marie's resources were the balance of her checking account, the clothes in her backpack, and an aunt ready to open her home.

Being a guest in the home of strangers also concerned him. And, he was also off of the pain meds and the discomfort of his healing injuries made him cranky. Still, he agreed to stop in Phoenix even though he'd rather not. Getting a plan together could only help them.

Marie squeezed his hand in return. He turned stiffly toward her. She wanted to touch his face, hold his cheek in her palm, but the cuts were still healing.

"They're going to love you," she promised of her family.

He lifted her hand and kissed the back of her fingers. Then, he rested his head back in the seat and closed his eyes, prepping himself for the moment the wheels would touch down.

At the gate, Marie and Ash gathered their bags, and made their way up the gangplank to the terminal. A burly black man stood a ways back from a gathering assembled to greet the arriving passengers. Marie smiled, held tight to Ash's hand, and pulled him through the crowd.

The moment she broke through the crowd, she released Ash and jumped for her uncle. He caught her in the air and held her, feet dangling, as he would one of his own daughters. She sobbed quietly, in sorrow for all she had lost, but also in gratitude she had not lost all.

"Oh, child." He hugged her tighter and let it linger. "You will be okay."

Finally, he put her down. She wiped her eyes and reached her hand out for Ash, who had been standing back and out of the way.

"Is this the young man your papa told me about?" Uncle Carl held his hand out to him.

Ash hesitated. She imagined he had spent much of the flight wondering what to expect from her Arizona family, but he clearly hadn't expected Uncle Carl to reach out to him while referring to him as a man.

"Ashton." He took Uncle Carl's hand and shook it. "It's an honor to finally meet you, sir."

"All mine, Ashton." Uncle Carl said before leading them out of the airport to take them home.

An hour later, when Marie sat down at Tia Sarita's glittery black granite kitchen island, she was overcome with a sense of oddness. It had been only two weeks since she sat in that exact spot, playing with a pair of apples, and pondering the fate of space travelers according to the Mormon doctrine of salvation, but it felt like months.

Tia Sarita leaned on the island opposite Marie, and after serving Ash a glass of the best bourbon in his liquor cabinet, Uncle Carl settled into the corner of the cabinetry between the sink and the stove. They wanted the whole story, so Marie gave it to them. From the moment she left Phoenix until the moment Signy told her to call Tia Sarita.

"Why California?" Uncle Carl asked.

"Warm sun. Beaches." Ashton shrugged. "People who get people like me."

Her uncle smirked. "Son, *I* get people like you. And it's not California you want. You want a place you're safe to be you, and California is the name you know."

Ashton's jaw fell open. "How do you—"

"I loved a woman once who ran away from Idaho looking for the same thing." Uncle Carl shoved his hands in his pockets. "I've had twenty years to think back on the ways I failed her, and…well, trust me. There's nothing in California you can't get in Phoenix. Except here, you don't have rent."

Marie shook her head. "We just wanted a place to stay for a few days. We couldn't—"

"The rehab has counsellors for gender dysphoria," Tia Sarita added, ignoring Marie's objection. "We refer to doctors and surgeons."

"Woah!" Ash sat up. "I'm not talking about jumping into surgery."

Uncle Carl left his corner and stood next to Tia Sarita. "Just ask yourself… would you like California to be the place you bury Ashley? Or the place no one ever knew her at all?"

Ashton sighed heavily. "Dammit. I got trapped in Coulter by logic, too."

Marie laced her fingers with his. "And look how that turned out."

He looked at her and briefly pressed his lips to hers before touching his forehead to hers. "I guess California can wait a little longer"

Tia Sarita introduced Ashton to a doctor at her rehab clinic. As the ball started rolling on his medical goals, Marie took a job in the pressroom of a newspaper. Ashton put on a green apron for Starbucks.

Back in Coulter, Jason and Sarah lived lean for few months. They saved enough for a deposit on a one bedroom apartment, two months rent, and grocery money for a month. The day they had the cash, they packed up the belongings they couldn't survive without and drove straight through to Phoenix. There were a lot more restaurants, more pianos, and more kids to teach lessons to. They made regular visits to Tia Sarita and Uncle Carl's house. Carmina took her first steps in their kitchen and learned to swim in their pool.

Not long after that, Neil and Raleigh made the move as well. They rented a house with a garage and soundproofed the walls. The band's equipment was installed there. They made a practice schedule, and when they had a setlist, they scheduled their first gig as *Cry Little Sister*. For the stage, Marie combined Neil's nickname for her with Ash's last name: Manita Clarke.

She missed performing in front an audience, she realized as their first set ended, but diving had never allow her to interact with them. She learned to command the energy between the stage and the audience. She *loved* singing, and the band's fans loved her.

Four years later, after an opportunity arose that the band really shouldn't refuse, the time had finally come to continue to onto California. Their car was packed. Jason's family was due at the house any moment. They all planned to follow the band's equipment trailer, so they were just waiting for Neil and Raleigh to roll out of bed.

Marie sat on the edge of the board cantilevered over the deep end of her aunt's swimming pool. Mounted low, it allowed her toes to touch the cool water below. As the sun rose behind her, her shadow stretched across the pool, darkening the water. But the sound of the water in the drains remained constant, tying every day she'd ever spent poolside together into one moment, almost stopping time.

The board jiggled. She grasped the edge to keep from falling. Strong arms wrapped her up as hairy legs lowered into the water on either side of her. Warm lips touched the spot where her shoulder met her neck and a furry chin rested on her shoulder.

"Are you okay." Ashton's voice was a deep purr across her ear.

"Yeah."

No, she didn't want to leave Tia Sarita and Uncle Carl. But she'd broken off an engagement, left her home, and quit a demanding church. She knew she could survive leaving.

"I just miss them already," she admitted.

"Me, too." Tia Sarita, Uncle Carl, and their girls were his family now as much as hers. "I'm amazed, every moment, by how lucky I am to have them. To have you."

She leaned back into his chest and dropped her head back. The sun behind Ashton lit up a patch of unruly honey blond hair like a slipping halo. She took his chin in her hand and rubbed his beard with her thumb.

Marie shook her head. "I've always been the lucky one."

Ashton kissed her gently. Enjoying the moment, she barely heard the sliding glass door open.

"Tia Maria!"

They both turned toward the squeal of a young girl. Carmina Swing, now four-years-old, bounded across the stone pool deck in denim shorts and a lime green halter-top. Her long blond hair was in pig-tails today and they danced around her head with every step she took. She climbed the two stairs and walked carefully along the board, until Ashton reached over his shoulders and picked the child up by her arms.

Carmina squealed as Ashton picked her up to fly over his head. Marie held out her arms to catch the girl and helped him bring her down gently. Once she was settled in Marie's lap, Ashton wrapped his arms around both them.

They sat together on the diving board until sitting still bored Carmina. Ashton flipped the child upside-down again and deposited her safely on the board behind him. She ran back into the house, leaving Marie and Ashton alone again. They cuddled, cheeks touching, and listened to the gurgle of the pool drains as the shrinking shadows became vibrant colors, until slammed vehicle doors and boisterous voices disturbed their peace.

"That'd be Neil and Raleigh." Ashton caressed her arm and kissed her cheek. "Time to go."

Thank you for reading a Life Less Perfect. Please leave a review—rave or scathe—on Amazon or Goodreads and share on your preferred social media channels.

About the Author

Wendy S. Russo got her start writing in the sixth grade. That story involved a talisman with crystals that had to be found and assembled before bad things happened, and dialog that read like classroom roll call. Since then, she's majored in journalism (for one semester), published poetry, and entertained her friends with Star Wars fan fiction and epic fantasy novels. Her debut novel, *January Black*, won silver in the Coming of Age category of the 2013 Reader's Favorite Awards.

A Wyoming native transplanted in Louisiana, Wendy is a wife, a mom, a Tiger, a Who Dat, and she falls asleep on her couch at 8:30 on weeknights.

Website: www.wendysrusso.com
Facebook: @wendysrusso
Twitter: @wendysrusso
Email: ALifeLessPerfectBook@gmail.com

Acknowledgements

First, always, my husband, Robert, and our son. They have being incredibly patient while I write. Robert has endured many more conversations about Mormonism than he could have anticipated when I unshelved this project. AND he proofread the final draft of a novel that is *so* not this thing. Also, many thanks to my aunt Sandy Giel, and my mother-in-law, Diane Russo, for being faithful cheerleaders.

Christine Ashworth read version 2.0. And version 3.0. AND she was on hand for hundreds of Facebook Messager DMs, ready to comment on snippets and to offer encouragement when I was down in the dumps about writing, publishing, the state of humanity, and whatever else got under my skin. Best crit partner ever.

Rainy Kaye, my editor, said she didn't find much wrong with the book. Just an obsession with italics and about six *thousand* missing words. Good editors are worth their weight in gold. I'm grateful she charges on the low side.

This book owes much to the input of my beta readers: Pike Martel, James Stryker, Roxy Krawczyk, Natasha Larry, and Erica Cameron. I'd like to thank Pike and James in particular for their enthusiasm and critical input, respectively, and for assuring me redeeming the manuscript would not require lighting it on fire.

Over the years, I have received support from other writers, including but not limited to: Nancy Brandt, Steven Brandt, Josephine Templeton, Kristin Lamb, Raidon Phoenix, Marie Sexton, Lynn Rush, and Kelly Seguin. Also Adam Skelter's "The Art of Story" was crucial in developing scenes in the third draft.

To research the LGBT threads of this book, I watched every video ever posted by YouTubers Alex Bertie and Ash Hardell.

For the Mormon arc, I owe much to Jeremy Runnell's *Letter to a CES Director*, Fair Mormon's rebuttal, and Runnell's response to Fair Mormon's rebuttal. Also, the story benefits from the critical analysis of Mormonism by the Mormon Research Ministry website, John Dehlin's Mormon Stories podcast, and I Am An Ex-Mormon YouTube channel.

And while I have read the *Book of Mormon* cover to cover, it was years ago. I cannot take credit for having found what Marie refers to as Jason's "black verses" on my own. I'm not sure if Evidence Ministries is the origin of "The Impossible Gospel," but I did get the list of verses from one of Keith Walker's videos.

Jason's "Black" Verses

1 Nephi 3:7

And it came to pass that I, Nephi, said unto my father: I will go and do the things which the Lord hath commanded, for I know that the Lord giveth no commandments unto the children of men, save he shall a way for them that they may accomplish the thing which he commandeth them.

Alma 11:37

And I say unto you again that he cannot save them in their sins; for I cannot deny his word, and he hath said that no unclean thing can inherit the kingdom of heaven; therefore, how can ye be saved, except ye inherit the kingdom of heaven? Therefore, ye cannot be saved in your sins.

Moroni 10:32

Yea, come unto Christ, and be perfected in him, and deny yourselves of all ungodliness; and if ye shall deny yourselves of all ungodliness, and love God with all your might, mind and strength, then is his grace sufficient for you, that by his grace ye may be perfect in Christ; and if by the grace of God ye are perfect in Christ, ye can in nowise deny the power of God.

D&C 1:31

For I the Lord cannot look upon sin with the least degree of allowance;

D&C 25:15

Keep my commandments continually, and a crown of righteousness thou shalt receive. And except thou do this, where I am you cannot come.

D&C 58:43

By this ye may know if a man repenteth of his sins—behold, he will confess them and forsake them.

D&C 82:7

And now, verily I say unto you, I, the Lord, will not lay any sin to your charge; go your ways and sin no more; but unto that soul who sinneth shall the former sins return, saith the Lord your God.

Chapter Playlist

http://bit.ly/ALLPWSR

Rotten Apple — Alice in Chains

Help! — The Beatles

Gotta Get Away — The Offspring

Wonderwall — Oasis

High Hopes — Pink Floyd

Jesus Forgive Me (For the Things I'm About to Say) — Concrete Blonde

Bullet with Butterfly Wings — Smashing Pumpkins

Don't Speak — No Doubt

River of Deceipt — Mad Season

Alive — Pearl Jam

Iris — The Goo Goo Dolls

Bonus Scene

The second draft of A Life Less Perfect *alternated between Marie's and Ash's POVs. After a beta reader gave compelling storytelling reasons for focusing on Marie, I removed the scenes in Ash's POV. This conversation between Ash and Jeannie Praetor, aka The Shrink, takes place on Friday night after Marie gave him the keys to her car at the coffee shop. Note: Marie's mother did not throw out her CDs in this draft.*

Marie didn't almost kiss you.

You didn't catch her flirting.

Neil's wrong about her.

She didn't laugh. She didn't roll her eyes, or play along with what she assumed to be a joke. When Ashton asked her to come with him to California, she confessed a desire in two dangerous little words.

I wish.

What the fuck was he supposed to do now?

Ashton rubbed his hand across his face. As he brushed his jaw, the skin her ice-cold fingers had touched hours earlier came to life. A shiver rushed through his flesh and down his spine. He dropped his hand and grabbed hold of the Camry's gearshift.

Mr. Baez didn't react at all when his daughter gave Ashton the keys to her car. Like cars were things the man let people borrow every day.

Well, he is a car salesman.

Ashton leaned on the driver's side door and chewed on his left thumbnail while tapping the right-hand fingers on the gearshift. The car had been detailed recently, evidenced by a strong, artificial vanilla scent. With the engine running, the heater blowing, and stereo pumping out tunes, the car was a cozy enough place to put off a decision.

The kitchen and living room windows beyond the windshield, glowing with gold light, beckoned. No, they were distracting him from his senses. What he wanted was to throw the car in reverse and drive. The tank was almost full. He estimated he could get maybe a hundred and seventy-five miles before running out of gas forced him to turn around.

Because Ashton didn't want to skip town. Not really.

No, he'd turn back time if he could. Two years. Turn right in Laurel, Montana, instead of left. He'd never have crashed in this town and he'd never met her.

All the while these thoughts tumbled in his head, the house in front of him waited, patient as the woman within its walls. He supposed it was rude to keep her waiting.

Ashton reached for the key in the ignition. Under the driver's seat, the CD changer snapped. The stereo filled the care with a bright melody played on piano keys. He stopped his reach and pulled his hand back.

Marie loved "Winter." It had been her favorite song since Jason Swing gave her this CD years ago. He was a bit of a piano prodigy, that guy. Ashton had long suspected talent was what set him apart from other boys in Marie's eyes while young, because without it, he was an average-at-best pale-faced geek with rosacea and rooster cowlick The Little Rascals would mock.

Ashton laced his fingers, pressed them to his lips, and listened to Tori tell him winter would end. Inside, his gut twisted as she begged him to make up his mind.

He threw away his cassette tape copy months ago because the woman's voice inspired ideas he shouldn't have. This song tempted him to push the repeat button so he could listen to it, only it, all night. The urge was so strong he gave thought to leaving the car here to escape it. Jump out. Run. And run, until everything reminding him of Marie Baez was far behind him.

I wish.

The living room windows glowed brighter as someone pulled open a curtain. The home tugged at him with its warmth harder. It promised if he went inside,

The Shrink would bleed the hemorrhage from his chest.

Tori asked him when he'd love himself as much as she did.

Ashton yanked the key down, shutting down the power to the stereo. The car fell silent. He blew his breath out and stepped out into the frigid night. Salt crunched under his tennis shoes as he walked along the driveway, up the steps, and paused on the stoop of the kitchen door. He didn't have the opportunity to knock.

A tall, stocky silhouette appeared in the storm door window as inner door swung open. As Mr. Praetor came into the light of the porch entryway, his eyes narrowed. "Neil's at Raleigh's."

There was a bit of inflection at the end, so Ashton answered the possible question. "Probably. Is Jeannie home?"

Mr. Praetor opened the screen door. Ashton thanked him as he stepped inside and followed his best friend's dad into the home's kitchen. It had a red, white, and black color scheme, and was accented with Holstein cows. They'd struck Ashton as strange the first time he saw them, but now, he really liked them.

As Ashton settled in a chair at the breakfast table, Jeannie put on coffee while her husband laid out leftover desserts. A plate of Christmas cookies wrapped in plastic. An apple pie with a slice missing. Half of a white cake covered in shredded coconut. Paper plates, plastic forks, and napkins with Christmas-y designs followed.

Mrs. Praetor returned to the table with two cups of coffee and her husband slipped out of the room. Ashton held his cup between his hands, breathing in the rich scent. When Jeannie's was properly spiked with Irish cream liquor, she departed as well, leaving behind her disgraced alter ego, The Shrink.

"Something happened today."

Ashton scoffed. "And happened." He laughed and sniffled back a sob. "And happened."

"Do you want to start at the beginning? Or is there something specific?"

Neil cussed. I saw Sam, in the flesh. Marie kissed my cheek.

The memory of his conversation with Neil crawled across the skin behind his right ear, leaving a furious itch in its path. Ashton scratched it. "How much do you know about the Mormons?"

"More than your average member." She shrugged off his incredulous stare. "The LDS Church is a good mommy bird. Most members never find themselves hungry enough to look for sustenance that hasn't been pre-digested."

The itch grew, millimeters per second, into his scalp. The reaction to religious talk started around puberty, when the spittle flying out of his stepdad's mouth mixed with Ashton's changing body in a multitude of undesirable ways.

Girls are the devil. Ashley wore jeans and sweatshirts to hide her body, feeling comfortable in her skin for the first time in years.

Boys don't like girls who dress like boys. She wore skirts so boys would like her, only to discover she didn't like boys. No one could ever find out.

Dress like a whore. You'll get what's coming to you. She kept close to her female friends, avoiding boys as much as possible, at which point she knew for certain she was worse than a lesbian. She was a *boy.*

God hates queers. She tried out for cheerleading and dated basketball players to keep up appearances.

Sluts like you go to Hell.

True to the pastor's word, Ashley got what was coming to *her. She* got the blame, and the shame, and death threats when the boys who pinned *her* down lost scholarships because *she* reported a crime.

It went on, and on, and on. Until he cut off his hair and burned *Ashley's* whole fucking wardrobe in the back yard. Until his parents sent him to a camp to *cure* him. Until Ashton came home unchanged, stole money from his mom, and drove west until he crashed until a light pole several states over.

"What do you want to know about the LDS?"

The woman's voice yanked him back into the present. Yes, Neil's rare curse in Valkyrie's break room got Ashton's attention. But the wacky interpretation of the New Testament "sun, moon, and stars" metaphor rattled the cage confining Ashton's inner Christian, and the startled bird was still squawking. He couldn't shut the damn thing up.

Ashton stumbled over his tongue before his question made it out. "Is it a cult?"

"Of course it is. All religions are."

"But, are they—?"

The Shrink filled in the blanks. "Dangerous? Abusive? Evil?" Ashton nodded. "Depends on who you ask."

Ashton raked his fingers through his scalp. She wasn't giving him answers he could do anything with.

"If you're thinking about trying to save Marie, I'd advise against."

He stopped scratching. "You just said she's in a cult."

"And she's happy there." The Shrink took a sip of her coffee and hummed. "You're leaving in…what, five months? Six at most? Would you yank her out and then leave her here to pick up the pieces."

"I asked her to come with me." Jeannie's eyebrow arched. Her silent judgment compelled him to explain himself. "I hadn't planned it. It just came out."

"And? What did she say?"

"I wish."

The Shrink softened, letting Jeannie come out. "Ashton, don't. For both of your sakes, let her go."

"Why? She's not happy. Content *maybe*, but…" The woman's eyes sharpened again, bored into him harder. Ashton withered a bit in their heat, but he didn't back down. "She's planning on throwing her life away over bullshit!"

"Worship isn't something we do, Ashton. It isn't a place we go. It's a part of us. It shapes how we see the world, how we function within it. When a person is content with the fellowship of a church, any church, losing faith is rarely a good enough reason to risk losing everything else the fellowship offers. And the LDS offer a hell of a lot."

The words inspired Ashton. "If she had a reason—"

"If you gave her one, you mean?" The Shrink couched her question in a tone straddling admiration and exasperation, like he was twelve years old, on his nth big idea, and he'd shown her plans for a nuclear reactor he wanted to build in his parents' garage.

He steeled his resolve. "How long do you think it would take?"

"Seven years."

Ashton's face tightened and shriveled around the words. She answered without hesitating. With a *number*.

As he stared at her in disbelief, The Shrink explained her answer. "Leaving is the easy part. Cult members often struggle for years with fear, doubts. Regrets. Have you overcome any of yours yet?"

"No." Ashton covered his face in his hands and exhaled. "Shit."

"And, let's get really real here. You've lied to her for two years about your gender. If you're not living your life the way you want, do you have any moral authority to challenge the way she plans to spend hers?"

Ashton shook his head, and his thumb brushed his jaw, reminding him of her cold fingertips on his skin. How could a touch so soft, so gentle, rip up a storm? He sniffled and wiped away the tears in his eyes.

"Oh, God. Why am I doing this to myself?"

Jeannie stood up and walked around the table. She wrapped her arms around his shoulders from behind. "Love leads to madness, Ashton." She kissed his head, as a mother would her struggling son, and held him in a way his own never had.

· ❄ ·

I hope you enjoyed this scene from the cutting room floor. — Wendy

61773663R10139

Made in the USA
Columbia, SC
27 June 2019